Cass Moriarty lives and writes in Brisbane. After completing a Business Communication degree at QUT, she worked in public relations and marketing. She began writing fiction after the birth of her sixth child. *The Promise Seed*, her first novel, was shortlisted in the Emerging Author category of the 2013 Queensland Literary Awards.

The
Promise
Seed

Cass Moriarty

UQP

First published 2015 by University of Queensland Press
PO Box 6042, St Lucia, Queensland 4067 Australia

www.uqp.com.au
uqp@uqp.uq.edu.au

© Cass Moriarty 2015

Cover design by Kirby Armstrong
Author photograph by Lenny Muthiah Photography
Typeset in 12/16pt Bembo Std by Post Pre-press Group, Brisbane
Printed in Australia by McPherson's Printing Group

Lines from *The Lacuna* by Barbara Kingsolver are reproduced with permission of Faber & Faber Ltd.

National Library of Australia
Cataloguing-in-Publication data is available at http://catalogue.nla.gov.au

ISBN 978 0 7022 5375 1 (pbk)
ISBN 978 0 7022 5563 2 (ePDF)
ISBN 978 0 7022 5564 9 (ePub)
ISBN 978 0 7022 5565 6 (Kindle)

University of Queensland Press uses papers that are natural, renewable and recyclable products made
from wood grown in sustainable forests. The logging and manufacturing processes conform to the
environmental regulations of the country of origin.

For the child who has no voice.

(And for Sean, who always told me I could.)

'I wasn't raised in this country.
Wasn't raised, really at all.'

'If a person is not raised, then what? He grows from a seed?'
Barbara Kingsolver, *The Lacuna*

The years teach much which the days never know.
Ralph Waldo Emerson

The morning my infant sister died, the sharp chill sucked the oxygen from the air and felt like it would strip the skin right off your face. Sparkling icicles hung like crystal daggers from the eaves. One policeman slipped in the dirty driveway slush, leaving bright red drops freezing in the puddle.

It was 1944 and I was six years old.

My mother's sister Kath found me holding the blanket over Emily's face. She bustled into the sleep-out and slapped my hands away, and she had this expression on her face that I'd never seen on an adult before, a sort of thrilled horror and irritation all at once. I almost expected her to say *Bloody hell, June, what's the little monster done now, I s'pose I'll be the one who has to sort out the mess.* In any event, it was close to the truth, 'cause Mum wasn't up to sorting out much, let alone a dead baby in a crib, and so Aunty Kath did all the wailing and calling of police and making of tea and so on. She was good in a crisis, Aunty Kath, as she never tired of telling us.

Like I said, it was her who called the police. Got right on the blower and blurted it out – *He's killed her! He's killed her!* she kept shouting into the receiver – and then glaring at it like it might come alive in her hand. She didn't like to use the telephone, Aunty

Kath; back then it was one of those new-fangled bits of nonsense that she could get along quite well without, *thank you very much*. I still remember the piercing sound of her voice, echoing through the cold, still rooms of that cold, still house.

Everything after that was a bit of a blur. There were police officers. Seemed like quite a lot, seemed like the kitchen and sleep-out and sitting room were all crowded with people in uniforms and smart hats. I even stumbled across one young fellow throwing up his breakfast into the basin in our mildewy bathroom. There were probably only two or three police officers but I was at eye level with a lot of unfamiliar legs, so maybe that multiplied them for me. And soon enough there were nosy neighbours popping over to help. Even that Catholic woman from next door, the one with about a dozen kids. She'd never said a word to Mum all the months we'd lived there, and her twin boys (who were about my age) had called me names and thrown dog shit over the fence. Even she appeared, saying wasn't it terrible, and was there anything she could do?

So there was a general palaver and people asking questions and then the doctor coming and looking at Emily, and noise and commotion and who knows what else. In the midst of it all sat Mum, real quiet, her eyes blank, like she was staring at something far away, as if she was trying to see something of great interest or importance but she couldn't quite figure out what it was. And she didn't say anything, not then anyway, and not to me. But I heard this keening, this high-pitched wail that seemed to come from no-one in particular, and it got louder and louder until it filled that tiny kitchen, bouncing off the walls and right into my eardrums, and I realised it was Mum making that sound, and I really wanted to switch her off and make her go quiet again.

They took her away, all wrapped up in a blanket for the shock. I think she went to the hospital and then she stayed at Aunty Kath's place. I know she never went back to that house. They took me to the hospital too, I think because they didn't know what else to do with me. I remember sleeping that night in a bed so huge that even with my arms spread out wide I still couldn't touch the edges. The sheets were perfectly white, and stiff like they'd never been washed. And they let me keep a light on all night, the lamp on the bedside table, like a little midnight sun burning.

If I'd known then what I knew later, I'd have fought harder to stay in that hospital room. I would've put on a cough or feigned an incurable disease or something. But I didn't, and so they made me leave … but that's all coming along further in the story, and I don't want to burden you with too much information right at the start. Suffice to say that life is a long, hard road, and I learnt that lesson early.

It may be that you're wondering where my father was when all of this drama was going on. Well, not two weeks earlier, Mum had broken down in tears as she told me that she'd received a telegram informing her that my dad was missing in action somewhere in the jungles of New Guinea.

So I suppose that didn't help.

···

Those years of enduring the cold of the southernmost bit of Queensland around the Darling Downs have made me appreciate the mild weather of the capital. Every year until I was sixteen, I spent at least five months freezing my balls off walking to classes or pedalling my clapped-out bike, my ears red as beets, my nose dripping and my eyes streaming. Too cold to snow, that was what the weather girl usually said. At least a bit of snow would've made a change. All we had was frost and numbing winds. Toowoomba, Warwick, they were all the same. The little towns around Stanthorpe that took their names from the battlefields of the Great War – Pozieres, Amiens, Passchendaele – growing up in those towns you could well imagine the men in France freezing their balls off in the same way.

Mind you, that was the least of my troubles.

Still, at least I can't complain about the weather at the moment. Sunshine is good for the soul, no doubt about it. There's a fresh chill in the morning even here in the big smoke, sufficient so you don't feel guilty for wanting to lie under the covers a little longer. Soon enough the thin sun spreads fingers of warmth creeping through my bedroom window, settling a pale golden blanket over me in my bed – that's when I get up, and not before.

At my age, getting up's a feat in itself, that's for sure. Truth be told, if I had one of those catheter thingamies like poor old Roger down on Boundary Road, I'd probably stay in bed even longer. But I'm not that far gone, not yet anyway, and the pressing pain in my bladder eventually persuades me to make a move. 'Course, once I make it to a standing position, and find my damn slippers, and manage to knot the dressing-gown cord and then shuffle down the hall to the loo, I usually stand there for a good few minutes, waiting. One more advantage of being old: your body demands one thing and then changes its mind.

But we should be thankful for small mercies, as my Aunty Kath used to say, so I'm grateful the days are mild. There's a spot out on my back landing where I like to have my cup of tea in the morning. I've got a chair out there, and a little rickety table, and I sit and read yesterday's paper while the sun's rays fairly burn right through my clothing. I swear I can feel my blood thawing and starting to flow again.

When the kids in the street are blessedly quiet, there are a couple of rainbow lorikeets that visit. Might have something to do with the fruit I put out but I like to think they come for the company. Bob and Noreen, I call them. No idea what sex they are actually, but they bicker and argue over the food like an old married couple, so that's what I've named them. Not that I would know anything about old married couples, bickering or otherwise, being as how I've never had the pleasure myself, but still. Just 'cause I'm old doesn't mean I've got no imagination.

So once Bob and Noreen have buggered off and I've read anything worth reading in the paper (I refuse to call it a *news*paper on principle), then the excitement of my day begins. Ha. If only. But, like I said, life's a long, hard road, and it certainly doesn't get any easier.

Kids today, they don't know how good they've got it. Larking the day away, no chores to do, no worrying about getting a clip over the ear if they're not done, or not done properly. No respect, some of these young ones. You pick out any handful of the kids around here, from this very street, yahooing and backchatting and smoking and swearing when they're still in short pants. Cricket on the road after school, balls going every which way, and those kids scrambling over your garden beds to retrieve them. Not a care in the world that they're on someone else's property. Wouldn't occur to them to ask permission. Like every backyard in the street is their playground. And the noise and all sorts of carry-on from some God-awful hour of a Saturday and Sunday. The kid next door dragging his stick along my side fence, making a din loud enough to wake the dead. Scaring my chooks. I've a good mind to have a word to that mother of his. Not that that would get me anywhere. Kid seems to do pretty much as he pleases. Bet he's never had a chilblain or a woodchopping blister. Bet he's never lain awake at night with his empty stomach growling, or had to fight his way through a horde of kids to get a seat close enough to the fire that your backside doesn't freeze solid.

That kid has no idea what life can be like. None of them do.

The boy felt the weak sunlight on his eyelids. He lay perfectly still, hoping that sleep might reclaim him. But the wretched cough hacking through his bedroom wall resigned him to relinquishing his haven. As if on cue, she called his name.

Be a love and bring us a cuppa, would ya?

The boy pulled back the thin coverlet, releasing a musty odour. He danced miserably from foot to foot on the wooden boards, looking around for a jumper. He discarded one as too smelly, but then took a whiff under his own arms and realised he smelt worse than the clothing. He dragged the hoodie over his head. The sleeves stopped a good five centimetres above his wrists. He pulled on two odd socks, encrusted with yesterday's mud.

In the living room, the television was still on from the night before. A blonde woman in a leotard demonstrated the Amazing Results of the Ab-Buster. He switched it off and made his way to the kitchen.

Thousands of dust motes spun merrily in the light that spilled through the dirty window. The boy paused for a moment, watching. When he was little, he used to think they were wishes, waiting to be captured and granted. At nine years old, he no longer believed in wishes, or fairy tales, or angels. But he did believe in the devil.

He pushed aside an old margarine container overflowing with cigarette butts and ashes to reach the kettle. He filled it from the tap and sat it on the hob. Lit a match and flicked the gas until he had a ring of blue flame. He rinsed the curdled dregs from a chipped *Star Wars* mug, put in a Woolies teabag and three heaped spoons of sugar straight from the packet.

The table was littered with dog-eared copies of *TV Week* and *Woman's Day*. He pushed aside a stiletto with a broken heel and a plate congealed with grease, and sat with his head in his hands. When he lifted his arms, his elbows stuck to the tacky surface. *Someone should tidy up,* he thought. He pocketed three lotto tickets peeping out from under an empty McDonald's packet, thinking he would go down to the newsagent later. A carton of milk stood lidless on the table. One sniff was enough; he tipped the gluggy contents down the sink. He reached hopefully for a plastic bag with a few slices of bread still inside, but wrinkled his nose at the fine green mould creeping across its surface, and shoved the whole lot in the bin. Searching through the fridge, he found a half-full jar of peanut paste. He scooped it out with his fingers.

The kettle whistled. He splashed water into the mug, dunked the teabag in and then sat it on a saucer for her next cup. He carried the scalding mug carefully down the hallway.

A tentative knock on her door. He pushed it open with his foot and peered into the room with accustomed wariness.

It's all right, love, he's gone. Left early. Oh, that's lovely and hot. You're a good boy for Mummy.

Her room smelt as bad as his, or worse. The same mustiness, a stale, airless quality – she never opened the window. Cigarette smoke, an overturned beer can leaking onto the carpet. The strong animal fug of the absent man.

Come here, baby, give Mummy a cuddle.

He let her hold him, briefly. Her body, warm with sleep, enveloped him in a feeling so familiar it made him faint with longing. Abruptly he rose.

Gotta go to the shop. No bread or milk.

She fumbled on the bedside table for her purse and handed him a ten-dollar note.

Here, love, buy yourself a Mars Bar or something.

He took the money. Paused at the doorway.

It's only eight o'clock in the morning, Mum.

...

Later he was squatting at the bottom of the back stairs, following a trail of ants that marched down the guttering and across the soil in a tidy line. He placed obstacles – a stone, a jagged tile – in their path, and they went around without hesitation, each one following the one in front. Ants on a mission. He tired of watching and decided to create havoc. With his bare foot he squashed a whole battalion of ants and brushed away their broken bodies. A sharp, sweet smell rose. The other ants panicked and scurried about, antennae waving. Some collected their fallen comrades and returned the way they had come, communicating with their fellows along the way. Others were nonplussed; they continued on their path as if nothing had happened. The boy thought about ants. He thought about their reactions. He wondered.

The soil was tightly packed underneath the sprinkling of dust that lifted with each breath of wind, catching in crevices. Nothing grew here. The boy squinted against the grit and wiped a finger under his itching nose. He sneezed out a globule of snot. The ants headed straight for it.

Further across the yard was a riot of vegetation, as if to make up for the bare patch around the house. Tangled weeds choked overgrown bushes. Ancient ornamentals long gone to seed struggled for space with native trees. The boy parted a section of matted green vine, snarled around grasses peppered with tiny, neon-yellow flowers. He lay with his cheek on the cool ground and heard the ticking of a bug's wings. He imagined himself small enough to swing on a grass stem, to sit cupped inside a yellow petal. He breathed in the smell of approaching autumn.

Next he investigated the turkey mound in the back corner of the yard. The male strutted in alarm, proprietarily scratching at leaves and soggy detritus, adding more height to the already enormous nest. The boy knew this was to regulate the temperature of the eggs incubating below. The father's anxiety was amusing but somehow admirable. The bird cocked its head and stared at the boy, one black beady eye appraising him, the risk he posed. The boy shook a stick to assert his dominance, and laughed as the turkey opened its beak in protest.

He ran the stick along the wooden palings of the fence. The sharp *crack crack crack* ricocheted loud in the emptiness of the morning. He saw a movement at the window of the house next door; the old guy peeked out, probably wondering what was making such a racket.

She appeared at the doorway behind the boy.

Come over here, love.

He struck a last reluctant crack to the fence and went to her, trailing the stick behind him in the dirt.

Sorry about school today. I didn't realise it was so late.

Doesn't matter. Didn't want to go anyway.

Yeah well, school's important. You know, I wasn't feeling too great this morning and the time got away on me.

She inhaled a deep draught of acrid smoke, pulled it into her lungs and expelled it in a hazy stream.

How about we do something together, the two of us? Want to see a movie?

He waited a beat before replying.

What about that new vampire one? It's on at Indro tonight at seven. I checked.

9

Another plume of smoke.

Sorry, love, not tonight.

She stood and pirouetted grotesquely.

Got myself a hot date!

He looked away.

Wanna do something else? Maybe this arv?

Nah, it's all right.

The turkey watched them, never straying far from his nest.

Come on, love. Don't be like that.

He didn't turn his head. She got up in disgust.

Jeez, aren't I allowed to have a life? It's not all about you, you know.

She stamped into the house and slammed the screen door behind her.

The boy lunged at the turkey, whooping loudly. He landed full force on the mound, and imagined the sound of eggs breaking.

Those first few days were pretty confusing, I remember. After that one night in the hospital, I somehow wound up in another house altogether. There were some other kids my age, and a rather large woman with a doughy face who was always forcing scones on me. I've never liked scones. But I suppose she meant well. There were quite a lot of people living in the house, and even more coming and going all the time.

Aunty Kath came by to visit. Just the once. We sat outside, under the mango tree, on a creaking swing set with faded cushions that smelt of damp. She cried a lot, which I remember thinking was kind of strange, 'cause Aunty Kath had never struck me as the crying type. She must've talked to me, but I can't say I remember much of what she said. She had this flowery handkerchief and she kept folding it into a neat square and then unfolding it and then starting all over with the folding again. I do remember that I asked where Mum was, and was she coming to visit me too? And Aunty Kath got this look on her face, like she was sad, and even angry, and she said Mum was at home and no, she wasn't up to visiting me, she was *too sorrowful*. I've always remembered that phrase, *too sorrowful*, as if Mum had drunk this big jug of sorrow until she was full, too full to see me and be forced to drink down another cup of sorrow.

There I was, surrounded by strangers.

Would've been nice to get a visit from Mum. I was still her son. Despite everything that had happened.

The next thing I recall is being collected in a car that was so shiny I could see my own face right there on the blue paintwork. We'd never had a car, so I was pretty excited to hear that it was me being collected and driven somewhere. We drove for what seemed like a long time, although it was probably only an hour or so. I had the window down and I kept sticking my face out so as to feel the wind whooshing past, so fast it made my eyes water. I was happy to be leaving those scones behind, I can tell you.

Simple pleasures, hey. No computer games or Play Boxes or X Machines or whatever the heck the kids have today so they're amused every spare moment. A simple ride down the highway in a blue car with the wind in my face, and I was happy. Despite Emily. Despite everything.

I didn't know where we were going, but I think I expected to see Mum or Aunty Kath or someone familiar at the end of it.

When we arrived, it was this massive grey building with lots of windows. Next to one wall was a great big weeping willow moaning gently in the wind. And the whole lot was enclosed with a fence: I'd never seen one that high. I wonder now whether it was to keep the inside people in, or the outside people out. In any event, there was nobody I knew, only an empty sitting room where I was told to sit, and wait, which I did. I wouldn't have minded seeing even the woman with the doughy face. But I waited an awful long time, and no-one came, not for me.

Unfamiliar faces streamed past, some kind, some mean-looking, and some strange and bewildered.

I had a lot of time that day to sit and think about what had happened. In retrospect, I can see that my six-year-old self had a lot of trouble connecting the dots. I only understood that I was in a mess of trouble.

That building doesn't exist anymore. I went down there once, in the seventies, and the whole place was gone: the buildings, the fence, even the willow tree. Half of it was made up of what they call spec houses, a whole lot of boxes with cream walls and red roofs and the exact same letterbox outside each one. The other half used to be a playing field, where we threw a ball around and had running races and rode our rusty bicycles; that was gone too. There was a little shopping centre there, three or four shops grouped together, selling stuff to the people living in the spec houses, I suppose.

I wondered whether they ever thought about the foundations of the Darling Downs Home for Wayward Boys, right there under their feet.

But at the time I arrived that spring of '44, that building felt as solid as rock and about as interesting. It was to be my home for the next eight years.

I shared a room with two other Wayward Boys. James was three years older than me and knew a heck of a lot for a nine-year-old. He was thin as a rake, and wiry, but he had some muscles in those puny arms. He gave a Chinese burn that left a red mark 'til the next day. James had what I suppose they'd now call Attention Deficit Disorder or Hyperactivity or some such. Back then he was just plain naughty. He'd been to four different schools and none of them could hold him. He'd kick the teachers and punch the other students and in the end his parents gave up and shoved him into the Home. James didn't seem to care; he continued kicking and punching all the boys that were smaller than him.

Derek was my other roommate. Poor Derek was a touch slow. Not the sharpest tool in the shed. He couldn't even say the alphabet all the way through, and he was only a few months younger than James. He was real shy too, wouldn't ever look you in the eye, if he spoke to you at all. Nice enough kid though. Funny thing, James took a shine to Derek. I guess they'd been together a couple of years before I came along, and he pretty much took Derek under his wing and watched out for him. Any of those other kids picked on Derek or made fun of him for the way he talked, James would be on them quicker than you could blink. As time went on, people knew to keep clear of the two of them. So when I arrived, and Mr McCready put me in the same room, I think the older boys thought I wouldn't be long for this world, being locked in there with James every night. But I survived. James didn't go out of his way for me like he did with Derek, but he did tolerate me, most of the time. Never missed an opportunity for a hard pinch or a swift kick up the backside, though.

I see that kid next door, mooching around on his own, tormenting the bush turkeys and playing games of make-believe with himself, and I find myself thinking he's lonely. But then I recall my youth, which was quite the opposite – never a moment to yourself, never a possession you didn't have to share or a dessert that wasn't fought over, always having to get a handle on a dozen different personalities and negotiate the friendship groups that formed and disbanded and re-formed like swarms of blowflies over a rotting carcass. And again I think to myself, he doesn't know how lucky he is. Him and all the kids around here. They haven't got a clue.

...

I was the youngest kid there when I arrived at the Home, and one of the oldest when I left.

There were some miserable years in between. Some nights I'd lie in my narrow bed in that close room, listening to the other boys breathing, and I'd weep with the uncertainty and unfairness of it all. The days stretched out in infinite monotony. Dull lessons by teachers so strict and nasty they made your hair stand on end just to look at them. The ceaseless routine of chores. Not so many when I was younger, although a six-year-old can still be made to sweep a floor. By the time I was nine or ten I was scrubbing pots and chopping wood. That's what I blame for my arthritis, all that time swinging an axe in the biting wind. I got so I had blisters on my blisters, my hands were that chapped and sore. I've still got the scar too. A pink jagged line in the webbing between my thumb and first finger on my left hand. I was steadying a chunk of wood and forgot to let go when I brought the axe down. Sixteen stitches. Never did that again.

It wasn't all bad though. I guess even in a place as dismal as the Home you've got to have a few bright moments, especially if you're there as long as I was. One of my best friends was a boy named Archi. His full name was Archimedes – can you imagine any parent inflicting that on a little baby? Archi arrived a year or two after me and we were almost exactly the same age, give or take a week. Birthdays weren't much celebrated in the Home, but you did get a day off your chores, and they served a sponge cake with sticky icing after dinner. So Archi and I got to have cake twice in the one week, which was pretty good. Archi had spiky ginger hair and so many freckles it seemed like he was one big freckle with bits of skin poking through. He was funny too. Always thinking up silly riddles and practical jokes. Most of the other boys liked Archi OK, but it was me he stuck around the most. *Joined at the hip,* Mr McCready used to say. We were good friends for quite a few years.

One morning, Archi didn't come down for breakfast and when I went up to his room, his bed was stripped, the bare mattress with bits of ticking showing through in tufts, and all his stuff was cleaned off his desk. Even the mouse skeleton was gone, the one I'd given him for his tenth birthday, so I knew something was up. His roommate, a loudmouth kid with bad breath who used to wet his bed a lot, I forget his name, he was useless. Said he *didn't know nothing* in this adenoidal whine that annoyed the heck out of me. I tried to ask Mr McCready but all I was told was that *young men should mind their own business.*

I never saw Archi again.

I heard a rumour that he got sick, but someone else told me that some relation finally came to claim him. So that's what I choose to believe. I like to imagine Archi growing up somewhere in a nice house with a family who cared about him. He would've liked that.

I wonder where Archi is now. Him and James and Derek and the rest, they'd all be old men now, if they're still alive at all. Makes you think, doesn't it.

Another good memory I have of the Home is the surroundings. The building itself was grey and depressing – I think it must have had rising damp, 'cause it was always so cold and clammy. And there was the accumulated smell of hundreds of meals of boiled cabbage and fatty pork. But once we were allowed outside, it was like being in another world. The air was fresh and sweet. I'd take great gulps of it, like I was thirsty for oxygen. In winter the sky was a fragile blue dome. Sometimes massive clouds would congregate, shifting slowly above us, before sending down icy drizzles. In summer the blue was brighter, it had more depth – an oil painting rather than the thin watercolour of winter. When those first days of spring came, the tips of the tree buds were tinged with pink or pale mauve, and the snowdrops had given way to colourful wildflowers and blossoms from the fruiting trees. It all seemed so alive, bursting with possibility, and made you forget, even for a little while, about the grey building and the cabbage and the chores.

It's a funny thing, but sometimes I miss those spring days. I do. Whatever else you say about the Home, I lived there longer than I'd lived in that house with Mum, the house that was cold and still even before Emily died.

The Home. For most of my childhood, the place was home.

It was a long walk from school. The boy reached his yard and pushed past the rusty vine-covered gate. Wedged firmly at an odd angle, it was not quite closed but not quite open enough to be welcoming either. He stopped when he saw the motorcycle, leaning as if it belonged there. He briefly considered leaving, but he hadn't eaten since the night before – a gnawing emptiness growled in his stomach – and he remembered he had less than a dollar in his pocket.

Besides, this was his house.

He went around the back and ascended the stairs on quiet cat feet, pausing to peer inside. From her bedroom he heard a rhythmic *thud thud thud* as the bed hit the wall. He stepped inside and foraged in the kitchen for something to eat, closing cupboard doors with a muffled click. He found a muesli bar and a packet of potato chips and put them in his school bag for lunch the next day. Half a pizza sat in a box on the table. He brushed away the flies, folded a whole slice and stuffed it into his mouth. The idiot had left a full pack of smokes too. The boy pocketed them. He would sell them to the older kids down by the creek after school. He guzzled from an open can of Coke, wiped his mouth on his sleeve and retreated to his room.

The thudding reverberated through his bedroom wall and he tried not to imagine what was causing the sound. Finally it stopped, and the house was at rest. His mother's boyfriends never hung around unless they were too drunk or stoned to leave; he crossed his fingers and hoped to hear the roar of the motorcycle. But instead he heard the toilet running and someone moving around the lounge room, and then raised voices, a man's grunt, and his mother's nasal tone. Suddenly his bedroom door was open and a man he had seen only once or twice before was glaring at him, intent.

Get out of here! You're not allowed in here!

Where're my fucking smokes, you little shit?

I haven't touched your smokes. Get out. Leave me alone.

I'm not going anywhere until you give me back my smokes.

The man walked through the doorway and glared about. He reached for a music poster taped to the wall and, in one slow deliberate stroke, tore half of it away and dropped it to the floor.

You bastard. Get out! Mum!

Oh, go on, cry for Mummy, little boy.

He swept his arm over the top of the dressing table, scattering books and Lego in all directions. The boy slid backwards on the bed under the man's piercing scrutiny.

Where ... are ... my ... smokes?

He lunged, catching the boy's wrist. The boy twisted his body on the bed, trying to wriggle free.

Where ... are ... my ... smokes?

This time he punctuated each word with a sharp slap. The boy's cheek stung and his ear rang.

He looked up and saw his mother standing in the doorway. Her eyes were blank windows. She chewed on a fingernail and glanced behind her as if she might have somewhere else to be.

The boy jolted forward, and the unexpected movement put the man off balance. His grip loosened and the boy slipped away from under him, onto the floor, and past his mother out the door. He didn't stop running until he reached the fence. He could hear the man's curses. He scrambled over the palings and into next door's yard, towards the shed. A couple of chickens scattered, noisily announcing his intrusion. The boy found a niche between the side of the shed and the ageing scribbly gum, flattened himself into the space, and slid onto his haunches, breathing hard.

The hens were still running around in crazy circles, squawking indignantly. He could see the man outside his own back door, and his mother too. The man was still cursing loudly. His mother said nothing.

He tilted his head at the sound of footsteps. The old guy was walking towards him.

Hey you! Bugger off! What are you doing, scaring my chickens!

The boy put his finger to his lips and pleaded with his eyes. The old man glared back at him in astonishment. His gaze shifted over to the shouting in the next yard, and the hairy, bare-chested man swigging from a stubbie. He stared from the man to the boy, and back to the man.

Hey! Old man! You seen a kid just now? Little bugger run off with me stuff. You see which way he went?

He motioned to the woman. *He's gonna get a fucking belting.*

The old man took a tottering pace forward.

No, he said in a firm and even tone. *I haven't seen anyone.*

He stared defiantly at the man, and then reached for the henhouse door.

Don't come all piss and vinegar on me, ya hairy galoot, he muttered. He waited as the man and the woman completed their desultory search of their own yard and then went back into the house.

The old man turned back to the folds of the tree. But the boy was gone.

I got three letters from Mum while I was at the Home. The first one was right after I arrived. Being only six, I don't think I could've read it. I suppose someone read it to me but I don't remember. The second one came around the time of my eighth birthday. I was reading pretty well by then. In it she said she was sorry she'd missed my seventh birthday and she hoped I'd have a happy day on my eighth. She enclosed a card with little cartoon chicks on it. It was babyish and I threw it away so the other boys wouldn't tease me. I didn't hear from her again until I got another letter when I was about eleven. Mum sounded real happy. She said she'd gone to Adelaide, which I knew was way down in the south of Australia, and that she had a new husband named Barry. He worked on the railroads and that's why they'd moved away. In hindsight, it does seem kinda funny that she just blurted it out like that after so long, like she was telling an acquaintance she'd bought a new hat. But then I suppose there was so much going on in my life that simply happened to me − I must've accepted it as merely one more thing. Mum's silences were nothing new. I still have that letter somewhere.

In between letters one and two, the war ended. I was seven at the time. Mr McCready had his transistor radio on all day and into the night, and we were allowed to crowd around him and listen as long as we didn't make any noise. We heard important people making important announcements, and snippets of recordings of soldiers cheering. A few of the teachers sat with their ears glued too, and classes were all but suspended for a day or two. To my young mind it seemed like cause for celebration, but some of the teachers got right emotional. Mr Elms, the maths master, had a brother who had died over in Europe some months before, and when peace was announced he went to pieces, blubbering like a baby and ranting about the senseless waste of life. I suppose that while the war raged, people put on a good face and kept up that fighting attitude, support for our men and all that, but when the end came, it was like that little Dutch boy taking his finger out of the plugged-up dyke … all those emotions finally came rushing through, the dam walls broke, and oceans of misery and sorrow about drowned us all.

He was given extended sick leave, Mr Elms. But he never came back.

After the war, life at the Home went on much as usual, with a few adventures along the way. One year there was a big flood. It started raining one weekend and that rain didn't let up for three whole weeks. The ground got all soggy. Nothing would dry properly. Mould started appearing everywhere – it blossomed on our bedroom walls and grew on our shoes. And little mushrooms sprouted in a big circle around the front of the building. The little kids thought it was a fairy ring. The older boys picked them and boiled them up to eat, thinking they'd get a buzz, but all they got was real sick. One kid even had to go to hospital. And in the midst of it all, that rain kept on coming. Our outside activities were cancelled and we played endless games of chess and draughts in the main hall. Then one night, one of the younger boys who stayed in the downstairs part, he got up to go to the bathroom and stepped out of bed right into a big pool of water. He woke us all up with his screaming. The whole building was flooded all through the downstairs. It was like a slow-flowing river, carrying shoes and papers and hats. We spent weeks afterwards trying to dry out the swollen pages of our books.

Another time we had a fire in the toilets and the whole building had to be evacuated. Big Johnno lit it. He was an unfortunate wretch, Big Johnno. He was only twelve but he had size-eleven feet carrying around a huge lump of a body, and he wasn't too smart either. The whole reason he was at the Home was for starting fires, so I suppose it was no surprise that he eventually lit one there too. In winter, when Mr McCready stoked up the fireplace in the main hall, Big Johnno would sit there for hours, staring into the flames. I asked him once what he was staring at. He said he saw all sorts of things in those flames, animals and people and whole cities sometimes, all dancing around in the blazing colours. Then he leant over real close to me and cast his eyes around conspiratorially, to make sure no-one else was listening.

Can you keep a secret? he whispered.

I said I could, of course. Secrets were valuable currency in the Home, and you did whatever you could to get a hold of them, whether you could keep them or not. So Big Johnno leant in even closer to me, his eyes shining brightly. I could see the reflection of the flames in those black circles.

They talk to me, he said.

Who? I said.

The fire creatures. They talk to me.

What do they say? I asked him.

They tell me stories. And they tell me to wait.

Wait for what?

They tell me to wait for their signal. And when the time is right, I'll join them.

Well, as you can imagine, I steered clear of Big Johnno after that little chinwag. I didn't fancy being around him when those fire creatures decided the time was right, you know what I mean? And sure enough, not a month or two after that, some boys came running out from the direction of the upstairs toilets, calling *Fire! Fire!* I was in my room reading, and by the time I got to the door to see what all the commotion was about, there were great billowing clouds of smoke coming from the bathroom. Big Johnno had finally done it. He'd nicked some matches from the kitchen and collected a week's worth of loo paper and set the whole lot alight. The worst thing was, he'd piled it up on top of one of the toilets and then locked himself in the cubicle. Apparently he just stood there, with his back against the door, watching it burn. By the time Mr McCready had found a ladder and bucketed water over the top of the cubicle, and Mr Harris the maintenance man had found a screwdriver to undo the lock, poor Big Johnno was semi-conscious from inhaling all that smoke. He suffered serious burns to his face and hands too, which didn't help his general appearance, even after they healed. The scarring made him look like one of those blackened stumps that you see standing after a bush fire.

He never stopped listening to those fire creatures though. Even after all that, every winter night when Mr McCready laid the kindling in the fireplace, and those first tiny licks of flame began to flicker, Big Johnno was always the first to bags the closest chair, and always the last to go up to bed.

Then there was the time that little skinny kid disappeared. That was sad, but still, when you're with a whole lot of boys living in a place like the Home, anything out of the ordinary is an adventure, sad or not. I don't recall his name. He was only seven or eight, with ears that stuck out from either side of his head like two handles. I must've been thirteen, 'cause it was a year or so before I left. A whole lot of us were playing hide and seek in the grounds. It was the beginning of spring and one of those beautiful warm days that arrives out of the nowhere of winter. We'd been cooped up inside due to the cold, and so when the day dawned sunny and bright we were all champing at the bit to run around in the fresh air. So we had this game of hide and seek going on, and Mr McCready must've been in a good mood that day, 'cause he'd said we could go anywhere at all within the boundary, even in the back orchard and out along the side amongst all the pine trees. I was real pleased about that 'cause my favourite place to hide was up in one of the pine trees, a big one with sturdy branches the right distance apart for climbing. Me and some other boys had even lugged an old wooden pallet up there, our attempt at a tree house. Anyway, so I was busy hiding up in my pine tree, and all the other boys were in their various hidey-holes, and the game was going on fine, except that after a few rounds we realised that no-one had found the little skinny kid. Quite a few people had been It, and I guess there were so many boys playing that we didn't notice before then that he hadn't been found. But it wasn't until Mr McCready called the end of the game and we all trooped back up to the grey building that we realised he wasn't being a good hider, he was actually missing. We were all sent out again to find him. We must've searched for two hours or more.

My roommate Derek was the one that finally located him. Stupid kid had levered the cover off a disused well right up in the back corner of the property. He must've climbed in and braced himself against the inner walls while he dragged the cover partially closed over the top of him. I don't know how long it would've been before the poor bugger realised he couldn't hold his own weight up like that, balanced against the sides of the well, but eventually he must've dropped like a stone, right to the bottom. It was a long way down too.

There was a big inquiry after that, into the Home and everything that went on there. Like I said, I left the following year, but the Home itself was closed down soon afterwards. I guess that even though they were happy to put all of us boys there and practically forget about us, they weren't too happy to be losing kids down wells.

That kid next door, the one who was scaring my chooks and hiding near my woodshed, reminds me of that skinny kid who fell down the well. He's got that same air about him, beaten down and bedraggled, but determined too, like he's the permanent runner-up in the dogfight of life. To tell you the truth, I hadn't taken much notice of him before today, other than when he's making a racket running a stick along my fence. Think it's only him and his mum, and she's a sorry creature; always a man or three hanging around like they're after a bitch on heat. Not nice types either. Driving motorcycles and drinking and cursing and carrying on. The pair of them moved in two or three months ago but you'd think it was yesterday – there're still stacks of half-empty cardboard boxes scattered all over the porch, and an old fridge that never made it past the bottom front stair.

He gave me quite a start today, hiding there. I was all ready to yell at the little blighter for disturbing my chooks – they won't lay, you know, if they're frightened like that. But that bloke with the filthy mouth got my dander up, and to tell you the truth, I kinda felt sorry for the kid. There was something in his eyes that stirred a memory inside me. For a moment, I was him, I was that boy hiding by the woodshed, and I figured that whatever he was hiding from, it had to be worse than an old man with arthritic fingers and a few frightened chooks.

The air was charged with that peculiar smell of electricity before a storm. A wind had started up from nowhere, whipping the uppermost branches of the trees and tunnelling through the side of the yard, sweeping plastic bags and discarded rubbish before it. In its wake, the bushes shivered. The gusts plucked a few late-flowering jasmine from their stems and tossed them into whirling white eddies. A subtle green shaded the afternoon light, washing out the colour of the sky. Everything was trembling in anticipation.

And then it began. At first, a few fat raindrops thudding to the ground. Then the clouds cracked open with a clap of thunder and the water fell like a solid mass, drenching the boy as he hurried across the road and in through the squeaking gate. He couldn't even hear it above the noise of the downpour.

Up the stairs, two at a time, and then he was under the cover of the verandah, shaking the rain from his hair like a wet dog. He wiped his nose against his shoulder and went inside the empty house.

His bedroom was at the back of the building. It had a sloped ceiling; his mum had told him she thought it probably used to be the kitchen, before it was renovated in the seventies. Once she'd told him that, the room's eccentricities seemed to make more sense. There were several circles of darkened wood on the pine floor, which the boy imagined were caused by a stove. At one point, though, the cooker would almost certainly have been in the tiny alcove that jutted out into the side yard, now fitted with a crossbar and home to his few clothes. Only one of the wardrobe doors remained.

The walls of the room were painted a soft shade of blue, and he loved to lie on his bed, half-close his eyes, and lose himself in the soothing colour. A previous tenant had painted a white cloud on the wall near the window. Usually it floated, light and fluffy, between the blue of the wall and the blue of the sky outside. Today, however, it seemed benign against the thunderheads storming across the vista of the window, the silver-streaked sheets of water plummeting into the ground.

The boy kicked off his dripping runners. Taking aim, he threw one towards the cardboard box on the other side of the room. It missed, but he tried again with the other shoe and this time it dropped agreeably into the box.

Yes! he shouted, and punched the air.

He rummaged under his bed and pulled out a battered shoebox. Sitting cross-legged on the bed, he took out the contents and placed them in a semi-circle. There were four marbles he had won off the fat kid. Three pieces of crystal quartz he had dug out of the dirt in their previous house. He fanned out his collection of Pokémon cards and counted them carefully. There were nine doubles; maybe he should try to swap them after school tomorrow.

He fingered a small gold ring. It had belonged to a stuck-up girl a year above him, who was always bragging about her big pool and her overseas holidays. He had stolen it when she'd left it on a communal basin the day they'd all done the tree planting. Probably didn't want to get it dirty. He wasn't sure if it was real gold, but it was pretty. He had planned to give it to his mum, but that was about five months ago now and here it was, still sitting in his box under his bed. The moment of his imagination, some special moment that culminated in giving her the ring, hadn't eventuated. Not yet anyway.

There were bush-turkey feathers and unusual rocks and a spent bullet; there were half-a-dozen wishbones and a pointy stick he particularly liked and a magnet; there was a miniature model train engine given to him by one of his mum's boyfriends and a birthday invitation he had received two years ago from a boy in his class. He had a Batman torch and an *I participated in Sports Day* ribbon and a matchbox containing his collection of dead bugs. And there was a note in his mum's spidery handwriting – *Gone to the pub for bingo. Leftovers in fridge. Love Mum xx*. He'd kept it 'cause of the *Love Mum* and the *xx*. He examined his treasures as if they were holy things. He squared the cards into alignment, rubbed a piece of quartz on his sleeve until it shone and then rearranged the bits and pieces into their appointed spaces in the box. Finally, he drew from his pocket a golden cocoon he'd nicked from his teacher's silkworm display. One end was splayed open where the moth had emerged. He peered through the hole. The inside – that dim place of mysterious transformation – contrasted sharply with the fine strands of shimmering gold surrounding it. He placed the cocoon gently inside the box, closed the lid and slid it back under his bed, his ritual complete.

He retrieved the latest John Marsden book borrowed from the school library and settled back on his pillows. The rain sluiced down his window and drummed a hollow rhythm on the tin roof.

It was the autumn of '52 when I left the Home. Not exactly voluntarily, I have to say. But once you reached fourteen, Mr McCready didn't like you hanging around the little kids anymore. He particularly didn't like me hanging around the little kids, even when I was one myself. And, as I said, there were a few dramas going on, what with the inquiry into the death of the kid down the well, so they were starting to move on a few more boys than usual.

I'll always remember the day of my departure. Unlike most of the state, autumn meant something on the Darling Downs. The whole area was surrounded by the most beautiful gradient of colours – bright reds through to pale pinks, a range of yellows from golden to pumpkin orange to amber to soft lemon, chestnut browns, caramel browns, chocolate browns, with even a few plum purples and the occasional stubborn green thrown in. It was a sight to behold. There was a slight wind that day too, and those leaves still clinging to the trees shivered like they were waving goodbye. Every so often the breeze would pick up and release a shower of colour. I wasn't going to miss the grey building, but I was real sorry to be leaving behind the trees and flowers and bits of nature I had learnt to love.

A few of the older boys were allowed to come out to the bus to see me off. My old roommates, James and Derek, were already long gone by then, being older than me. Someone told me James ended up in juvenile gaol for stabbing some girl with a penknife, but that could have been hearsay. Anyway, there were one or two kids who'd been there almost as long as me, and they came out to say goodbye and good luck and all. Though I'm not sure any of us knew what we needed good luck for, or where we would be going to get it. Still, it was nice that they bothered.

I was off to the unsettling prospect of a *normal high school*. I had no idea what that might mean – how these new kids would be more normal than me, or normal in a different way. I needn't have worried. The two years I spent boarding at the Christian Path Academy in Ipswich were so normal as to be dull to the point of monotony. The school was populated with adolescent boys from good Christian families and run by an evangelical group that offered several scholarships each year to wayward boys who – the church elders felt – might have just enough salvageable soul to drag them back onto the Path. I was seen as a good candidate.

Mostly my past didn't matter. They knew where I'd come from.

But every so often the rumours would circulate. I'd catch a trio of boys whispering, or find some hurtful words scrawled across my locker. Once, not long after I arrived, I returned to my classroom after the bell and found my maths teacher and the new science teacher engaged in a furtive discussion. As soon as I entered the room, they clammed up. I remember the new teacher stared at me, open-mouthed. I saw a flicker of fear and curiosity cross his face.

Gradually, though, the rumours petered out, and once I'd left school altogether, they stopped following me around like a bad smell. I could look a bloke in the eye without him flinching. I no longer felt like I was being watched. People's memories are short, and thank God for that. Living on your own as an old fella's bad enough without giving folk any extra ammunition to hurl at you. Every time I consider opening my mouth to tell those kids in the street to pipe down, or that boy next door to stop making such a racket, I remember those days when people had heard the rumours, the apprehension flitting across their stony faces, and I think better of it and shut my mouth. No point courting disaster, inviting nosiness when indifference serves me just as well.

But back at the secondary school, the gossip still had legs and the speculators still had plenty to speculate about. Those two years were not the most comforting of my life. The day boys had families to go home to each night, and although there were quite a few boarders from distant properties, most of them went home for the holidays or even sometimes for weekends. There were only a few of us that lived permanently at the school, which had been named as our legal guardian for the term of our enrolment. There were a couple of orphans, and one kid whose parents were both in gaol, and two more – like me – who refused to speak about their families at all. At first I gravitated towards these boys in the mistaken belief that they would be kindred souls, seeking the gruff rough-housing camaraderie I had shared with the kids at the Home. But other than the fact that we all received welfare bursaries, there didn't seem to be any other ties binding us, and I soon realised I was more comfortable with the regular boarders or, more often than not, with my own company.

The religious angle was something new to me and for a while I threw myself into reading the Bible, listening to all the stories, learning the hymns and trying to work out how to get my prayers heard.

I prayed a lot for my sister. And I prayed for my own flawed soul.

But despite all the hype, the energy I saw devoted around me to the Path didn't seem to materialise into any actual results, and I became a tad dismayed and bored with the whole process.

The boarders were nice enough. One boy, Tom, invited me to his parents' property a few times. And eventually the school relented and said I could go. It was the Easter break. Tom and I took a train and then a bus to get to the little township near where he lived, and then we had to wait on the side of the road until his dad came along in this filthy banged-up ute with a hyperactive border collie straining at the leash in the back. Boy, was that dog pleased to see Tom. I thought he was going to lick him to death. Tom's dad told Bluey (that was the dog's name) to get back in the tray so we could drive to the house, but Tom pleaded with him to let him sit on our laps in the front, and so he did. Tom's dad pretended not to like it, but I saw him smiling when he thought Tom wasn't watching.

Tom's family consisted of his dad, his mum, his big sister Therese, who was living in the house with her husband, her belly full of their baby, and Tom's ten-year-old sister. I never did find out her real name but everyone called her Bump. Their house was this huge, rambling farmhouse with about seventeen rooms. They even had a music room with an upright piano. Not that they were rich or anything, or not so as they boasted about it. I got the impression the whole family worked pretty hard, and even Tom and me were expected to chip in with the chores.

That week was the best out of all my time at Christian Path, and probably one of the best times of my life. I suppose that's sad, seeing as I was only fifteen or so and I've lived so much more of life since then, but there you go. It was the first time since I'd left that cold house of my memory, with Mum's wailing filling the air, that I'd stayed in a real home with an actual family. Tom's parents genuinely seemed to like each other, which I have to say was somewhat surprising for me. Most evenings they'd switch on the radio and dance around the living room, pretending they were at a ball. Then Therese's husband might get up and say to Tom's mum, *May I have the pleasure?* and his mum would blush and say *Of course, kind sir,* and Therese would erupt in a fit of giggles. Everyone adored Bump, and Bump adored Tom. She followed us around the whole week, wanting to do whatever we were doing. Eventually Tom would get jack of it and tell her to go play with her dolls (which annoyed her 'cause she hated dolls and told him so), but most of the time he put up with her good-naturedly, and let her tag along. We took her swimming in the dam, where she was like a fish back in its natural habitat. She put me to shame.

Sometimes I'd look at Bump – watch her catching bugs or playing the fool – and think about how my sister Emily would have been just about her age.

Once I caught Tom watching me watching Bump. I was careful after that.

Tom's mum could cook up a storm. I must have put on five pounds. We were allowed as much fruit as we could eat; Tom and I had seconds at every meal, and dessert after dinner every night.

We went for long rambling walks through the countryside, exploring and finding all sorts of stuff. One day we found a fox skull and Tom let me keep it to take back to school. I even got to ride a horse. I watched the shearers at work. I saw Tom's dad get up each day and head off to a different corner of his land to do all kinds of strange and wonderful things – mend fences, tend to sick animals, discourage foxes, and cope with the problems of whitefly and weevils, of canker and leaf rust.

But the week had to come to an end. Tom's mum was good to me when we left to board the bus and the train; she gave me a huge slab of orange cake in a tin and told me I was welcome to come back anytime. Bump gave me a necklace she'd made herself out of cow's teeth. I don't mind admitting I felt the sting of tears that day, saying goodbye to them all.

After we got back to school, Tom and I stayed close for a time, and I was finally starting to think that maybe he was a friend, a true grown-up friend, not like the little kids I'd known in the Home.

Unfortunately, fate intervened in the form of a dysentery outbreak at the school in early 1954. Dozens of students fell ill and many were transferred to the local hospital. One boy died, an eleven-year-old named Stuart Little; his name had been lost for many years in my subconscious, but a few years ago, when that film came out, the one about the mouse, I remembered that kid, Stuart, and it's stuck with me ever since. They said his mum went mad with grief – she came to the school one day, shouting and cursing, her husband trying to get her back into their car, and eventually the ambulance came to take her away. After that, the school closed for a few weeks and all the boys were sent home. Not us, of course, the bursary boys, seeing as we had no homes to go to. We were all put into the one dormitory and had to endure endless games of Monopoly in which the supervising teacher, Mr Heslop, played with a competitive streak bordering on viciousness. Apparently he had drawn the short straw among the staff, and resented us for preventing him from being at home.

In any event, the crisis blew over, the school reopened, and the students drifted back, except for poor little Stuart. And Tom. He sent me a letter saying his dad had decided he needed more help on the property and, as Tom was now sixteen, his family thought it was more important for him to be earning his keep than continuing his education. His letter was full of unspoken disappointment. We corresponded a few times after that, and he even invited me back for another visit, but since he was no longer a student, the school couldn't see its way clear to paying my way, and I had no money of my own. Eventually we stopped writing altogether. A Christmas card that year was the last I heard from him.

I was lonely at the school after that. Whenever I got close to someone, something happened to get in the way. I became more and more isolated. At sixteen, I was wondering what to do with my life. When the recruitment people came to the school to consider kids interested in training for an apprenticeship, I put up my hand.

I'd had about enough of formal education as I thought could matter, and I was dead keen to learn a trade and make my way in the world. That was the one time in my life I was truly hopeful. I didn't realise at the time that no matter how big that balloon of optimism, all it takes is one small prick to burst it to nothingness.

The boy struggled to wake from his nightmare. His eyelids quivered and beads of sweat dotted his forehead. His bedsheets were twisted around his legs. He was in a murky, close space that smelt of earth and wet leaves. He could see twigs and feathers. But it was the sound that disturbed him … the sharp cracking of eggshells, over and over. He focused his eyes into the dark and saw two red pinpoints glaring malevolently back at him, growing rounder and larger as the creature to which they belonged crept closer. He tried to shrink away, but the outline of the creature came slowly into view: a half-formed turkey chick, its feathers slimy, its beak misshapen, its red eyes fixed on his. The boy cried out.

He raised himself up on one elbow and rubbed the vision from his eyes, blinking into the morning sunlight. He could feel his heart racing. He breathed deeply, waiting for calm to settle. Outside his window, the twittering of squabbling honeyeaters was interrupted by the mournful cry of a bird on the wing. A butcher bird swooped into the bush, and the smaller birds mushroomed upwards in a frightened cloud.

The boy planted his feet on the floor and applied the smell test to a pair of underpants.

It was a Monday, which meant his mum would be sleeping off her Sunday hangover. She played the pokies on Sunday afternoons with some girlfriends, but this always led to a counter meal with the girlfriends and some drinks with the girlfriends, which further led to meeting up with some of the girlfriends' boyfriends, and various other hangers-on, and that led to drinks with the boyfriends, and that led to … well, he didn't want to think about what that led to, but it usually meant she slept late and soundly on a Monday, and not often alone.

So it was a surprise when he entered the kitchen to find her sitting at the table, already dressed, nursing a mug of instant coffee and apparently *not* nursing a hangover. She smiled at him brightly and asked if he had slept well.

Yeah, he lied, wondering what was going on. His mother continued to gaze at him expectantly. He circled the table and made for the fridge, where he was further surprised to discover a fresh container of milk and a large tub of Greek yoghurt with mango flavouring, his favourite. He brought both to the table. He poured a tall glass of milk, levered the lid off the yoghurt and began spooning it directly into his mouth before whoever had taken his mother and replaced her with this stranger changed their mind and brought her back.

She was still staring at him, the twitch of a smile playing around her lips. *Well?*

Well what? he muttered.

She suddenly looked crestfallen and he remembered his manners.

Oh, thanks. Thanks for the yoghurt.

She sighed and rolled her eyes. *No, not that. I can't believe you've forgotten! Today's your special day! Happy birthday, my little man. Happy birthday.*

As she threw her arms around him, he could smell her first cigarette of the day on her breath.

He was surprised that he'd forgotten, but he was more astonished that his mum had remembered. Last year she'd been working, although she did take him to Pizza Hut after she'd finished her shift at eight o'clock. He'd been so tired by then that he'd barely summoned the energy to enjoy it. The year before she'd slept until lunchtime. The boy had waited in the house for her to wake up, his stomach a knot of anticipation. When she woke but didn't mention it, he knew she would say something after her shower. While she smoked a cigarette, he was certain she would produce a present after she'd eaten. By the time she'd dressed and left the house to meet someone, calling out to him that if he wasn't going to bother going to school, he could at least tidy the house a little – by that time he'd stopped waiting, and the knot in his stomach had dissolved into shame for having expected anything more than what had happened.

So it was startling to find her awake and sober.

My little boy, ten years old. Ten! I can't believe it. It seems like yesterday you were causing me so much pain trying to enter the world and now here you are, all grown up, taking care of your old mother.

The boy squirmed to escape her clinging, cloying embrace. He returned to the yoghurt. His mother sat down opposite him, staring at him.

So … he ventured after a while, into the silence. *So … you wanna do something today?*

Maybe today would be the day, the moment of his fantasies, when they would spend a happy day together and he would give her the stolen gold band.

His mother's eyes dropped to the table top and she scratched anxiously at a hardened lump of food stuck there.

Well, no, see, that's why I wanted to get up early, see, because I wanted to tell you myself that I have to go out today, you know, with Tobias? You know, the guy I've been seeing? He's taking me somewhere special today, had it planned for ages, and I didn't want to disappoint him, you know, he's taken the day off specially and everything. So, no, we can't.

The boy lowered his spoon.

Could we ... he began evenly, *could we ... maybe ... do something together then? Like, the three of us? Could I maybe come with you?*

His mother laughed, not unkindly. *Oh, no, I don't think so. I don't think what Tobias has in mind would be very suitable for you. No, that wouldn't work at all.*

The boy's grip tightened on his spoon until his knuckles glowed white. He hated himself for allowing his hopes to rise; he hated his mother for pretending. He pushed back his chair and threw his spoon into the sink.

Well I'm not going to school, if that's what you think. I don't care what you say.

She moved to his side and ruffled his hair, ignoring his outburst. *I wouldn't dream of letting you go to school on such a special day. That's the other thing I've got to tell you! I have a surprise for you! Something special, come and see!*

She grabbed his hand and began pulling him towards the back door. He allowed the bruised bud of excitement in his stomach to unfurl as he hurried behind her. Of course he didn't hate her. Of course.

She opened the door with a flourish and practically pushed him through. There on the verandah was a very shiny, very complicated, very expensive-looking bicycle. The paintwork was metallic blue. He counted the gears – twelve. He circled the bike like he would a spooked animal, fearful that it might lurch away into the morning. His mother stood in the doorway, beaming.

I hope you like the colour. They had red too, but I thought this was more like you. And you can adjust the seat here, see?

She began touching the bike's various workings almost in awe.

And these are the gears, and this is the brake, and it even has a water bottle, see? On its own little attachment here. And listen, here's the bell.

The bell tinkled merrily.

Well? she asked, after he hadn't spoken for several minutes. *Well? Don't you like it?*

His face changed in an instant from incredulity to adoration. He sprang at her, wrapping his arms around her and burying his face into her blouse.

I love it! I love it! Thank you so much! It's the best present ever! This is the best birthday I've ever had! You're the best mother in the world! Thank you, thank you, thank you!

His mother laughed and tickled him around his ribs. *I'm so glad you like it, baby. You can spend all day riding around, getting used to it. Try that big hill over by West Street; that would be so cool to go fast down there. Or you could ride around the park and over to the old quarry. I've gotta run and get ready, but you be careful and have fun now, OK?*

He gave her one last squeeze. *I will. Thanks, Mum, you're the best.*

As she disappeared back into the house, the boy struggled to drag the bike down the back stairs, cautious not to scratch the bright blue paintwork on the iron railings.

Walker and Co., Printers and Bookmakers, had operated out of the ground-floor offices of the Caxton building in the main street of Warwick since before both wars. It was situated between a bakery on one side and a fancy tea shop on the other, and to this day I can't smell the aroma of baking bread without conjuring up the waft of guillotined paper and wet ink.

There had been several apprenticeships on offer, but I had bypassed the building yards and barber shops to huddle over a lino-type machine at Walker's. My work was fiddly and slow, picking out the individual metal letters to line them up side by side, back to front. Any mistake earned me a clip over the ear from my supervisor or a dock in that month's pay. I learnt to be meticulous with those letters.

The concentration I needed to keep a steady hand and a keen eye kept my mind from wandering. I tried not to think about the past. I tried not to think about Emily, her harsh cries and the silence that followed. Her cooling skin, her half-closed eyes. I focused only on the future.

For the first time there was no-one dictating the parameters of my life.

I took lodgings with a family named Robinson. Mrs Robinson was a tough old bird with a cigarette permanently hanging out of the side of her mouth. She drank endless cups of tea and moaned about the lonely life of a war widow. Her husband had perished in the Great War, so I guess she'd had forty years for that loneliness to fester. She made ends meet by taking in boarders of the young, red-blooded male variety. She scared most of them off after the first month or so by wandering nonchalantly along the common hallway in nothing but her undergarments and a sheer lacy night-gown, emitting squeaks of feigned embarrassment when one of us ran into her unexpectedly. Like I said, she was lonely. But I didn't mind her so much, and it would take more than what she presented me with to turf me out of the first room I could truly call my own.

I say the Robinson family 'cause there were a few hangers-on. She had a son, Bert, who must've been pushing fifty – a completely useless bloke who couldn't change a light bulb, let alone a tap washer, and spent most of his time and his mum's money down at the pub. Then there were a couple of kids who were around a lot, although I could never quite figure out if they lived there or not. I think they must have been Mrs Robinson's grandkids. There was a sallow slip of a girl who was about four or five, and a couple of skinny boys around nine or ten that come to mind every time I catch sight of that skinny kid next door. And there was a moody teenage girl around my age who liked to act all high and mighty around us boarders, and hang her silk stockings out to dry above the bathroom tub for us all to see. Took after her grandmother in that respect. Anyway, I'd heard stories about Mrs Robinson having a run of bad luck with her own kids. The mother of some of the grandkids, Gloria, apparently dropped them at Mrs Robinson's door one day, announcing she'd left their prick of a father and was going off to America with a sailor. That's what I heard, anyway. So all in all, I figured she was doing what she had to do, and getting on with it. And like I said, I could put up with her shenanigans if it meant having my own space.

Not that the room was anything to write home about. It was at the rear of the house, overlooking the backyard dunny, and when the wind blew the wrong way I could practically diagnose the stomach complaints of anyone in the house. But it did have another double-hung window with a view out towards the park, and Mrs R had tried to make it nice with some homemade calico curtains. The bed was sturdy, but the mattress was saggy in the middle and had so many stains on it that I didn't like to look at it when I changed the sheets. With my first pay cheque, I went down to Acton's and bought myself my own pillow, the first time in my life I'd ever had one brand new. I had a pine wardrobe with hanging space, and a chest of drawers that doubled as a bedside table. There was a gooseneck lamp with a shabby greying fringe on the shade, and two pictures on the walls – a melancholy rendition of a forest glade, and a copy of one of those famous Vermeer paintings with a homely girl sitting in a parlour, engrossed in needlework. At least I assume it was a copy; I don't think Mrs Robinson would have been in a position to afford the original. So that was my room, and for a while there, with my room and my new job and my relative freedom, I was what I suppose you would call happy.

But like I said, it doesn't take much for the bubble to burst. And in my case, all it took was Maybelline Frost.

I often wonder what my life would've been like if I hadn't ever set eyes on Maybelline, or if she hadn't flashed her lashes at me, or if her uncle hadn't happened to be a local copper, or if she didn't turn out to have a husband.

But then I think about my life up to that point, and its trajectory since, and I honestly think those factors probably didn't make a blind bit of difference.

West Street was quiet at that time of day, the rat run of peak-hour morning traffic long since passed. A clear path. The slight incline at the north end of the street quickly descended into a downhill run worthy of a ski resort before flattening out to a wide plateau. The boy was on his fifth run. He pedalled furiously until the drop began, and then held on for dear life as the bicycle careened down the asphalt, swerving past parked cars and the mad dog with the death wish that kept materialising halfway down, barking frantically. The road angled hard to the left but the boy continued straight ahead, towards the scraggly triangle of nature strip that hugged the footpath. Finally the bike and the road parted company, the boy shouting in triumph as his bike leapt over the kerb, landed forcefully on the gravel and grass, and coasted to a halt among the trees. It beat school any day. He dropped his bike to the ground and sprawled beside it to catch his breath. He closed his eyes and could feel the wind whooshing past his ears, his hair flying around his head, the amazing sense of freedom of the downward rush.

What a fantastic present. Now he had wheels, transport. A means of escape from the gang that hung around the fish and chip shop. A way to get as far away from the house as quickly as possible, should the need arise. He felt a rush of warmth towards his mother, and decided to check out the gardens on the way home to see if he could find any flowers and put together a bunch for her.

One more go down the hill, and then he might cycle all the way out to the old water tower.

...

Two hours later he was pushing towards home, his aching legs like lead. He was happy and exhausted in equal measure. Hadn't ended up as such a bad day after all.

The air was crisp with late-autumn dusk. A flock of rainbow lorikeets, screeching on the wing, chased a pair of noisy mynahs before perching, victorious, upon the large branch of a eucalypt shading the footpath. The boy stopped to watch the mass of colourful birds hanging upside down, swaying, bickering over the seeds in a bird feeder.

He slowed as he approached the old man's place next door. A bush inside the fence was a riot of purple, the blooms boasting cheeky yellow bursts at their throats. The boy hesitated. There was no sign of the old man, no twitching of curtains at the front windows. He stood astride the bike, sensing the air. He swung his leg over, laid his bike gently on the ground and jumped the fence. The flowers were sturdy bells complete with intricate black tracery decorating the yellow. He picked four, breaking the stems as far down as he could.

A movement caught his eye: the old man was standing beside the wooden front steps. His trousers were pulled up almost to his armpits, and his faded grey shirt had frayed cuffs. He stared calmly at the boy.

The boy froze, undecided whether to bolt back over the fence with or without the flowers.

Nice bike, the old man said.

The boy took a possessive step backwards, his eyes fixed on the old man, his mouth a tight line.

Is it new?

The boy nodded mutely. He'd been bursting to show it off to someone, anyone.

Mind if I take a gander?

The old man made his way towards the gate and out to the footpath. The boy noticed the way he shuffled along, as if his feet hurt. For one apprehensive moment he was afraid the old man would kick the bike or haul it back into his yard, but he merely hunched over, his hands planted on his knees, and inspected it.

The boy wanted to stand next to him, to demonstrate the bell and explain the brakes, but he stood paralysed with the flowers in his hands. Eventually the old man swung his head up and gave the boy a grimace.

Well, come on then, I can't stand here all day. Are you going to ride it for me or not? Give me those flowers, will ya, you'll squash them into mush the way you're gripping them. Give them here and I'll mind them for you while you show me what this machine can do.

A cheeky grin found its way onto the boy's face. He approached the old man and tentatively handed him the broken blooms. The old man accepted them, shaking his head at the crude way they had been wrenched from the bush. The boy lifted the bike and sat astride it. He rode a little way up the street, returned and sped past the old man, his hands in the air, his face aglow. He skidded to a halt, circled, and jumped the bike in a series of sideways leaps he had been practising all day, before speeding up again and riding across the street and around the old man in a victory lap. His eyes were glittering spheres.

Well now, that's mighty impressive. You know, I had a bike that colour when I was your age. 'Course I was much more skilled, but I expect you'll get the hang of it.

His teasing expression stopped the boy's protest.

It's new, you say.

Yeah, birthday present. Today's my birthday.

You don't say. How about that. What are you, nine?

Ten. Ten today.

Ten. That's a mighty fine age for a boy to be. Ten. Believe it or not, I was ten once. Long time ago now, though.

He handed the boy the flowers.

Who're they for?

My mum. To say thanks. For the bike.

Hmm. Well, how about you come inside and I'll find some proper shears and we'll go round the back and you can choose some more, hey? Get yourself a decent bunch instead of these looking like something the cat dragged in. I might even find you a lemonade.

The boy hesitated.

I'm not supposed to go into a stranger's house, he said finally.

Hmm. I see. Quite right too. Although we're hardly strangers now, are we, we're neighbours. But anyway. Hmm. Well, how about this then. How about you come round to the side there, and stand right there near your fence, and I'll go inside and get the scissors and then we can choose some flowers together round the back. Would that be all right, do you think? If you don't come in the house?

He turned and made his way gingerly to the stairs without waiting for a reply.

The boy smiled. *That'd be OK, I guess.* He added, *And … I'm sorry. For taking the flowers without asking.*

The old man paused momentarily but did not look around, so the boy didn't see his lips curl into a smile.

Hmm, he said.

Maybelline Frost was a looker, no doubt about it. Tall for a girl, about five foot nine, with an hourglass figure she didn't bother to hide. Curves in all the right places. She liked to wear tight skirts and low-cut tops that didn't leave much to the imagination. Nowadays she'd probably blend right in, but back then she certainly turned some heads. Red was her favourite colour. Red lips, red nails long as talons. Bleached blonde hair that cascaded around her face. Pale skin, like she didn't see enough sun.

She worked in the bakery next to Walker and Co. Well, I say worked there, but her colleagues might have disagreed. Situation was, Maybelline Frost – a mere twenty-one years old and in the prime of her life – was married to Colin Frost, the baker, who must have been fifty if he was a day. Old Colin never saw the sun either. He was at work kneading dough and firing up the ovens from 3 am. He'd emerge about lunchtime all covered in flour, like a creepy snowman, and he'd amble off home and sleep until the early evening. All this I found out later, of course. Their routine. At first, all I knew was Maybelline Frost, the look of her, the scent of her perfume as she leant against the wall outside the bakery, luring in the customers. Being one of the youngest apprentices, I used to do the lunch run. I'd go around Walker's and collect everyone's change and then I'd go next door and purchase whatever they'd all ordered – sausage rolls, pies, thick white-bread sandwiches with ham and pickle fillings.

They should've warned me. It was sport to them, I suppose. The new boy, doesn't know jack. I'll bet they all sat back and watched, laughing their heads off, while I proceeded to make a complete fool of myself. She was like a painted fly, that woman, and I was the sucker fish all too keen to take the bait.

Sugar, she'd call me. *Sugar.* Like in the movies. *Hi, sugar. How you doing this morning, sugar?* with the faint trace of her Oklahoma roots. I heard later that Maybelline had grown up like a wild blossoming weed in the midst of her southern family's carefully manicured flowerbed of a life. They were church people, I heard, Baptist, and real strict. But apparently at thirteen Maybelline was drinking and all, and by fifteen she'd hooked up with a sailor and got herself pregnant. I never did quite work out how the family sorted out the intricacies and inconveniences, but the upshot was Maybelline got transported halfway across the world to her aunt and uncle in Australia. I guess her parents figured some distance wouldn't hurt and, with her uncle being a copper and all, I s'pose they thought he'd pull her into line. Seems maybe Maybelline's mother hadn't seen her brother in a while, 'cause while Jack Summers was a policeman all right, that's about as far as his reputation ran – in title only. Uncle Jack was on the take left, right and centre, in tight with all the local mischief-makers and petty crims. And when he got bored doing deals, he'd slap his missus around a bit. She was long-suffering, that one. Anyway, to cut a long story short, Jack owed Colin Frost a favour. There were many a morning Uncle Jack would be at the bakery before sunrise, and if anyone thought it was strange that the local police chief was helping the baker unload his flour, I never heard anyone voice the opinion, although rumour had it that there was more than self-raising in those daily deliveries. But Colin turned a blind eye and so, to even things up, Jack introduced his fresh-off-the-boat niece – Maybelline – to his old pal Colin, and within three months they were married. Life with Colin must have looked more attractive than going back home to Ma and Pa. And if that was the case, then home in the States must have been real bleak.

Actually, with the clear vision of hindsight, I feel a touch sorry for Colin. His first wife had run off with the fishmonger early in their marriage, and he'd had to deal with a lot of jokes about loaves and fishes. And while getting hitched to twenty-one-year-old Maybelline might have seemed like a sweet piece of luck to old Colin, she was quite a handful. At the time of my Maybelline troubles, she and Colin had been married a year or so, and he was in the throes of protective jealousy. To look at *her*, though, you'd never even tell she was spoken for.

It ended badly, of course. Me with my newfound job and income and aspirations, Maybelline starting to realise that maybe escaping to Colin and the bakery wasn't such a grand idea after all. Add some flirtation from her and an eager response from me, and before I knew it I was pinned against the wall in the alley behind Thommo's pub, with two big galahs in coppers' uniforms holding me down while Jack Summers delivered well-aimed punches to my face and stomach with each sentence of the lecture he was giving me about keeping my eyes off other blokes' women.

When dawn broke the next morning, the sunlight bored a hole right through my skull and I was sure I could feel my brains oozing out. My left eye was swollen shut, my lips were stuck together with dried blood, and my ribs hurt like at least three were broken.

And then the day got worse.

I stumbled up the path to Mrs Robinson's, hoping for a bath and some sympathy. I found my bags, roughly packed, sitting on the porch. The teenage girl who had been practising sneering at me had perfected it – she informed me that fighting was not allowed and that as only young men of reputable character were welcome in their home, I was out on my ear.

When I arrived at work later that day, full of apologies for my tardiness, I was regretfully informed by Mr Walker that he had decided to *let me go*.

Go where? I wanted to ask.

I very quickly discovered that the long arm of the law could reach out its grubby tentacles very far indeed, and that when a no-hoper like me was down, there was no limit to the kickings that could be inflicted.

The morning was grey and chill, and by late afternoon the weather had not improved. Sudden flurries of wind brought a scattering of leaves and timid raindrops. The boy was immersed in the adventure and danger of *Treasure Island* while huddled on the verandah. Every so often a rent in the ominous clouds would allow a shaft of sunlight to pierce through with ferocious warmth. The boy wriggled his toes. He rested the book against his chest, leant back and closed his eyes, picturing the scene in the book as clearly as a movie at the cinema. The clouds parted again. The warmth on his face made him drowsy. He marked his page and made his way towards the fence, the book dangling from his hand.

The old man was out in the yard again. The boy couldn't imagine what he found to do out there all day. He seemed to have a never-ending routine of weeding and watering and pruning and chicken feeding. His garden certainly seemed much better cared for than the boy's patch of tangled weeds and gnarled bushes. But it wasn't formal or overdone – just sort of *loved*. The boy found a place behind a clump of trailing vine that shrouded an old hibiscus. He wrapped his arms around his knees and the book, and watched.

The chickens were out of their pen, strutting and pecking at whatever small bugs were brave enough or stupid enough to be wandering about the yard in broad daylight. The boy listened. Amongst the scratching and occasional clucking of the birds, he could hear another sound – a steady cheeping. He crept closer to the fence. Definitely the peeping of new chicks. He quickly scanned the yard. The old man had disappeared into the shed. The boy could hear him humming, and the muffled sounds of implements being shifted around. The old man reappeared carrying a large pair of shears, then climbed the back stairs in his lopsided gait and went into the house.

The boy scrambled over the palings, dropping with a soft thud to the ground. He wedged his book into the forked branch of a scrubby bush, out of reach of the chooks, and made his way closer to the henhouse, peering into the murky interior. As his eyes adjusted to the gloom, he could make out five, no, six baby chicks in a small wire enclosure at the back of the structure. They circled in a panic as he approached, chirping and flapping their wings. Three yellow, two with brown and white markings, and one the velvety black of a night sky, its round eyes sparkling like two stars. The boy searched the wire netting until he discovered a crude latch. He unwound the wire securing it, reached in and attempted to grab the black chick. The six small creatures went mad, hopping and cheeping loudly. He didn't want to grab too hard or too fast and hurt them. His hand chased them around the enclosure. He gave up on catching the black chick – he would settle for any of them – but the soft, slippery down of their coats eluded him.

After a while he stopped trying. He sat and watched as they calmed down, their urgent chirps quieting as they practised pecking the ground and fluffing their feathers.

Very slowly, the boy returned his hand to the cage, gradually edging closer and closer to the birds, until his fingers sat in their midst. The chicks hurried against him, their warm bodies brushing his skin. His patience paid off – the black chick, as oblivious to his hand as to the old bit of corn cob beside it, settled backwards into his embrace, contentedly pecking at the ground. Slowly … slowly … and then the boy closed his fingers around the chick and lifted him triumphantly.

He settled back on his haunches against the henhouse wall, the black chick cupped in his hands. He lifted one finger, then two, and peeked in at the tiny animal nestled in his hands. He could feel its scratchy feet grazing his palm. He could feel its heart beating fast. The boy didn't know if that was normal, or if the poor thing was panicked. Its glittering eyes stared up at him. Gradually he splayed his fingers open. The bird hopped cautiously, and then fluttered upwards in an abrupt flap. The boy caught it and laughed as the chick stretched its wings and jumped from one hand to the other, cheeping noisily, its siblings answering from below.

I see you've met my new girls.

The boy glanced up nervously. The chick saw its chance and plunged into the void, landing with a bruised squeak on the ground. The old man strode forward and scooped it into his hand before it had time to decide which way to run.

Firm but gentle, that's the key, he said. *Don't give 'em a chance to think.* He dropped the chick back into the boy's hands. *Like chicks, do you?*

Are they girls then? the boy asked. He patted the downy feathers with one outstretched finger.

That's right, girls. No use for the boys, only grow up to be noisy buggers. Not real good egg layers, either, he said.

The boy glanced up, and caught the old man's wink.

A beat of silence.

I've never held one before, he said quietly.

The old man took a step back in mock horror. *Never? Never held a chick? Aarr, what a deprived life you youngsters lead nowadays.*

Here, I'll tell you what. How about we let them all out into the yard for a bit of a scratch?

The boy's eyes widened.

On one condition though, mind. My legs aren't what they used to be, and I'm in no fit state to be running after them. That's why they've been stuck inside here the last few days. Be good for them to get out, get some sunshine, maybe find a worm to worry. But we can only do it if you promise to help me get them all back in again once we're done watching them have some fun. What do you reckon, deal?

He held out his hand. The boy cradled the chick with his left hand against his chest, and shook the old man's hand solemnly.

Deal, he said. A small smile curled around his lips and ignited his eyes.

After the business with Maybelline Frost, I drifted along for a time, homeless and unemployed, all that pain behind me, and my dead sister like a millstone round my neck.

I took in labouring work when I could get it, or fruit picking with foreign workers on the outlying farms, where the owners didn't much care what you'd done as long as you could fill up a basket without bruising the fruit.

I still caught sight of her every now and then when I went into town, craving a cold beer to wash the dust from my throat. And I'd see her, red nails flashing in the sun, her long hair bouncing down her back. I don't think she was a bad 'un, not really. She can't have had an easy life, banished from home, losing the baby, winding up married to someone old enough to be her father. I guess she didn't know any better. She'd catch my eye, and there'd be all sorts of things passing across her face – a timid hunger, like she was starving for some more of those stolen kisses we'd shared, and maybe regret at the thought that she wasn't going to get any more. 'Cause I'd learnt my lesson, well and truly. I kept my distance. I'd still get the evil eye from Jack Summers and his mates from the constabulary if ever I strayed too close, and after a few months of feeling like an intruder in the place, or at least a visitor who's outstayed his welcome, I decided to move on.

I caught a lift with a truck driver who was transporting a load of grapes. I still recall the scent of the fruit, and the sound of Doris Day on the radio singing 'Que Sera Sera', and thinking, yep, that's it, whatever will be will be.

There's something to be said for the kind of freedom that allows a man to up sticks and leave town, all his worldly possessions carried in his two hands, to go wherever the wind blows him.

At the end of that long, hot drive, I climbed down from the cab and the truckie threw my two bags after me onto the dust at my feet. I raised my hand but the rig was already rolling.

The city of Melbourne was churning with people for the Olympics and I joined the throng, taking work where I could and laying my head wherever I found a soft place to fall. I knew nobody and not a soul knew me. Thoughts of the Home and the school, even thoughts of Maybelline Frost, all seemed so distant. Another world, another life. Only Emily persisted, creeping through my dreams. The memory of my father, the shadow of my mother, and Emily, observing my every move, a silent witness to my unfolding life.

...

At first I watched the woman in the department store from afar, but as I became braver, I hovered around the confectionery counter. Miss Edith Flower, her name tag said. I was self-conscious; children with sweet-streaked faces avoided me, and their mothers stared hard, distrustful, until I walked away.

In appearance she was as opposite to Maybelline as you could get – polished olive skin, jet-black hair cut into a bob, and large dark eyes that seemed to absorb everything around her without reflecting anything back. Later on I'd gaze into those eyes and see nothing but a pool of black and brown, an endless whorl of chocolate. She wore a cute little uniform – a figure-hugging black skirt with a crisp white shirt and a candy-pink scarf knotted jauntily around her neck.

I'd dawdle beside the book counter opposite, pretending to be interested in the latest bestseller, and glance up from time to time when I heard her serving customers, so she wouldn't notice me staring. After a few weeks of that, of me reading lots of covers but never buying anything, she called me over. It was pretty funny really: she called out *hey mister*, and I looked around, to my left and to my right, like on a cartoon, trying to see who she was talking to. *You,* she said, pointing right at me. *We've got free samples of rock candy today. Would you like to try some?* And that was the beginning of Edith talking to me, although it was still a few weeks before I started talking back.

Speaking to her blotted out the awfulness that had gone before.

I'd never eaten many sweets 'til then, no money for them as a kid, and no inclination as I got older, but I swear I damn near became addicted to sugar, seeing as how I always felt the need to buy whatever she was recommending that day. Addicted to Edith Flower too, if I'm honest.

One day I was at the confectionery counter, and Edith and I were involved in our usual routine.

Morning, mister. Your usual selection? Let's see, fruit jubes ... saltwater taffy ... atomic fireballs ...

But this time I opened my mouth and the word tumbled out.

No.

Sorry? Did you say something?

I mean, no ... no thanks. No atomic fireballs.

I could feel my heart hammering in my chest. I wiped my sweaty palms on the sides of my trousers.

But you always have atomic fireballs.

I don't really like them. They're too hot. They make my mouth feel like the inside of a boiler.

Edith sat back on her stool, and she shook her head in disbelief.

Well, if you don't just take the cake, mister. Nearly every day now for weeks you've been coming in here and I've been making you up a bag of your favourites and putting in atomic fireballs and it's only now you tell me you don't like them. Jeez, I didn't even know you could talk. I had you figured for one of those mute people who can't say nothing.

And that's where we started.

The boy and the old man stood side by side in the wells of dank shade thrown by the giant avocado tree. It listed crazily to one side, where its beginnings had grown under the graft twenty years earlier. Glossy leaves hid the burgeoning fruit. The boy stared up through its branches at the intricate patterns of light and shadow forming and re-forming over the china blue of the sky.

It's like a kaleidoscope, he said.

The old man followed his gaze. *Yep,* he said, *that it is.*

The chicks sure like it under here.

Too right. Lots of leaf mulch and rotting avocados – perfect conditions for grubs and bugs and all sorts of creepy crawlies. You'd love it too if you were a chicken.

The six chicks were busily investigating under each fallen leaf and inside every hole in the soil. The older birds were rather selfish, the boy thought, as he watched a particularly strident hen pull a reluctant caterpillar from the underside of a weed and gulp it down.

A buxom cloud scudded across the sky.

The man rummaged through the leaf litter, plucking out avocado seeds. He collected a handful and threw them beyond the shed and out of the hens' reach.

Seeds make 'em sick. Give 'em the runs. Skins too. Stupid hens'll eat 'em though. Don't know what's bad for them.

He shaded his eyes with his hand.

Ever lie on your back and look up at the clouds?

Sometimes.

I used to do that a lot when I was a boy. Get away from the others for a spell. I'd lie down and stare up into that endless sky until it felt like the ocean, and I was in danger of falling right off into the depths. Used to have to hang on tight to the weeds to stop myself!

Sometimes I see shapes, said the boy.

Yeah? What type of shapes?

Animals, trains, fruit ... once I saw a map of Africa, I swear!

I don't doubt it, my boy. You live long enough, you see a lot of strange things in the clouds. In fact, you live long enough, you see a lot of strange things, full stop. I used to think that maybe there was a whole other world up there, cloud world, with cloud buildings and cloud animals and all, and little cloud people lying on their backs gawking down and thinking they could make out the shapes of people and cows and such down here on earth. Wouldn't that be something, huh? Cloud world. I haven't thought of that for quite some years.

The boy watched the clouds as they panned across the sky. He thought he saw a chicken.

Best be getting these ladies back inside before the sun sets. Remember your promise, now. The old girls'll go in themselves with a little persuading, but these youngsters, you'll need to pick them up. And you gotta catch them first. That's it ... gentle now, like I showed you. Cup her in your hands, that's the way.

The boy allowed himself a secret smile as he squatted and shuffled after the lively chicks.

They go everywhere except where they're supposed to! he protested. *How come they don't follow their mums, anyway?*

Well, for one, they're not too smart. And second, I bought them direct. Those girls are no relation.

The boy thought how lucky the chicks were to have ended up in the old man's backyard, scratching in the dirt, watched over by a clucky group of females, none of whom were their mothers.

At last the fowls were all back safely in their henhouse, except for the black chick. The boy was giving her one last reluctant stroke.

Hold on there a minute, will you? said the old man. *I'll be right back.*

The boy sat in the cool henhouse, the smell of hay dust and chook poo combining pleasantly in his nostrils. He wondered if the old man would mind if he came again.

The old man stooped as he entered the lean-to. He shuffled over to the boy, holding a small tin of something in his left hand.

Hold her still now, he instructed the boy.

He reached down and with a shaking finger, crooked with arthritis, he daubed a spot of yellow paint on top of the chick's black head.

Just hold her there a minute 'til it dries, he said.

There. All done. You can put her back in with the others now.

The boy lowered the cheeping chick in with her siblings and fastened the wire latch. *Why the paint?*

So you can tell your chick from the others.

The boy stared hard at the packed dirt floor. Particles of chaff floated in the air, drifting up with each flap of a hen's wing.

Mine? My chick?

Sure. You like her, don't you? I'll make you a deal. You come visit her regularly, any time you like. You can let them all out, give them a run around, so long as you latch that wire properly when you leave. How does that sound?

The boy's smile changed the countenance of his face, disappearing the anxious lines and worried features into an expression of pure joy. He grinned as he squinted up at the thin frame of the old man leaning against the rough-hewn wood.

Shit, he exclaimed. *Awesome.*

Yeah orright, watch your language. The old man lifted his hat and ran a hand through his thinning hair. *When I was a lad, I lived for a time with a group of boys; there must've been ... erm, let's see ... about fifty or sixty of us. And there was always the danger of whatever you had being pilfered by some other fellow who took a shine to it. So we took to dabbing a spot of paint on our belongings, to identify them, you see. My colour was a shade of purpley-blue that I mixed up myself so it was hard to replicate. They couldn't copy it, I mean. Yellow was the colour of my best friend, Archi.*

The old man rested his hand for a moment on the boy's hair, the weight of it no more than a touch. His rheumy eyes stared off at something the boy couldn't see. He blinked, then rubbed his knuckles into his eyes and cleared his throat with a raspy sputter.

Damn dust. Well, that's enough of that. You mind that latch, you hear?

He shuffled out the door as the boy lay on his stomach and touched his chick through the wire.

But you're different already, he said quietly. *You're the only black one.*

...

Autumn days slid soundlessly into a mild Brisbane winter. School was out for two weeks and the boy could stay home with not a twinge of guilt. It wasn't that he disliked his teacher or even the learning; more that, once inside the perimeter of the noisy throng of children, he felt disconnected and alone – far more alone than during the days he spent by himself riding his bike or reading. His family and his life seemed so far removed from what he heard discussed in the playground at break. He had never gone to a match at Suncorp or the Gabba, no-one read to him at night, if he wanted a clean shirt he often as not had to wash it himself, fast food was not a treat but a staple. Unlike most of the kids in his class, he regularly lit the gas and used the stove, frequently stayed home alone, and was almost never questioned or reprimanded.

Sometimes he felt childlike and naïve in his estrangement; occasionally he felt a superior maturity.

The result of this paradox was that being at school was like an unnatural confinement. He persevered because of the books and the library, the timelines and the experiments, the questions and the answers. He enjoyed the excursions, when there was money enough to attend – or when he had slipped it unnoticed from his mum's purse. He hated the sports, despite the fact that he could catch a ball and run as fast as anyone. Whenever he started at a new school, he was always the first picked for teams, once the leaders had spotted his potential. But he quickly developed a reputation for sullenness and contrariness: he took a catch only when it suited him, and crossed the line as the mood took him. He wasn't a *team player*. This strange combination of ability and reticence, skill and defiance, seemed to bewilder the others, and in response they retreated from his company.

Which suited him fine. He was happy to wander alone or sit under a tree with a book. He knew he wouldn't stay long anyway, and what was the point of making friends if you only had to leave them? It was an early life lesson that had proved itself to him over and over again.

But the arrival of school holidays provided a respite from the vagaries of the playground. He was free. No-one to answer to, no-one to impress or please or accommodate.

He had spent the day exploring the tracks of Mount Coot-tha, surprising bush turkeys, perfecting jumps on his bike, staking out the boundary of Channel Nine to see if he could spot a celebrity. He disturbed a brown snake and it slithered into the brush, the dry leaves crackling; all that remained was a wavy line in the sand. He had found more than four dollars in the vending machines and splurged on a chocolate ice-cream. On sunset he had set down his bike on the uppermost lookout and stood with a dozen tourists, draped over the railing, gazing down through the failing light at the city spread out like a quilt, puckered in places by its hills and gullies, and with the river – a silver-blue vein – flowing through its heart. Behind him a kookaburra called raucously.

In the distance he could see the towers of the CBD. He tried to count the floors on one building but only got to twelve before his eyes blurred and shifted. Jet-black crows swooped within arm's reach, and a cluster of cockatoos with startling yellow plumage soared forward before landing proprietarily on a tall gum, distorting his sense of space and distance. He felt for a moment that he could climb up onto the railing and – with arms wide and knees bent – spring upwards and outwards, take flight into the endless space above the city, and coast with the currents on outstretched limbs. It was a pleasant thought. Appealing. Perhaps he had been a cockatoo in a former life.

A woman in a uniform and a red beret flourished a triangular flag and shouted instructions to a group of Japanese tourists. Chatting and pointing, cameras aloft, they followed her to their bus.

Bye bye! they exclaimed, to no-one in particular. The boy waved.

The bus roared away, leaving a cloud of grey exhaust in its wake. Most of the other sightseers had departed. One couple still sat in the covered gazebo at the highest point, kissing, making out as if they were alone in the entire world. A man surveyed the brass compass etched into the pavement, his cigarette a bright pinpoint in the gathering dusk. Staff left the café, their voices vanishing into the distance.

Lights began to twinkle in the buildings far below. Streets threaded through the city, stitching together the shadowed nest of the cemetery, the steely span of the Story Bridge, the illuminated ferris wheel. Beyond, the coastal islands were shrouded in violet.

By the time he skidded his bike to a stop in his yard, scattering gravel in its wake, it was truly dark. A single bulb burned dim from the old man's house, while his own lay still and quiet. As he approached the back stairs, the dry leaves beneath crackled as a small shape scurried. He paused, unnerved, thinking of the snake he had seen earlier. He stared intently into the blackness but whatever had passed had dissolved into more blackness. He pounded up the steps, which vibrated under his feet. The noise – he hoped – would alert anything or anyone to his presence. He felt better as he locked the door behind him, and then went from room to room, switching on lights, chasing the shadows. In the kitchen he found fresh strawberries. He heated water for two-minute noodles and set about mixing leftover sausage and grated carrot to put on top. He opened a can of tuna and threw that in too. He heaped his plate with food and settled on the couch to eat. *Deal or No Deal* kept him company.

When he opened his eyes some time later, a black-and-white western flickered on the TV, strobing the room. He blinked into the glare, confused, shivering. His plate had slid onto the carpet. A small pool of noodles sat jelly-like on the floor. He scraped the leavings onto the plate, carried it into the kitchen and dumped it in the sink, flipping switches as he left each room.

He peed into the toilet, a long, satisfying stream, and then made his way to his bedroom. The boy slipped under the covers and jiggled his legs with the cold, his skin retreating from the clammy sheets. Gradually his body created a warm, comforting spot, and he relaxed once more into sleep.

...

He woke with a start. The hall light was on. He could hear his mother's voice, laughing, faltering, thick with alcohol. He heard deeper male grunts. All of a sudden the three of them were in his room. His mother wore her tight black skirt. It had slipped around her waist so that the zip was near the front, off centre, half-undone. Her blouse gaped open and he could see her large breasts

66

spilling over the top of her bra. Her hair had been piled up on top of her head, but now it fell around her face in untidy spirals. Her lipstick was smeared. He could smell her sour breath as she teetered towards him and fell with a rough groan onto his bed.

This here is my boy, she crooned. *Darling … my precious baby … my best boy, aren't you, darling?*

One of the men extended his hand in mock politeness, laughing as he overbalanced and landed on the floor. The boy had never seen him before.

The other man's head was haloed in a pale yellow glow from the beam behind him. He stayed in the doorway. The boy couldn't make out his features.

It's the middle of the night, Mum. Get off. Go to bed. You've been drinking too much.

Oh, he's a self-righteous bastard, isn't he? The first man got to his feet unsteadily. *Not very welcoming, hey?*

The boy's mother lifted one manicured hand and stroked her nails along the side of his face, then threaded her fingers through his hair. *You leave him alone; he's a good boy, aren't you. Come on,* she said, grunting as she hefted herself off the bed, *let's continue the party elsewhere. Let my boy get his beauty sleep.*

She clung on to the man by the bed, and the two pushed past the other man and lurched out the door. The boy pulled the covers around himself and watched the second man. He took a step forward. Where the first man was bulky and uncoordinated, this one was slight and wiry, the sinews in his arms shining like scales. His eyes were the colour of road tar. They bored into the boy, and he felt like a rabbit frozen in headlights, or a rat pinned beneath the death stare of a cobra. The boy could not say he saw the man move, but in a moment he was there, leaning over him. His glare remained unbroken. The boy stared back, mesmerised by those unblinking eyes. The man reached out his hand and touched the boy's face, his fingertips skimming so delicately that the boy felt all the hairs on his skin tingle. Slowly, the man's nails scratched a fine trail from the boy's forehead to his chin.

In a voice smooth like molten chocolate, he parodied the mother's words.

You're a good boy, aren't you … but I don't think you need any more beauty sleep …

The boy stayed entirely still, his whole body tense, transfixed by the fact of the man, his nearness, his pulsing power.

Come on, big boy, we're wai-ting … called his mother in a lilting voice. We're lonely in here, come and liven up the party …

Without haste, the man withdrew his hand and tilted his head closer to the boy as if he was about to whisper something, but only a ghost of a smile tightened his lips. He drew back, and then was gone.

Edith lived with her parents in a tidy stucco workers' cottage in Footscray. Her two brothers had already moved away. Her father was on a disability pension and mostly sat around in his singlet, watching the football. I had a lot of time for her mother, Edna, a busy, rotund woman with a ready smile and a bucketload of patience for her indolent hubby. *Call me Mrs E,* she told me, the first time we met.

I began walking out with Edith. Before too long her infectious talking wore down my defences. She'd chat about the weather or the football or the people she worked with, and I'd try to keep up my end of the conversation. Never mentioned my days at the Home, though, and certainly never mentioned my sister. That was too raw and too hard for me to even think about explaining. Sometimes there are rooms in your mind that are places of long-ago sadness or despair, and you lock them up tight and throw away the key, or at least hide it pretty good. I had a few such rooms and I wasn't planning on entering them for anyone, not even Edith.

Sometimes I see the lad next door and I recognise that he might have a few of those rooms himself. I picture him wandering around there, inside his head, peering through keyholes and then backing away real quick before the door swings open. It's not pleasant, that recognition, but I figure what with all the disasters and wars and family squabbles that go on in the world, there's probably quite a few people with sorrow locked away in the gloomy recesses of their minds.

The kid's a closed book. Barely says boo. I knew kids like him at the Home. Carrying around secrets and lies enough that he's got the weight of the world on his shoulders. I suppose I was a bit like that myself. Perhaps that's the connection that binds us together. Or the fear that keeps us still apart.

Makes you think, though. What I know about kids you could fit on the end of a pin. Space left over. I wonder about Emily, and how she might have turned out. How the two of us would've coped there with Mum. I reckon the pair of us would've had a weight on our shoulders. I catch the boy's eye sometimes and I see a shadow across his face. A hard edge to his features. At least Emily was spared that.

No, I didn't tell Edith about my sister. Or the Home. I couldn't. Those were things I was unable to put into words. But even without sharing my past, Edith and I gradually got to know each other. We danced in other people's kitchens and made new friends. I started to believe that I had found someone I could confide in. I found work with a printing company again. The familiar smells of kerosene, linseed oil and fresh ink on paper. The rhythmic thumps of heavy machinery.

And then she got pregnant.

...

They say it only takes once. With Edith and me, it was five times, not that I was counting.

Edith was much more confident than me in the area of intimacy. She had no problem holding my hand in public or throwing her arms around me for a cuddle when the mood took her. So

I suppose it was natural that she'd take the lead. Truth be told, I reckon she was more experienced than me in that department, though given my history, I suppose that wouldn't have been difficult.

The first time it happened was in March. I recall it was the first chilly evening we'd had after a scorcher of a summer, the temperature plummeting and raindrops whipping against my face as I waited on her parents' front porch. Through the window I could see her mum hurrying out from the bathroom, wiping her hands on a towel. She threw a scowl at Edith's dad, who gave the impression of being nailed down to that sofa, like he wasn't getting up for nobody. She opened the door and beckoned me in with her usual kindly words, asking about my work and tut-tutting about the weather.

Are you sure you want to be out in this? Why don't you young people stay home here with us tonight, I've got a jam roly-poly in the oven and we were thinking about a game of Scrabble, weren't we, dear? Dear? DEAR?

Mrs E always claimed her husband's hearing got damaged in the war, but I wasn't so sure. There were times she was nigh on yelling right in his direction, and he wouldn't even twitch a muscle to indicate he'd heard her, but I swear I'd see a glint in his eye when he finally turned his head. More than once I thought that maybe Old Joe had heard enough of Mrs E over the years and figured she didn't have anything new to say, so he simply tuned out.

Anyway, the idea of a night in with Mrs E's cooking sounded all right to me, and I was just saying so when Edith appeared from out the back where she had a little bedroom made out of what used to be a pantry.

What's all this talk? You promised to take me to that new place for a meal and some bingo!

Well, the weather's so bad, I thought … I drifted off when I saw her adorable face all puckered into a frown, and I knew I'd lost.

'Course I did! Come on, get your coat, we'll make a dash for the train while the rain's slowed.

But once we were outside and out of view of the house, Edith led me in the opposite direction to the train, back towards the bus.

Let's go back to your place.

But ... I've only now come from there. I thought you wanted to play bingo?

Stuff bingo, I want to play with you.

She said that last bit in a voice she used sometimes when we were alone, a voice so sultry that I felt myself stiffen right there in the middle of the footpath.

But what about Mrs E? You know she doesn't approve of us being alone over at my place, even during the day.

What Mum don't know can't hurt her. Come, on baby, pleeease? I think it's time we got to know each other a little better ... don't you?

She reached up then and put both her arms around my neck and began nuzzling my ear, right there in front of whoever chanced to be passing by. Her warm tongue was flicking in and out of my ear and I thought I would collapse with pleasure. I grabbed her hands and made for the bus stop.

By the time we reached my place I was worked up pretty good. Edith had chosen the back seat of the bus, me trailing behind, and she had her hands all over me during the ride home. I kept glancing towards the front to see if the driver had noticed. I could feel my face, warm and flushed. At one point another young woman shot us a disapproving glare. I think that might've been after I groaned a little.

I'm sure the driver took the long way round 'cause that bus ride seemed to last forever. A cold drizzle left tracks on the other side of the steamy glass. Edith wrote our initials inside a clouded heart.

At the flat, I couldn't seem to fit the key into the lock and eventually Edith took it from me and did it herself. I wondered if she was feeling as het up as me, and if so, how she could act so calm and capable. Once we were inside I thought I should at least offer her a drink, but she would have none of it. She was a woman with one thing on her mind.

Don't get me wrong, we'd fooled around before, but I'd always made sure we didn't get carried away. I'd never let things get as far as they did that day. We were always careful.

We ended up on top of the faded chenille bedspread, wrestling and scratching and pulling at each other. Before I knew it my trousers were off and Edith was pretty much naked and we were under the covers, skin to skin. She was soft and silky, but her breasts were firm under my hands, and she kissed my throat and my chest and ran her fingers down my abdomen until I thought I might pass out. Then she took my hand and placed it between her legs. I could feel the soft mound of hair and under that a moist tender spot that yielded under the pressure of my fingers. Right when I thought I was surely having a heart attack, she manoeuvred me around somehow and slipped me inside her and I got this surge of energy and passion and heat. I recall thrusting and bucking so hard that afterwards I thought I might have hurt her.

So that's pretty much how it went after that. Edith went at it hell for leather whenever she got the opportunity, and I went along for the ride. And each of those four more times I couldn't believe my luck. A fella surely wasn't gonna complain.

I know what you're thinking – what about protection? Surely he wasn't that stupid. Well, I'm ashamed to say that yes, I was that stupid, or maybe naïve if you were being kind about it. Truth is, each time it happened I was that caught up in the moment – that unbelieving and grateful that we were even doing it at all – that the notion of protection never even crossed my mind. In the light of day, of course, like sitting on the bus the next morning, a thought would niggle in the back of my mind. I'd wonder about the workings of a woman's body, and I'd consider what Edith might be doing to prevent those workings, but I knew so little about it myself that I wasn't exactly sure what I should be concerned about. And despite our nocturnal fumblings and exchanges of bodily fluids, I was much too embarrassed to ask her directly.

We were in the cinema when she told me, the old Esquire in Bourke Street – gone now. Some years later they incorporated it into yet another shopping centre. Apparently under that ghastly grey cladding, the original Edwardian façade lies hidden, crying out to be uncovered. It was a true old lady – stately, cavernous, with as many decorative bits and pieces as a grand dame's overskirt. We were watching some film about a homely girl who couldn't get a boyfriend but she had this sweet, sweet voice, and then she finally found a man and he got himself killed and she was all alone again. Right depressing it was. And Edith whispered something in my ear and I only caught the word *pregnant* and I sat there confused for a moment, thinking that I must have missed that bit in the movie, when I noticed Edith's eyes shining out at me and I realised she was talking about herself. And me. About us.

My education about all things sexual got brought up to speed right quick, I can tell you.

Her parents were pretty decent about it, I have to say. Mrs E spent the first few weeks crying every time Edith so much as glanced at her, and she avoided my eye altogether, but then once she'd come around to the idea, she started crying every time she saw me, in between taking me in her arms and squeezing the life out of me and telling me how I was one of the family. I hadn't been one of the family, any family, for so long – not since that one week with my friend Tom. So that was rather nice.

Old Joe took me aside after he heard the news and gave me the token speech about carelessness and a woman's honour and a man's responsibility, but it lost its sting when he gave a chuckle and mumbled something about *sowing wild oats* and *best days of your life*.

Mind you, didn't stop him insisting that we had to get married.

The boy woke to the sounds of a howling wind tearing viciously through the house; the walls creaked and groaned in protest. Outside his window the fig tree swayed sideways under the assault. Gusts of leaves eddied in great clouds. The sky was the overcast hue of an elephant's hide.

Sunday. The last day of the holidays. School tomorrow, should he choose to go. *She* wouldn't notice or much care if he didn't. He thought he might. He liked the routine of it, the rules. Unlike the blurred lines surrounding schoolyard banter and games, he knew where he stood with the rules. Raise your hand before speaking, treat your possessions with respect, no running on the concrete, no leaving the school grounds without permission – he liked that these rules were there, that they existed, and that he was expected to follow them. He liked that there were consequences if you broke the rules. Discipline meted out. Justice dispensed. Sometimes the boy deliberately did the wrong thing purely so he would be reprimanded. So another kid would notice and tell on him. So a teacher would speak to him sternly and remind him of his responsibilities. He often wished the rest of his life operated under the same rules, the same structure.

He peeked into his mum's room on his way to the bathroom, but the bed was cold. She hadn't come home.

In the toilet, he tried to aim without looking down. It was a disgusting way to start the day, having to stare at that dirty bowl with its rust-coloured watermark. One morning, when he couldn't stand it any longer, he had taken the brush and scrubbed hard, willing the bowl to sparkle like the one on the TV ad. But the brush had come away with bits of crap stuck all over it and he couldn't see any way of removing it from the bristles without picking it off with his hands. He had eventually thrown the whole thing in the bin. This morning, the empty brush container still stood alone, a rank pool of gritty water sitting in the bottom. He peered closer. Tiny mosquito wrigglers rippled the surface.

The boy tensed as a cramp gripped his stomach. His tummy had been unsettled all night, growling and roiling. He searched under the sink. A large brown cockroach scurried away from the light, through a trail of black specks. He found a tube of hair-removal cream, the contents crusted around the top. Several rusty razors, empty cans of hairspray and deodorant, dozens of old lipsticks and mascara tubes leaking onto the grimy shelving. He pushed aside stray tampons and bobby pins, a jar of face cream and one of Vaseline. He pulled out a damp packet of home-brand paracetamol but the silver sleeve was empty. Eventually he stood and contemplated his choices – in his left hand a small white bottle that could have been aspirin, the label faded beyond reading, containing three tiny white pills; in his right a box of capsules for muscle pain, prescribed for B. Silk. The boy didn't recognise the name. He replaced the box, tipped two of the white pills into his hand and swallowed them down with a handful of tap water.

He returned to his bedroom and collected an armful of clothes from the floor and the end of his bed and went out the back to the laundry. It was the coldest room in the house. The wind tunnelled through the large gap under the outside door. He lifted the lid of the washing machine, an ancient Westinghouse. A sour smell assailed his nostrils. He reached in to remove the slimy mass of sodden clothes, dumping them into a washing basket. The spinner had been broken for months. He loaded his own clothes into the drum and poured in a generous shower of detergent. The machine came to life reluctantly, water trickling.

His stomach churned violently as he entered the kitchen, the greasy smells from last night's chicken pervading his nostrils. A blackened fry pan sat on the stovetop, half-filled with murky oil. As he emptied the pan into the sink, the oil spattered onto his jumper and left a dripping trail across the bench. The chicken had been a disaster anyway. The oil had got so hot so quickly that he had been afraid the whole pan would catch alight. He had taken the pieces out as soon as they began to crisp; too soon, he realised when he bit into them — each piece was pink and gelatinous near the bone, slimy in his mouth. The skin had tasted like paper towel absorbed with grease.

He tried to find something more to settle his stomach and settled on some crackers from the pantry. The packet had been left open and they were stale. He washed them down with lemonade.

He wondered briefly whether she would be home in time — or in any condition — to go to the shops and get something he could take to school for lunch the next day.

When he opened the back door, the wind crept down inside his collar and curled around the space between his shirt and the top of his jeans. He pulled his beanie down low over his ears and strode across his yard towards the chicken coop.

The birds could hear or maybe sense his presence. Their cackles intensified into squawks of anticipation as he scrambled over the fence and wormed his way inside the hut. Spider webs feathered the wire, grey with feed dust, adorned here and there with fluffy down. The older hens strutted towards him expectantly. He rattled the lid off the beaten tin drum, extracted a handful of seed and scattered it. The hens darted about, pecking at the ground, their eyes bright.

He slipped the wire loop over the catch and cupped his hands under his black chick. Midnight, he had named it, even though the old man had said that was *a stupid name for a chook*. It seemed bigger than yesterday. He snuggled Midnight close to his cheek and smelt its warm chicken smell. He held one small foot in his fingers, the claws pricking his skin, the scaly leg fragile as a dry twig. A correlation between Midnight and the chicken from last night began to coalesce in his mind, but he sidestepped the thought.

The old man never ate his chickens. He had told him that. He kept them only for the eggs, and when they were too old to lay, he let them *live out their retirement in peace*. The boy was glad.

A noise at the door and he was there, his hunched shadow.

Thought I saw you come in. How's that bird with the damn fool name?

She's OK. Aren't they cold, but? Out here with the wind?

Nah, they got all those feathers. Not like us hairless critters, exposed to all the elements God sends.

But the chicks, their feathers aren't so thick yet.

Don't you worry about the chicks. They fluff themselves up, get a real warm buffer of air all around them. Warmer than you in your bed, I'll bet.

The old man peered at the boy's face.

You look a bit peaky. What's up? You crook?

Ah, my tummy's upset. Feel like crap. Reckon I ate something.

Yeah well, watch your language. You got anything to take?

The boy hesitated. *I took some tablets but I'm not sure if they were the right ones.*

Well, for the love of God. Don't you have more sense than to go taking medicines you're not sure of? Didn't you check with your mother?

No, she wasn't … she … she was asleep. I didn't want to bother her.

He returned to the chick, chastened by the lie that had fallen from his lips, and slowly stroked its soft head.

The old man made his way out of the hut, muttering. The boy couldn't catch the sense of his words.

Goddamn it ... more useless than tits on a bull ... only a young'un ... for Christ's sake ...

He stopped abruptly.

Well, don't just sit there. Put ol' Blackbeard back in there with the others and get yourself on up to the house. Best thing for a wonky gut is some of that fizzy powder. Got some in the cupboard. Fixes me right up every time.

The boy gave him a blank look.

And don't give me none of that can't-talk-to-strangers nonsense. Been living cheek by jowl with you for long enough now not to go standing on ceremony. I'm not the big bad wolf and I don't bite.

He headed back towards the house. The boy heard him muttering again.

Somebody around here got to do something ... may as well be me.

The boy snuggled the chick to his face, then returned it to the enclosure, its small wings flapping hopefully as it dropped to the ground. He rose and followed the old man out of the henhouse.

The yard was compact and neat. A row of gnarled hibiscus, as old as the house itself, lined the perimeter on two sides. The leaf litter under the avocado tree was an anomaly in the tidy lawn – the boy wondered who mowed the grass. Several bushes grew up through white painted tyres. Off to one side, a rough woodshed held stacks of timber. A passionfruit vine climbed voraciously along the other side fence, and had made its way across one end of the sagging clothesline and onto the peeling verandah railings. The boy mounted the stairs in the shadow of the old man. He glanced back towards his own yard. His house looked forlorn and lonely.

The screen door banged shut behind him. The old man's kitchen was as neat as his yard. A single sink with a cupboard either side, and on the draining board an upside-down mug. The old-fashioned upright gas stove was black with use, one knob missing. The gleaming fridge jangled in its newness. The boy had never before seen a fridge that wasn't covered in photos and cuttings and vouchers held on with magnets. But the old man's fridge was devoid of clutter, a vast white space in the crowded room.

Well, sit yourself down. Make yourself at home. Now where did I last put that stuff ...

The boy pulled out a wobbly wooden chair and sat at the table. A salt shaker, a bottle of Worcestershire sauce and a chipped mug half-full of sugar stood on a plastic doily.

Ah! Here it is. Bit of Alka-Seltzer'll fix you right up.

He retrieved a glass from a cupboard and shook it into the sink. A dead spider fell out. He filled the cup with tap water and spooned in several teaspoons of the white powder. It fizzed impressively as he stirred. He placed it in front of the boy.

Drink that quick, now, while it's bubbling.

The boy gulped the liquid and coughed, wiping his streaming eyes.

It goes right up your nose, doesn't it? Go on, get it into you, do you the world of good.

The boy held his nose and emptied the glass.

Thank you.

No worries. The old man pulled out the other chair and lowered himself into it. *You don't say much, do you?*

Not much to say, I guess.

Hmm. Quite right. Too many people yakking away without anything worthwhile to say. I quite agree with you.

The boy met the old man's steady gaze in silence.

So, do you fancy a game of chess?

I ... I probably should be getting home. Mum'll be wondering ...

The old man opened his mouth as if trying to decide how to reply. The boy noticed specks of white spittle caught in the whiskers at the sides of his mouth. His face was mapped with criss-crossing lines. The loose skin hanging under his chin reminded the boy of a turkey's wattle.

Well now, you said your mother was sleeping, right? So I reckon what she doesn't know won't hurt her, and you could have one game of chess and keep an old man company for a spell. What do you reckon?

The boy pushed his chair back and stood up.

I gotta go. Thanks for the drink.

He paused at the screen door, his eyes fixed on a spot in the yard.

Anyway, I can't play.

The old man waited a beat before replying. *What's that?*

Chess ... I don't know how to play.

Oh ... well, you see, that would be on account of that no-one's thought to teach you. I suspect a boy like you would pick it up real quick. It's not hard to learn, chess, but it takes a lot of practice to get good at it.

The boy turned.

You'd need to practise, and you'd need to be patient, with yourself I mean, while you're learning. And you'd have to be prepared to be regularly and thoroughly thrashed, of course. I'm the former Footscray champion, you know.

He raised himself up and shuffled towards the boy, his hand outstretched.

Whaddaya say, we got a deal?

The boy smiled, a shy smile that shone from his eyes before it reached his mouth. He walked back into the room and took the old man's hand. It was dry and smooth, and trembled slightly as he gripped the boy's fingers.

We didn't though. Didn't get married, that is. Not in the end. Don't get me wrong, I was ready and willing. I assumed that would be the natural progression, you know, after me getting Edith in the family way. So during one of those early man-to-man discussions with her father, when he suggested rather insistently that it would be *the right thing to do*, I acquiesced real quick. I had no idea what that would entail, of course. There was some talk of Old Joe fixing up the back room at their place for me and Edith to live in, at least until the baby came, although to be honest I couldn't see Joe getting up the wherewithal to fix up a good deal of anything. But it didn't much matter, because Edith took a stand. She said there was no way that she was going to marry anyone because she had to, not even me. She said she was a modern, independent woman and she'd have the baby herself, and she was sure I would ask her to marry me when I was good and ready, but she wouldn't be forcing me into it. Oh, she could be quite forthright when she put her mind to it. Mrs E cried and raged and threatened and sulked, but nothing swayed my Edith. She was determined to do it her way. Mrs E tried to enlist the support of Old Joe, but he crumpled in the face of his daughter's onslaught. Whenever the subject came up, he'd mutter something about having things to do and he'd be off, leaving Mrs E to fight her own battles. She even tried to appeal to me, gave me lots of speeches about accepting my responsibilities and such, but I put the truth out there – that I would've married Edith in a heartbeat, except she wouldn't have me.

I've asked her 'til I'm blue in the face, Mrs E, I'd say, *but she says it doesn't matter how many times I ask her, she won't be saying yes until she knows I'm asking her for her, and nothing to do with the baby coming.*

Mrs E wrung her hands and said, *But how will she know when that is, the silly girl?*

I don't know, Mrs E, I just don't know. She says she'll see it in my eyes and hear it in my voice.

But it didn't seem to matter how I looked at her or how I phrased the question, she kept repeating it wasn't time, and that she'd know when it was.

So that was how things stood. Edith stayed living at home, and I shifted into a closer boarding house so I could be nearby and drop over if I was needed. Mrs E took up knitting with a fury that was something to see, producing a pile of booties and blankets and matinee jackets enough to clothe an orphanage. She had expected Edith to quit work, of course, and sit home with her feet up, contribute to the knitting, but Edith knocked that idea on the head real quick.

I'm perfectly capable of continuing work, Mother. I'm not frail or ailing. I'm healthy as a horse.

And she was, too. Never a day of morning sickness, and an appetite to match a footy player. As her stomach grew, she had to get the confectionery department to order in a specially made uniform, with a white shirt that she hung over the top. Mrs E said it was indecent, but I thought she looked right fine. And she still wore her jaunty pink scarf.

I started to be more cautious with my money. Not that I ever had a lot left over, but what I did have, now I'd save instead of spending it on the pictures or going out to eat. We spent more time with her parents, and they were mighty good to us, feeding me whenever I came over. I was extra diligent at work too, and put in for overtime whenever I could. I was trying to squirrel away as much extra cash as possible so that when the baby came, I would be ready.

Edith started getting bigger and bigger, and more and more tired. But she kept on working; she never complained. She was a real trooper.

In the beginning, I kept asking her to marry me. I'd ask her two or three times a day, and in all different ways. Got to be a joke between us. I'd put on funny voices, or stand on my head, or write it down. But the answer was always the same. *No.* After a while I was asking her only once or twice a week, but still no luck. In the end, she had a serious talk with me and asked me to please stop asking her, it was upsetting her to have to always say no. I said, *Well then, why don't you just say yes?* But she was adamant. She said she didn't want me asking anymore, until the day I felt from my heart that I wanted to ask her for real, without anything to do with any baby, and then she would know, and she would most probably say yes. I said, *Heck, Edith Flower, why can't you say yes now and forget all about the mucking around in the middle?* But that only upset her more and she wouldn't speak to me for the rest of the evening, so after that I stopped asking her. I wanted to sometimes, but I didn't.

The baby was due to arrive in the weeks before Christmas, which pleased Mrs E no end. She kept telling all her friends that there was nothing quite like Christmas with a new baby in the house. Old Joe was pressed into service with the task of getting the house ready. She wanted a real tree, at least six foot high, and coloured bulbs strung up all around the eaves. By this time, mid-December, Mrs E's knitting had filled the linen cupboard and was spilling out into the living room, so she'd started baking for Christmas, and when that got too much, she began stewing apples and pears and canning them up for the baby. Edith would laugh and laugh and say, *Mother, he won't be eating stewed fruits for quite some months yet,* but Mrs E ignored her and kept right on cooking. I guess she figured you could never be too prepared for a baby.

Edith always called the baby *him.* She said she had a feeling that she was carrying a boy. Mrs E agreed, said she was carrying high and out, like she did for Edith's brothers. I always suspected a girl, although how I thought I could know was a mystery.

But despite all that preparation and planning, when the time came, it took us all by surprise. I guess that's the way of it – nothing can ever really prepare you for the experience of bringing a new life into the world.

It was a Friday and I was at work. I got called into the office by my supervisor to take a phone call, and I knew what it would be, 'cause I never got phone calls at work. It was Mrs E. She spoke in slow and measured tones. She said, *You need to come home now, the baby's coming,* and then Edith herself got on the phone and said, *Don't be in any hurry, this baby's not coming for hours yet. Finish your shift and just stop by on your way home,* and then Mrs E grabbed the phone back and her voice was now high and squeaky – *Don't you listen to her, she's not in her right mind, you get here as quick as you can* – and she hung up before Edith had a chance to answer to that. I suspect Mrs E was a touch anxious herself, and sure enough when I got there, Old Joe was puttering about in the back shed being no help at all, so I suppose she wanted another body there to order around and get organised.

Edith, though, was calm as anything. She was walking around the house and stopping every now and then when the pain hit her, breathing real slow and deep like we had practised. Mrs E was checking her bag and getting me to haul it to the door and then haul it back so she could check it again, and in between pains Edith was telling her to sit down and to make herself and me a cup of tea. Eventually, when Edith decided the time was right (and not a moment earlier), I called a taxi and the two of us headed off to the Footscray Hospital, leaving her mother on the footpath, wringing her hands and looking uneasy. I'm not sure Old Joe even knew we'd gone.

The boy's days took on a steady, comforting rhythm. Early in the morning, with the world still asleep around him, he would slip from his bed, dress silently amongst the dim, shadowy outlines of his room, and make his way to the henhouse. The fowls would cluck at his arrival. He would throw open the door and the birds would zigzag around him to make a break for the open yard, while he sat on the fence and watched, rubbing the cold from his stiff fingers and stomping the feeling into his feet. Some mornings the old man would appear on the verandah, holding a steaming mug. He would raise a hand in greeting, or simply nod. The boy knew they had reached an agreement of sorts, although he wasn't sure exactly what.

Soon enough the light would creep across the dew-dampened grass and the boy would hustle the hens back through the opening and secure it tight.

Most mornings he would go to school, riding his blue bike into the cutting wind.

Occasionally he would wag, returning home only briefly before slinking back towards the henhouse. The old man never spoke to him during school hours, no matter if the boy stayed in his yard half the day. But he knew; the old man knew. And the boy knew he knew, and the old man knew that the boy knew he knew. The boy sensed the old man's reluctance to acknowledge him when he should be at school. That would somehow constitute a failing, an absence of diligence on the old man's part. But every so often, the boy would peek up at the house to see a glint of glass behind a window, or a silhouette disappearing through the doorway.

The afternoons were different. That was their time, the old man and the boy, together. After three, the boy would pedal uphill in a fury of legs and motion and skid through the fence and into the side garden, dropping his bike beside the passionfruit vine. Or slip across the yard striped with shadow and up the steps, two at a time. A perfunctory knock. A glass of ice-cold milk on the table. (A quiet complaint – *Hot milk would be nice for a change* – and the chuckled rebuke – *Drink up, it'll put hairs on your chest.*) Next to the milk, a couple of arrowroot biscuits or a shortbread cream. Occasionally a slice of homemade chocolate cake. (Who would have thought the old man made cake?) Once or twice a store-bought chocolate bar.

Balancing the snack and his glass, the boy would pad into the living room, where the old man was waiting.

I thought you'd never arrive. Tell me, what interesting thing did you learn today?

The old man would wait, patient, for the boy to fill his empty belly. He would wait for two minutes or ten; he seemed to have all the time in the world.

One afternoon, in between mouthfuls of biscuit, the boy related his day.

We did an experiment about condensation.

Oh, yeah?

We picked leaves and put them in plastic bags and left them for a couple of hours. When we checked later, there was all this foggy mist on the bags.

Hmm. You don't say.

That's condensation.

It is indeed. Used to do the same experiment when I was a boy.

Plastic was invented then, was it?

I wasn't born last century, kiddo.

Yeah well I bet you never grew grass heads.

Sure we did. We had grass growing all over the place.

No, a grass head.

Had a few friends who were grass heads, he muttered.

Huh?

Never mind. All right, tell me. What the blazes is a grass head?

You fill a stocking with dirt and grass seeds. You make it into a head shape and draw a face on. Then you stick it in a pot and water it. When the grass seeds sprout, it's like hair.

Humph. Grass heads. Nope, never did grass heads. Only things filling stockings were women's legs. And we only had to look around us to see the grass grow. Grass heads. Fool idea.

It was an unsettled afternoon, the air crisp and tinged with the smoke of a wood fire. The boy surveyed the room, his gaze falling on the three ducks fixed in formation on the wall, the film of dust coating the surfaces of the shelves and the side tables. The lace doily, grey with grime, peeping from under an old-fashioned porcelain figurine – a wide-eyed child sitting cross-legged in a wheelbarrow, her arms filled with flowers. The colours faded with age. The girl missing the tip of one foot.

The boy licked his fingers, one by one.

So. How come you don't have kids. Or grandkids.

How do you know I don't?

Just know. No pictures. No photos. No kids' drawings stuck up anywhere.

Maybe I just don't like photos.

And maybe you just don't have kids. Actually. The boy's gaze intent. *Actually, you don't have any photos, of anything. How come?*

Told you. Don't like photos.

But everybody has photos of something. Or someone. Jeez, even my mum has photos of me stuck up on the fridge. And last year's school photo in a frame. And she has a whole album of photos of my grandma and grandpa before they died. And them with her and her brother when she was little. That's one of her favourite things to do, look at those photos.

Yeah, well. Not me.

Don't you have any pictures? Any at all?

Why're you so curious about pictures all of a sudden?

Just am.

Yeah, well.

The old man stared into space for a moment. He pushed himself out of his chair and reached for his wallet on the sideboard. The wallet shook with the palsied tremor of his hands as he searched. He held out a yellowed rectangle of card to the boy. It was soft with age, the corners dog-eared, the photo a black-and-white blur, faded with time to the sepia hues of an ancient thing, a relic, worn with the viewings of so many years.

The boy took it and squinted hard to make out the subject. A child. A girl of no more than a year.

She your daughter?

Yes. A beat. No. I mean no. Not my daughter. My sister. That was my sister.

Huh. That's a really old-time tricycle. I saw one like that at the history museum.

The old man peered over.

How about that. So it is. Never took much notice. I guess that would've been mine. I must've been about five at the time.

She's cute.

She was. She was very cute.

She still alive?

No. She ... she died.

How'd she die?

90

The bluntness of the question seemed to astonish the old man. He quivered and his rheumy eyes filled with tears. He pulled a crumpled handkerchief from his trousers pocket and blew his nose, a loud honk.

She ... she just ... she just died. Kids died back then. Here, gimme that. I need a cup of tea.

He snatched the photo from the boy and headed into the kitchen.

The boy watched his retreating back. He wondered what it would be like to have a sister. He wondered if it would be worse to have a sister who died, or to have no sister at all.

...

The boy was thorough in observing his surroundings each day. He wanted to have something of note to share with the old man in the afternoon. He related funny things he had seen or a witty comment made by the class clown. He described his teachers' shortcomings and his classmates' odd habits.

He spoke rarely of his mother and the old man didn't ask.

One day he broached again the subject of the photograph.

So when did your sister die, anyway?

What? The old man alert, nostrils flaring.

Your sister. In the picture. Was she, like, an old lady? Did she live around here? Did she have kids and stuff?

The old man appeared to shrink inside his skin, his body retracting into a smaller space.

No, he whispered. *No. She didn't have ... she died a long time ago, boy. A long, long time ago.*

Was she a grown-up?

Was she what? No, she never ... she died when she was a baby. I told you. Not long after that photo was taken, actually.

Oh. That's sad.

The boy sniffed and dug at something inside his nostril.

So you were only a kid when she died?

The old man pulled at a thread on his cardigan.

Yes, he whispered, without looking up. *Six years old. Yes.*

So do you even remember it? I mean, what happened? Was she sick or what? I don't remember anything from when I was six. Well, not much anyway. How do you even remember her if she died so long ago?

The old man gathered his breath. *Oh, I remember her all right. I remember everything.*

He was still whispering, his raspy voice thin and trembling.

So how'd she die—

He cut off the boy with a fierce glance, his eyes suddenly hard and glittering. *She died, all right? She just died. I told you before, that's what happened back then. Kids died. They were born and they hardly had time to draw breath before something bad happened. There was always something bad that could happen.*

He had raised his voice and it carried through the frigid air. His hands gripped the armrests tightly, his knuckles white. Spittle flecked the corners of his mouth. He glared at the boy. Then his demeanour shifted, as if he was a balloon with the air escaping. He sank back.

Bad things happen, he said, his voice lowered again. *You should be careful. You think you can trust people, but … but bad things happen.*

The boy shivered, though he couldn't tell whether from the creeping cold in the room or from the chill in the old man's voice.

...

Yet on his next visit, the warmth had returned to the old man's expression.

Fancy a game of chess?

It was a slow, lumbering game, especially at the beginning, when the boy didn't know a pawn from a bishop. Their first game had stretched into the late afternoon, with the old man trying not to win, trying to teach the boy the rules and rudimentary moves. The boy had grown frustrated at his ignorance, his short-sightedness compared to the old man's skill. But gradually, as his knowledge of the game increased, so did his confidence. The games picked up pace, battles between more worthy adversaries. And then, after weeks of sitting opposite each other across the chequered board, the games had become slow and ponderous again, but filled with a completely different energy. Now, each opponent drew with vigilance on his mental resources, played the game ahead in his head, foresaw moves, planned sacrifices. The game's slowness became a thing of beauty, a dance, a silent and thoughtful battle. When the old man rose to flick on the overhead lamp, banishing the shadows, the boy would wonder where the time had gone, how it had passed so quickly.

The day he brought his treasure box, he had thought about it for weeks beforehand. He had pictured himself bringing it out from under his bed and carrying it under his arm, over the vine-covered fence and up to the old man's back deck. But each time a niggling anxiety had prevented him from getting the box any further than the bedroom door. Until today.

As they sat in the lounge room, the old man looked from the box to the boy and back again. The boy waited. Waited for the question about interesting things. He sat on his fidgety hands. Sat and stared at the faded lettering on the box.

The old man said, *Fancy a new game then? I only just beat you yesterday. That was a good game, that. Three days, wasn't it?*

The boy squirmed until the old man put him out of his misery.

I'm only teasing you, son. Let's see what you've got there. Something interesting, I'll bet.

The boy removed the lid and, one by one, placed the objects on the arm of the chair. The old man leant forward, his eyes bright with interest.

May I? he asked.

He handled the contents with reverent care. He ran his fingers over the surface of each rock, commenting on the type of rock it might be, or what sort of country it might have come from. He tested the give in the wishbones, and blew softly on the feathers. He rolled the ring in his cupped palm, and raised his eyebrows at the boy, an unspoken question. He admired the toy engine and the marbles and the drawings. He examined keenly each and every treasure, as the boy had hoped he would.

The boy's apprehension faded with the sharing.

Afterwards, as the boy was packing away the last of the feathers, the old man heaved himself off the couch, with a creaking of joints as of something rusted being wrenched loose. He made his way to the solid oak dresser, opening one drawer and then another, muttering to himself.

Now where did I put it? I know I had it here somewhere …

At last, with a triumphant hoot, he reached into the back of one of the drawers and retrieved a brown paper packet. He slipped his finger under the flap and peered inside before emitting a satisfied grunt. He gestured to the boy, his rheumy eyes flashing.

For you, he said, and placed the packet into the boy's hands.

The paper was yellowed with age. Disintegrating sticky tape fell apart as the boy lifted the flap. He tipped up the envelope and some small, dense objects fell into his hand.

They're … they're like letters, little letters, but in 3D … and they're backwards. What are they?

The old man gave another snort as he settled back into his chair.

It's type. Linotype. That's what they used back in the old days, before computers. That's what they printed newspapers and books and such with.

But how?

By hand! All by hand. Some poor fellow had to sit there and pick out each little letter for whatever it was you wanted to say. I'll show you.

He collected a few in his hand.

94

Say you wanted to write Big Storm in your newspaper. Well, you'd get this upper-case B, see, and then next to that you'd put a lower-case i and then a lower-case g. Then you'd use a spacer. I don't have any of them here, but they were blank, to leave a space like. And then you'd start again with the S for storm, see? And they'd all sit on a special holder to keep them nice and straight, and the ink would go onto them, and then the paper, and when you pulled the paper off – he mimed with his hand – *the writing would be the right way around! See?*

The boy held the letters in his palm, felt the weight of them. He was silent with astonishment.

In fact, said the old man, *I used to be one of those poor fellows, huddled over the type. But no longer. That was all a long time ago. Keep them. Add them to that box. They're yours.*

Other than my night in hospital as a lad, I'd never been inside of one before, not into the real workings of the place anyhow – and I found it a little on the disturbing side, to be honest. Strange mixture of sounds and smells. Ungodly clatter and hoo-ha one minute and people shushing you the next. The smell of antiseptic, so cloying it made me feel nauseous. Lots of officious nurses in starched white uniforms, their sneakers squeaking on the green lino that was all over the place, even halfway up the walls. I wondered what circumstance would require them to hose down the walls that far up. Decided not to think about it. We were bustled through the maternity entrance and I was made to feel like the fifth wheel right from the get-go. Basically told to get myself a cup of tea and wait. Which suited me just fine, I have to say. By that stage, the pain had set in, and Edith's eyes were frightened, like a horse when it's spooked. Thank God Mrs E wasn't there; she would've about fainted on the spot, I reckon. I had one last moment with Edith before they wheeled her in. She gripped my hand so tight I thought for sure she'd broken a finger or two, but I didn't say a word about it. I figured that whatever she was about to go through would be a helluva lot worse than a couple of fractures. The moaning had pretty much become screaming by then, and I don't mind saying I was relieved when those double doors swung together and I could massage my fingers and drink my tea.

The waiting room was set aside for expectant fathers, and there wasn't another soul there, so I guess there weren't that many babies planning to be born that day. I drank my tea and read a six-month-old *Women's Weekly* and drank more tea and paced around and drank more tea.

Finally, after a few hours that seemed like days, a busy nurse with a face full of smiles marched right up to me and said, *Congratulations, you're the father of a healthy baby girl. Seven pounds, six ounces. All her fingers and toes. You can go right on in. Third door on the left, room number five.* And she swivelled on her heel and left.

Now this next bit is kinda hard to explain without me seeming like a complete idiot.

I'd had about seven months, since Edith had told me, to get used to the idea of the baby. I'd had many discussions with Mrs E and Joe about the subject, and my role in it. I'd escorted Edith in the taxi to the hospital. I'd watched her face transformed with the pain, and I'd heard in her voice the uncertainty and the fear.

And yet, when that nurse announced those words to me – *you're the father* – I couldn't for the life of me take in what she was saying. The word *father* reverberated in the sterile air and it seemed devoid of meaning or context. In my mind's confusion I thought she was speaking of my father, lost to me so many years previously. The word echoed around my head … *father* … *father* … *father* …

No images, positive or negative. Just a great void. *Father.* It was like I had no experience in which to place that word so that it meant something to me. It was quite unsettling.

But I needn't have worried. Not at that stage, anyway. Once I knocked on the door of room five and ventured inside, any idea of me being a father and what that might mean went right out of my head, pushed out by the vision of the little miracle before me.

Edith was sitting up in the bed, drawn and tired but with a grin plastered all over her beautiful face. And in her arms she held the tiniest, most delicate elf-like creature I'd ever seen. Her skin was mottled and her hair could've done with a good wash, but her round blue eyes were tinged with soft, dark eyelashes and her smudge of a nose was cute as a button. Sure enough, she had ten fingers and ten toes (I counted, to be sure) and when she opened her mouth to yawn I could see her pink tongue. She looked for all the world like she was saying, in a bored sort of way, *OK, here I am, enough fuss, what's next?* I felt a surge of love tug at my heart.

Isn't she beautiful? Edith whispered. She held her like she was a piece of fine china that might break if you dropped it. She stroked the pearly shell of our daughter's tiny ear; she touched the delicate fingernails.

She sure is.

And her arms. See how strong her arms are already.

Yep. Strong arms, that's for sure.

I think we'll call her Sarah.

That's a fine name.

Yes, Sarah. Sarah Emily.

Sarah ... Emily. That's ... that's a mighty fine name.

Welcome to the world, Sarah Emily. Welcome home.

Edith was staring down at her, captivated. And I stroked the soft downy skin on Sarah Emily's cheek and I thought about all the hundreds of thousands of baby names in the world, and I thought of the other Emily I'd had in my life, and I wondered at the chances of Edith choosing to give our baby the name of my dead sister.

It had been a harsh winter. The biting winds continued to tunnel through trees and whip their branches almost horizontal. Birds huddled in their safe places, their heads tucked protectively under their wings. Dogs planted themselves in the dust and dirt under verandahs; cats hid in washing baskets. Occasionally the wind caught in a treetop or under an awning and called out to itself in a cold, sad moan.

The boy dropped his bike and scuffled his way through the piles of brittle leaves that danced across the yard in ever-changing patterns. He spotted a piece of scribbly-gum bark amongst the detritus, and stuck it in his pocket to add to his collection. He took the front stairs two at a time, avoiding the dodgy one. Last week it had partially given way under a bloke's hefty tread, his leather motorcycle boot the only thing stopping the wood from piercing his calf.

The front door was closed to the elements, the screen banging noisily in the wind. He turned the knob and went inside.

The boy sensed the man's presence before he saw him. He hadn't come around since that night, but now he was sprawled on the lounge, the TV remote in one hand and a beer in the other. When the boy stopped in the doorway, the man flicked his eyes from the television, dropped the remote onto the couch and shifted slightly.

Hey.

The boy stood, mesmerised by his strange stillness. *Hey,* he replied.

Then silence.

Want a beer? The man gestured to the can in his hand.

No. No, I'm … I don't drink beer.

Aw, come on. Bet you do. Bet you'd like it if you did. I'd sure as hell had a few beers by the time I was your age. How old are you, anyways?

The boy's eyes shifted uncomfortably from side to side. *Where's Mum?*

Where's Mum? Now that's a good question. Well, see, your mum has to work this arvo and later on tonight, so I kindly offered to come over and sit with you after school, watch out for you.

I don't … I don't need looking after. Mum's always out. I look after myself.

You do, huh. Well … I thought we could get to know one another better. Your mum thought it was a good idea, to have a man around. You're growing up. You need some time with the big boys.

The man extended his hand. *Snake's the name.*

On account of the tatt, he added.

It was so obvious the boy didn't know how he had missed it the first time. The snake wound around the man's torso, appearing and disappearing through the boundaries of his singlet, and vanished in a coil around his neck.

Snake had an expression on his face that the boy was unable to decipher. He glanced around again, judging the distances, considering the safety of his bedroom, contemplating what food might be in the kitchen. His stomach growled. Then, he walked backwards slowly – one step, two steps – before throwing open the door and bolting down the front stairs. He could hear the man calling to him.

He dashed into the street and hid behind one of the hibiscus shrubs that dotted the footpath. When he was certain that Snake was not making any attempt to follow him, he circled around to the old man's side yard and snuck through the tangled bougainvillea on the far side of the house. He had never gone this way before; he swore quietly as the thorns needled his skin. He finally pushed through to the familiar space of the backyard. He didn't risk even a glimpse at the chickens, creeping immediately up the back stairs and into the house.

It was then he remembered that it was only one-thirty on a Tuesday, and the old man never expected him before half-past three. Their unspoken agreement was about to be tested.

Inside the house, he could hear the wind buffeting the weatherboards. There was no milk waiting. The boy hesitated. He could leave, slip out as silently as he had come, and go back towards town, or down to the creek. But he would need his bike, and that would require going back across to his front yard to get it. He lifted each foot and tentatively placed it down, feeling like an intruder, even though he had been inside the tidy kitchen dozens of times before. He reached the archway that led to the living room and peered inside. No-one. The chessboard was still set up from yesterday's game. This was as far as he had gone before – kitchen, lounge room. It felt wrong to linger. He called softly. Nothing. He called again, a little louder, and then let his foot drop with a thud. Something – a sound, a muffled sound. He crossed the room and stood before a door that was ajar. After a beat, he pushed it open and peered inside.

It was a bedroom, musty with the smells of unwashed clothing and sour breath. Dust motes hung in the air. At first he thought the room was empty, but another sound, a faint sigh, came from the direction of the bed. The boy moved closer. The old man lay curled up in the middle of the bed, covered with a worn, discoloured blanket. He hardly made a bump in the huge bed; he seemed so much smaller than when standing up. The boy listened for the old man's laboured breathing and was relieved to discover he wasn't dead. The old man's eyes opened a slit and regarded the boy wearily.

Water.

Eager to be useful, the boy hurried out of the room and into the kitchen, and returned to the old man with a plastic tumbler of tap water. The old man tried to raise his head to drink but sank back onto the pillows with a moan. Even in the dim light, the boy could see the sweat shining on his forehead. He reached behind the old man's head and lifted it to meet the cup. The skin beneath his hand was hot and slippery. The old man sipped and then sank back again. He was shivering, his teeth clattering. The boy rearranged the covers, pulling up the bedspread and tucking it under the old man's whiskery chin. He hesitated, and then touched the old man's cheek, feeling the warmth leach into his palm. The grey stubble was rough against his fingers. He must have knocked his head; a scab had formed on his scalp at the peak of a thin trail of dried blood. The old man's swollen eyes opened a fraction before sliding shut again, as though it was too much effort.

The boy perched himself on the chair beside the bed, willing the old man to wake up and give him an instruction. He sat there for over an hour, his eyes travelling around the dim room, lingering on the faded curtains, the faded prints on the walls, but always returning to the old man's ashen face, his shallow and irregular breathing creating only the tiniest movement in the bedclothes.

When a hacking cough disturbed the stillness, the boy's fear solidified. He watched wide-eyed as the force of the old man's coughing lifted his torso. He hunched over, struggling for breath, his thin frame wracked by shuddering spasms. The boy rushed to the living room, picked up the telephone and dialled triple-zero.

The day I escaped from that cesspit they call a hospital, I bought myself a lotto ticket. Told the boy I'd share the winnings with him, half and half, fair and square. Told him I was bloody lucky to live next door to a kid with such good sense. Couldn't stop telling him how much I appreciated him coming in like that and phoning for the ambulance. Pneumonia takes no prisoners at my age, I can tell you. A few more hours with that fever and the chills and I might not have seen the next dawn. Even told the kid I was glad he skipped school that day. Not that I want him to make a habit of it. Now that I'm well, we can go back to our regular routine of him sitting out there with the chickens and me in here pretending I don't know he's there 'til three-thirty comes around.

I couldn't get out of that building quick enough. Hospitals are full of sick people. Terrible places. I read in the paper about all those superbugs they have now, so strong that there's no anti-biotics good enough to stop them, and where do you get infected with them in the first place? That's right, hospitals. Nasty germ-incubating cesspits.

Mind you, they did get rid of my pneumonia, so I suppose I should be grateful for that. Whacked me straight on the drip, gave me some drugs, and before I knew it I had stopped hallucinating about giant one-eyed jellyfish and was feeling more like my old self. Three days was long enough though. Couldn't wait to get back to my own house and my girls. I needn't have worried. The boy had fed them and taken real good care of them for me. They hardly even missed me, stupid chooks. But it was good to hear them clucking around my feet again.

I've only had two experiences with hospitals and neither of them positive. I suppose that's where my obstinate feelings spring from. The overnight I spent as a youngster wasn't too bad, but the circumstances that sent me there soured the incident. The other time I was inside those sanitised walls was when Sarah Emily was born, when I was sitting in there minding Edith and marvelling at that baby girl. And I had the same feelings even back then. Seemed wrong to have such a beautiful, precious little life existing in that cold, sterile environment, with all those uniforms and charts and bad smells. And the twilight. Never fully black, never fully lit, always a dim sort of dusk.

By the time her confinement was up and they condescended to allow Edith to leave with our baby, she was practically pawing at the door. Said she couldn't breathe in that room and I didn't blame her. So I took her home to Mrs E and Old Joe.

Well, you've never seen such a palaver. Joe had balloons strung across the front porch, and a big sign *Welcome home Edith and Bub* in the window. Mrs E had cooked for a cast of thousands, though it was only us and a couple of neighbours who popped in to coo over the baby and tell us how pretty she was. As if we didn't know.

I see now what a special time that was. There was a lot of love in that house that summer and into the autumn. That girl was a breath of fresh air. Nobody could get enough of her. And for the first few weeks, that applied to me more than anybody. I was proud as punch that I'd played a part in the creation of such an amazing little creature. Every compliment and murmur of adoration seemed to rub off on me, and for the first time in my life it seemed like I'd done something good. Something worthwhile.

...

It couldn't last, that sunbeam feeling. I should've known and I should've prepared myself better. I didn't. And it was a shock. But it seems that no matter how many setbacks and disappointments a person has in life, when that bit of sunshine arrives you greet it like the day ain't never gonna end. You're always surprised when the darkness creeps in.

I remember clearly. It was after Christmas, and Sarah Emily was about a month old. It must have been a Sunday, 'cause I wasn't at work. It was late morning and the day was heating up. I remember the stripes of sunlight coming down almost vertical through the branches of the old liquidambar. Edith and I were sitting on a couple of lawn chairs out in the backyard, trying to stay under the tree's shade. That corner was the coolest spot during the summer, up until about noon when even that got too hot and the best option was to sit on the verandah with a wet towel and a fan. Edith was real fussy with the baby, adjusting the muslin cloth over her bassinet and checking that no bugs were hovering. We were quite contented there, the three of us. And then the bub started to fret, you know how they get when they're hungry and angling for a feed. Edith lifted her out and tried to shush her against her shoulder, but she was rolling her little head this way and that and snuffling into Edith's blouse. Edith was trying to stall her, muttering something about not wanting to feed her out there in the open for any man and his dog to see, and the baby was working herself into quite a state. And then she started up with that newborn wailing sound, and something in that sound stopped me dead. I was overcome, all dizzy-like, and had to shut my eyes. For a moment there I could've sworn that this was Emily, my baby sister Emily, making that noise. With my eyes closed, I could picture in my head, clear as day, my mother in front of me, holding Emily to her breast. That sound, that mournful cry, it did my head in. I must've let out a wail myself, and the next thing I knew I was up and out of that chair and making for the house, putting as much distance as possible between me and that sound.

After that, it was like something had switched on somewhere deep inside my memory and for the life of me I didn't know how to go about shutting it off again. Every time the bub cried or started fussing, my insides seemed to close in. I tried to hide it at first. I tried real hard. I couldn't even understand how I was feeling myself, so I knew there'd be no chance I could explain it to Edith. At first it was gradual. Little things. Those mewing cries the bub made, like a tiny kitten, them I couldn't cope with. Seemed to dredge up something from the past, something bubbling up inside me like black oil, and no matter how I tried, I couldn't put a lid on it. Then it was the smell of her. Oh, I don't mean only the bad smells, the dirty nappies and the stringy lines of sick down Edith's back. I mean even the good smells: her skin, like slightly sour milk … her hair, sweet and tangy … her breath when I held her, so warm … the whole of her smelling like Edith when we made love and her breasts were full, dripping and sticky. When she first arrived, those smells had been like heaven to me; I could inhale so deeply and yet never get enough. But then, when the noises were starting to get on my nerves, the odours did too. I can't explain it. She sounded and smelt … too much somehow, too new, too fragile, too baby-like. Thinking on it now, I realise that doesn't make a lick of sense, and in fact probably sounds kind of crazy. But at the time, the feeling was creeping up on me in this slow, insidious way, and there wasn't a damn thing I could do about it.

I began avoiding her. Used to be I couldn't wait to get over from work so I could sit with her awhile, just sit and hold her in my arms and watch her sweet face. But it got so I not only avoided that precious time, but I didn't even want to do my duty. Edith would ask me to hold her while she took a shower or fixed us something to eat, and I'd come up with a hundred excuses why I couldn't do that. My hands were dirty, or I smelt bad after work. I thought I was coming down with a cold and didn't want to pass it on to her. I needed to go help Old Joe chop the firewood.

At first, no-one seemed to notice. Mrs E was always hovering around in the wings, and she never tired of nursing the little one. But one day, when she was out shopping for groceries and Joe was in his workshop, and Edith and I were alone with the bub, my reluctance stuck out like a sore thumb.

It was one of those rainy days you get where the clouds have been gathering all day without doing very much, until suddenly they decide to let loose a deluge. The bub had been fretful and Edith reckoned she was developing a fever. Edith didn't feel that good herself actually, complaining about sore breasts and a head-ache, and Mrs E was worried she'd got herself a dose of milk fever, which was one of the reasons she'd gone out to the shops, to get some cabbage leaves. Anyway, Edith handed me the baby like it was the most natural thing in the world and said she was going off to have a lie-down, and before I could open my mouth to protest, she'd gone.

Now I don't hold much by all the doctors nowadays talking about anxiety and depression and all the modern ills of the world, but what I felt that day was akin to a panic attack, or what I've heard about them anyway, and I haven't experienced anything like it before or since. I sat there in the chair like I'd been struck dumb, that baby girl gazing up at me like she was placing her entire trust in me, like I was the one person that stood between her and the rest of the trouble in the world.

My breathing started getting faster. I could hear myself almost panting. My heart was racing and I could feel the blood pulsating through my body. Sweat started beading on my forehead, and my hands and feet went real cold and clammy. My breathing got so hard I thought I might hyperventilate or even pass out. I couldn't tell you what it was that was having this effect on me – Sarah Emily was lying there calm as could be; she wasn't even fretting anymore. But it was the whole look of her, her smell, the weight of her in my arms. I began to feel that I couldn't stand to be near her one minute longer. Plus I was shaking so bad I was worried I might drop her. I got up, real slow, and put her down on the floor. Simply put her down on the cold, hard floor. I backed out the door and down the stairs and caught a bus back to my bedsit and got under the covers. And that was it. I just left.

It wasn't good, I can tell you.

'Course, it was worse, much worse, when Mrs E arrived home with the groceries to find the bub thrashing about on the floor and not a parent in sight. She dropped her bags right there on the doorstep – broke a good number of the two dozen eggs she'd bought – and rushed in thinking that we'd all been kidnapped, with the little one left to fend for herself. Apparently Edith had put earplugs in to get some shut-eye, and Old Joe's hearing wasn't all that great, as I've said, so God only knows how long the poor thing lay there. According to Mrs E, she was so red in the face from screaming she almost couldn't breathe, and her limbs were all uncovered from squirming about. Mrs E told me later that it was a wonder she didn't catch her death.

Once she'd quieted the baby and calmed herself down enough to think straight, she was mighty frustrated with Old Joe for being out there in the yard and not hearing a damn thing, and she was none too pleased with Edith either, for going off to bed with earplugs in (*What if there'd been a fire?* she kept shouting. *You'd all be burnt to a crisp!*), but the person she was angriest with, of course, was me. Not that I blame her, not one little bit.

But as bad as Mrs E's reaction was, and let me tell you, it was pretty bad, Edith's manner was even worse. She didn't yell or scream or tell me off for leaving the way I did. She didn't even cry. When I finally saw her the next day, she only gave me this blank look of incomprehension, almost of resignation. As if she'd been expecting something like this from me all along, and now I'd fulfilled her low expectations. Or like she'd suspected there was some flaw in my character, and so she wasn't at all surprised when I revealed my true self. She accepted what had happened with an inevitability that was heartbreaking to see.

It had taken all my willpower to go back the next day. Mrs E's threats got the better of me and I went back to face the music. I got off the bus at Edith's stop, and I tell you, walking along that road towards their house was about one of the hardest things I've ever done. You know how when you put two magnets together the wrong way, and they repel each other? That's how I felt. Every step was an effort against an invisible force trying to push me back in the opposite direction. By the time I got to the stairs, I practically had to haul myself up by the handrail as if I was climbing a mountain.

The feeling got stronger, worse, when I went inside. I stood there in the living room, staring at the faces staring at me. I couldn't speak. How could I begin to explain what I didn't even understand myself? Mrs E was jabbering on and on about the poor bub and my irresponsible actions, and how now we were parents we had to put the bub first, and all the time Edith was sitting there silently on the sofa, with Sarah Emily in her arms.

I didn't say much. I don't even remember much of what I did say. I know I said sorry. I apologised to Old Joe, even shook his hand. Shook his hand! Like we were in a meeting or sealing a business deal. He seemed a touch shell-shocked himself, poor guy; must've been the ear-bashing from Mrs E. She was still yakking away, and I was so embarrassed I stared at the floor mostly and said *yes ma'am* and *no ma'am*. And then she delivered me an ultimatum. I looked up at her, finally. She had her hands on her hips and she was obviously waiting for my response. I expect she thought I was going to fall on my knees and beg, or sob into Edith's shoulder and ask to be forgiven. I can't even recall now what she was demanding, but I knew, with a certainty in my bones that was chilling in its ferocity, that I couldn't stay in that room, in that house, one moment longer. Every fibre of my being was telling me to get as far away as humanly possible from the house, from Mrs E, from Edith, but most of all from that baby.

And so I mumbled some meaningless tripe, stole one last glance at Edith, sitting stony and resolute as she held our daughter, and I walked out that door.

And I never went back.

Now that I'm older, I see that I was absolutely terrified to love that child. Frightened to allow her to stoke that flame in my heart. Seeing that trust in my own child's eyes, I remembered Emily, and how loving my sister had ended so badly. How I had lost her.

I told myself I was shielding my daughter. Or was I shielding myself?

The black chick, half-grown, its feathers a scrawny mixture of downy fluff and scraggy pinfeathers, followed the boy around the yard like a small dog. Every so often he would squat in the dirt and gather her into his arms. She would sit like this for minutes at a time before the stirring of some insect in the grass would claim her attention and she would flap her wings and struggle to be free. The boy petted the few smooth, glossy feathers coming through; her claws tickled his skin. He dug into the soft ground under the mess of the abandoned turkey mound, unearthing a buffet of wriggling brown worms and black beetles. His chick couldn't peck fast enough, her head bobbing up and down in an attempt to catch the bugs before they escaped back into the soil. He liked bringing her into his own backyard; he thought of it as a mini hen holiday. Different ground to peck at, new territory to explore. He was careful to watch that she didn't stray too far.

The boy sat under the shade of the verandah awning, his legs extending into a patch of sunshine beyond the steps. Although spring had begun, the house still held the chill of winter. He focused on the columns of numbers in his homework book, chewing his pencil until the tip was in stringy shards. He'd decided he disliked maths. He didn't like the way there was only ever one answer. Even when he knew the correct answer, he hated having to show how he had arrived at it. He much preferred to read. But his teacher had finally had enough of him losing his homework and not completing tasks in class, and she had phoned his mother and spoken sternly to her about his lack of application. The boy had crouched behind his bedroom door, listening. He could hear his teacher's voice echoing through the line, and his mother's equally forceful responses. He had a bad feeling as she hung up the receiver. He made a dash for the open back door but she was too quick for him, grabbing his ear so hard he thought she might pull it off.

You listen to me. Who is it that pays for that uniform? All those goddamn school books? Who goes out to work to put food on the table? Me, that's who. So you'd better pull your socks up, do ya hear me? Start fucking listening in class, all right? And do your bloody homework! I don't need some jacked-up teacher with a stick up her arse balling me out and telling me how to raise my own kid, got it? Now piss off and finish whatever it is you're supposed to be doing.

She gave his ear one last tweak and stormed off. When he rubbed the tender spot, his fingers came away smudged with blood.

And so he was attempting to concentrate on the figures dancing before him, trying to manipulate them into some sort of order.

He was glad the old man was back at home. Each evening he was in the hospital, the boy had contemplated the empty house, thinking how lonely it seemed. He hadn't known where the ambulance had taken him, or when – or even if – he would be back. He had fed the hens every morning and checked on them every afternoon. And then, on the fourth day, he had been mucking out the henhouse and putting in fresh straw when he saw the old man standing on his verandah, one hand raised to shade his eyes from the sun, mumbling something to him about a lotto ticket.

The boy had released a long sigh. It hadn't occurred to him until then that he had been holding his breath.

A shadow passed across his book. He turned to see Snake with his mother in the kitchen. He had her back pushed against the sink, his hands on her behind. They were kissing, his mother with her hands inside Snake's shirt.

It was the first time he had looked closely at the head of the snake tattoo. It covered the whole back of the man's neck – the serpent's jaws open wide, forked tongue flickering, fangs poised and ready to attack. The boy could almost hear it hissing.

His mother had one leg cocked up, her hands pulling at Snake's shoulders. He must have had his tongue halfway down her throat. The boy spun away, glad of the weak warmth and fresh air outside.

There was a noise as Snake landed heavily on the step behind him. The boy kept his eyes on his book. He heard a frustrated groan and imagined Snake adjusting his crotch.

His mother came out with three glasses of lemonade and a bottle of gin on a tray. She handed a glass to the boy, and then splashed a generous amount of gin into the other two before giving one to Snake and taking a deep draught from her own. She sighed in contentment. The boy watched her, her limbs sprawled on the verandah, and felt the hot bile of disgust rising in his throat. He closed his book and tried to get up.

Hey, where're you going? Sit yourself back down.

Snake caught the boy's leg, pulling him back onto the dusty boards.

Where are your bloody manners, hey? Your mother brings you a drink and you don't even say thank you? Show some respect, you little shit.

The boy remained silent. He stared at the book in his hands and willed the man to lose interest.

Hey, I'm talking to you, boy. You hear me? I'm talking to you!

The boy mumbled something.

What? What did you say?

The boy raised his head and forced himself to look into the man's dark eyes. He spoke slowly, enunciating every syllable.

I said, why don't you go fuck yourself.

The man moved so quickly, the boy didn't realise what was happening until he was sprawled in the dirt at the bottom of the stairs, with Snake on top of him. He tried to twist his arms, but the man had pinned them to the ground with his knees. The boy's legs kicked uselessly into the air. Snake brought his face closer, until the boy could feel the man's breath on his own mouth.

Now you listen to me, you little shit. And you listen good. I don't take that shit from nobody, especially not a snot-nosed kid like you. I think maybe you need to be taught a lesson.

He murmured into the boy's ear. *Your mother and me are good together. We like spending time together. You and me, we could be good together too. We could get to know each other better.*

The boy flinched as the man's tongue flicked into his ear. Snake was almost panting. He shifted his weight and the boy felt the man's hardness against his stomach.

You be nice to me, the man whispered, *and I'll be nice to you.* He raised his voice again and said, *But you continue to be difficult and disrespectful and I'll have to teach you a lesson. Won't I? Huh?*

The man raised his hand above his head and brought it down, hard, onto the boy's cheek. The boy felt his head reverberate with the shock. The hand came down again, this time connecting fiercely with his ear. The whole side of his head throbbed with pain, and the ringing in his ear was so loud he thought he could hear a bell. Snake jumped up and delivered a solid kick to the boy's ribs. He stood over him, his hands on his hips.

Had enough? He spat into the dirt. *Little shit.*

The boy curled up, cradling his head in his hands, pulling his legs up towards his chest. Waiting for another blow. Hot tears stung behind his lids but he squeezed tight, refusing to allow them out. After a minute with no further outbursts, he rolled over and gingerly got to his knees, crawling on all fours away from the house and the man. He could hear him laughing. His mother was quiet. When he risked a backwards glance, her gaze swept over him. Pleading. She pulled at Snake's sleeve, murmuring something about going inside.

The black chick tiptoed out from under a tangled bush and pecked at the ground beside the boy. He unclenched his fist to reach for her. Too late, he realised his mistake.

Snake wrenched free of his mother's hold and strode across the yard. Before the boy could rise, the man reached down to grasp the chicken. The boy cowered, scrabbling backwards in the dirt, holding on to the bird firmly. The man had a hold of the chick's head. The ghastly tug-of-war continued for a moment before the boy saw that Snake was not going to let go and Midnight was in danger of being pulled apart. With an anguished cry, he released his hold and the man staggered back, the chicken flailing in the air.

The man's eyes were blazing with fury. He held the chick by the neck and swung it in an arc above his head.

You stupid little bastard. You think you can protect a fucking chicken? What are you doing out here with the fucking birds, anyway?

His arm circled in a frenzy. The chick was a black blur. The man spun around viciously and then let go – like the discus throwers the boy had seen on TV. His chick flew through the air, fast, before colliding with a tree trunk. There was a sickening thud. It fell to the ground and lay still, a mound of feathers quivering in the breeze.

Poor little bugger didn't stand a chance. I had no choice. One of its legs was snapped like a twig and there was blood oozing out its eyeballs like something was broken real bad inside. I tried to tell him. I tried to explain to the kid that it wasn't any use – the chick would never walk again for a start, let alone what else was wrong with its busted insides. But that boy, he kept staring up at me with this hopeful expression in his eyes, like he truly thought I could magic it whole again. He didn't look too good himself. Tears rolling down his dirty face, washing tracks into mud. I reckon a big bruise was coming up on the side of his head, there were smudges of blood on his face, and he was standing like he couldn't hold himself in the one place for too long. But I knew I wouldn't get any answers, he was too cut about Midnight, as he was calling her. Stupid name for a hen.

I did what I could. I made a show of cradling her and pretending to check under her feathers. But there was only one thing to be done and I knew that as soon as I saw the little mite.

She's not gonna make it, I told him.

She will, he said, *she will, she's not that bad.*

She's bad, son.

116

She'll be OK. I'll take care of her. I'll carry her everywhere. I'll make special mush for her to eat, I'll feed her myself. She'll get better, I know she will.

I shook my head. *She won't get better, mate. There's no coming back from injuries like these. She's in a lot of pain. You don't want her suffering, do you?*

The boy stomped away and grabbed the nearest thing to hand, which happened to be my rake, and he hefted that thing in the air and brought it down so hard I thought it might break in two.

Bastard! Bastard! Bastard! he was screaming. He wasn't directing the curses at me, I knew that much, but at that point I hadn't yet put the pieces together. The bird, the boy's face, his anger. It was all I could do to deal with his anguish without trying to work out the circumstances that had led to it.

I thought I was doing the right thing. He was distracted, and it wasn't something I wanted him to have to see. Chicks' necks are easy to wring, especially when they're in no condition to struggle. I thought he'd understand. But when he'd finished killing my rake, he reached up to take that warm bundle of feathers from me, and he realised I'd done it. He glared up at me with such outrage that I thought he was going to pick up the damn rake again and go for me.

You killed her, he wailed.

I didn't know what to say. I thought he knew it had to be done. Maybe I should've let him do it himself, but surely that would've been even crueller.

It near broke my heart, seeing him all bloodied and filthy, cradling that chick like it was his most precious possession. What do I know, maybe it was. What do I know about kids? Bugger all.

He took off then. Stuffed the chicken into his jumper and hopped on his bike and rode away, snot trailing behind him in the wind. I picked up my rake, and a lone feather that shone like wet ink on the grass. I wasn't real happy, him taking it out on me like that, acting like it was partway my fault, but I could understand his sadness. I know all about grieving.

I had a gander next door, and I could see that mother of his sitting out on the porch with a drink in her hand, rolling the glass around on her cheek like it was hot out, even though the day was mild enough. She must have been there the whole time, watching. A man's voice shouted something from the house and she got to her feet, wearily, and went inside. The screen door slammed like a slap.

The wind picked up. I could feel it winding around the space on my ankles above my socks. I wiped the chicken blood off on my trousers. It left a brown smear.

...

Funny thing, but it was after all that with Sarah and Edith that I headed northwards, back up here. Can't explain why, even now. Hadn't been that many years before that I'd been running away from Queensland, away from that mad baker and his siren wife, and then there I was, running away from my own family back in the other direction. I guess it's like a homing pigeon. Instinct kicks in and you follow your nose, and before you know it you're back in your old stomping ground, familiar territory beneath your feet. By the time 1960 came around, I was renting a room by the river over at Norman Park, having got myself a job hauling fruit and veg off a ferry service that delivered produce to businesses up and down the river. It was exhausting work, and smelly, but it got me up early and out of the house and kept my mind occupied for most of the day until my body collapsed at sundown with a few beers and I was too tired to think much anyway. After a while, Edith and that little girl seemed a long way in the past.

...

My life rolled on, nothing to boast about but nothing to be ashamed of either. I kept my nose clean. I worked long days and put in for all the overtime they had going. Wasn't long before I'd collected a reputation as a good worker. Occasionally the others would tease me about having no life to go home to, especially when I put my hand up for the shifts nobody else wanted, Christmas and whatever, but I guess my silence on the matter made my point, and eventually silenced them. After a couple of years of that backbreaking work, my body was stronger than ever and my skin was brown as a berry from the Queensland sun. I could do the work blindfolded if I had to. Once I found I didn't have to concentrate so hard on the job, that I could let my mind wander without being at risk of falling into the water or dropping a bloody great crate on my foot, well then my brain began to ache for something more challenging to think about. All that work I'd done in the printing industry, the skills I'd learnt, started to play on my mind and I began to think about giving it another go. I'd never finished my apprenticeship, of course, and I was too old by then to consider going back to it, but I figured there'd always be places for people who worked hard. So that's how I came to work for *The Telegraph*. The newspaper had not long relocated from the city out to offices in Campbell Street in Bowen Hills, and they were expanding and hiring new staff.

The butterfly effect, they call it. You know, how one small incident can trigger a whole host of changes until it influences the final event? I guess if I'd never worked at *The Tele*, I'd never have met Pete, along with Sandra and the rest. And if I'd never met that gang, I wouldn't have ever got interested in their type of music, and I wouldn't have even noticed the ad. As it was, it jumped out at me and I was moving forward before I knew it.

That was all a long time afterwards. Plenty happened in the meantime. But all those years after that butterfly flapped its wings, the breeze it created was growing into a wind of hurricane proportions, and almost twenty years later the effect would be complete.

It was quiet down by the creek, quiet enough to hear the shushing of the reeds, the bubbling of water over the stones, the occasional splash of a darting dragonfly. The late-afternoon sun was settling onto the horizon, leaching the sky of light. Pale grey clouds hung suspended like sheets on a giant washing line. The afternoon chill had sent the kids scurrying, their bikes racing, soccer balls under their arms. Only a few determined joggers circled the oval. An older woman in a red jacket called to a huge dog, a Great Dane maybe crossed with something long-haired, with the unfortunate result of bearing a resemblance to a large, ungainly sheep. The woman threw a tennis ball and the dog bounded after it, slobber glistening.

The boy sat cross-legged by the creek bed, the cool air creeping across the surface of the water and spreading goosebumps up his arms. The black chick lay in his lap, its glassy eyes beginning to cloud over. He had started digging with a sharp pointed stick, and then used a flat rock to scoop out the soil underneath. Now he was using his bare hands, his fingers aching in the cold, damp earth that had also gathered under his fingernails. He smoothed out the cavity, picking out stray rocks and twigs. It smelt of mulch and rotting things, a rich aroma that filled the boy's nostrils and settled, thick and sweet, in his lungs.

The grave complete, the boy sat for a moment, listening to the sound of a kookaburra chortling, the stark laugh slicing through the silent afternoon. He shaded his eyes with one hand, searching. He found the bird on a low branch of a spotted gum, glaring at him accusingly. He dropped his arm and the bird took off, swooping across the empty sky. The boy lifted Midnight and cuddled her close to his cheek, her body cooling, her feathers already losing their sheen. He could feel that she had gone from him. With the tip of his index finger, he stroked her one more time, ran his finger over her beak, and petted the down on the top of her head. Then, with infinite care, he placed the small body into the hole, adjusting her until she looked comfortable. His hands shaking, he pushed the mounds of soil over the edge, watching as they thumped onto his chick, watching until the last clod covered one exposed beady eye. He quickly filled in the hole and patted down the surface until it was well packed. He got up and walked around the bank, collecting leaf litter and small branches, which he used to cover the spot. He searched again until he found two sticks of the right size that he broke in four and shaped into an M, and then stuck these firmly on top.

By the time the boy returned home, the sky had darkened to purple, like the passionfruit that grew on the old man's vine. A light shone from somewhere inside the house, and the boy could imagine him there, hunched over a tray of food, or perhaps watching the telly, a blanket on his stick-thin legs. He went towards his own house. The front-porch lamp, burnt out months ago, had been replaced; it illuminated the entrance with a false welcome. The boy stood listening, but could hear no sound from within. No car sat in the driveway. He wheeled his bike around to the back, propped it against the verandah post and made his way cautiously up the stairs.

His mother was sitting at the kitchen table, a cigarette in her hand. The smoke spiralled lazily upwards, dissipating into the film of ceiling dust. A half-empty bottle of vodka sat opened. The remains of a microwave meal had congealed in its plastic tray. A thin line of tiny black ants threaded across the table and into the food, then back again towards the table leg. Three bags of groceries sat, unpacked, on the floor. He could hear a game show on the TV in the other room.

He stood uncertainly at the door. His mother held out her arms to him, and he moved into her embrace. Her eyes were red-rimmed. She put the cigarette into a dirty saucer and pulled back to look at him.

It's late. I was worried about you.

It sounded to the boy like something she thought a mother should say.

I buried her, he said. When there was no response, he elaborated. *Midnight, my chicken.*

Oh darling, I'm so sorry about the chook. He shouldn't have done that. I didn't know you'd given it a name. You silly thing. Come here. Let me cuddle you.

Her hands stroked his cheek. He flinched. She pulled him close again and spoke into his hair.

You shouldn't provoke him, sweetheart. He didn't mean to do it. He feels terrible. He couldn't stay here and face you, he felt so bad. He's not a bad person. He just ... he's very protective of me and he doesn't like it when you sass me. If you could show him more respect, listen to him, do what he asks ... then there wouldn't be any more of this trouble.

She took his face in her hands and looked searchingly into his eyes.

Don't you want Mummy to be happy, baby?

Yeah, mumbled the boy.

Couldn't you try harder, for me? I'd do anything for you, you know that. We all need to try harder to get along, OK?

The boy sighed and allowed himself to melt deeper into her embrace. He wound his arms around her and relaxed into her chest. He could feel the tension draining from his limbs. His mother. All he had. All he knew. He didn't want to upset her. He tried to imagine his life without her, but couldn't. It had always been the two of them, together. She was rubbing his back and rocking him from side to side in a way that felt familiar and soothing. Some long-forgotten childhood comfort.

I'll try, he said quietly. *I'll try.*

She pushed the chair back with a scrape.

Well, I'm bushed. What a day. There's another chicken and rice thing in the freezer if you want it. Don't stay up too late, now. Don't want that bitch of a teacher on the phone again.

She gave his shoulder a squeeze and loped down the hall to her bedroom. The boy fingered his cheek, testing the bruised flesh, and then put his hand to his side. His ribs still hurt. He opened the freezer door and searched for some ice.

Pete was a music journo at *The Tele*. He spent his evenings going to gigs and drinking copious amounts of alcohol. He was into all sorts of music, as much at home in a Valley basement listening to some head-banging grunge band as he was spending a night at the opera. One of the perks of his job was free tickets to anything and everything, and sometimes he'd pass the tickets to me. The first time, I didn't realise he actually wanted me to report back on the music until he casually suggested that I might like to jot down a few notes, speak to people, grab a few comments. So that was my first journalistic assignment. The band was some one-hit wonder up from Adelaide. I'd never heard of them, and after the gig I never heard of them again. Pete took my notes and constructed some sort of sense out of them, and the article was printed under his byline. That's how I became an occasional accidental journo.

Pete was a big guy, well over six foot, with a head of hair on him like a grizzly bear and huge fists like ham hocks. Beats me how he ever managed those typewriter keys. He'd had a few fights in his day, mostly with other drunken patrons at the gigs. He was supposed to be representing the paper, so it didn't go down real well the next morning when Sandra had to go and bail him out. She stuck by him though. They sure had something, those two.

Sandra was a telephonist; she managed the switchboard and took messages. Never put up with any nonsense. Pete was no match for her temper. We all knew who wore the pants in that relationship.

Still, I think we all envied them a little bit, what they had together. Most of the others in the group drifted in and out of relationships or, like me, stayed pretty much single. Not that there wasn't a lot of sex going on. I mean, it was the decade of free love. I had my share of one-night stands, just like the next man. Many mornings I woke up in an unfamiliar room with my arm draped over some girl without having the foggiest notion of who she was or what we'd done the night before. Like the man said, though, the times were changing. Mostly the girls didn't seem to know or even care who I was either.

I worked as an operator on the offset printing machines, huge mechanical monoliths that had to be lifted in by crane through a hole in the roof, and serviced by specialists that came from Sydney. Despite their size, they were delicate and finicky to work on. You had to be sure of what you were doing. I was lucky to get the job at all, considering my lack of experience in recent years, but as I said, the paper was expanding, and what with half the young men going off to Vietnam and the other half dodging that very same circumstance, hard workers with any experience were difficult to find. I was happy to be given the chance, even though I started with a wage so low I may as well have still been loading vegetables.

The years unfolded around me in a blur of colour and music. Harold Holt disappeared amongst a host of conspiracy theories. I was listening to Normie Rowe, the Easy Beats, the Bee Gees, and of course the Beatles, young people's music, even though I was headed for middle age myself. Girls wore skirts so short they were nothing but scraps of material clinging together with a tantalising promise.

125

With a steady income again, and a secure job, I decided to take the plunge and buy a house. I was tired of renting, tired of sharing with strangers, sick of having to up sticks when a landlord wanted to sell. I bought this house in 1970 for under nine thousand dollars. Seems incredible. An unrenovated dog box in Bardon wouldn't go for less than half a million today. Inflation. Makes you think, doesn't it. I recall when that house next door went on the market a few years back, they wanted offers over seven hundred and fifty thousand. Seven hundred and fifty thousand! And it's not much chop to look at. Always been a rental. The owners seem to do the bare minimum of maintenance to stop the place falling down. What it needs is someone permanent to give it some TLC, instead of the array of tenants that stay for a couple of months and then disappear to who knows where.

Mind you, this place wasn't much to look at back then, either. But at thirty-two I was full of energy, and with a good job I had plenty of cash to fix up my own house. I bought it from an old couple who were retiring and going up to Cairns to live with their daughter. I remember they told me they wanted to see more of their grandchildren and dip their toes in the water occasionally. I used to wonder what happened to them, whether they were happy up in the tropical heat, with their ankle biters. They'd be long dead now. They seemed old to me then, and that was over forty years ago. I thought of them often because there were so many little things around the house that reminded me of their presence or, rather, their absence. She had stuck a plastic air freshener on the wall in the toilet. It was well past being useful, all cracked and yellowed with age, but I couldn't prise it from the wall without fearing that the whole sheet of plaster would come off with it. And every so often I'd find a button or a hairpin or a tin of half-used something or other at the back of a drawer, and it would bring to mind that couple, and the life they made in this house. In my house. They'd raised two sons and three daughters here. The place only has three bedrooms, even now, and one of them is more like an oversized cupboard, so I'll be blowed if I know where they put them all. But I suppose that's how things were back then. The chookhouse was theirs too, although I've had to do so many repairs over the years that it may as well be new. But it's in the same position as when they had their own hens scratching around. They were keen gardeners and the place was kept up nicely. Most of the plants I've got here today are similar to what they had growing then. Why reinvent the wheel, I thought. Mind you, my interest in gardening hasn't always been paramount. I neglected it for many years, 'til one day a friend came over, Sandra's sister actually it was, and berated me for letting it go to seed like I had. She told me I was lucky to have a house and even luckier to have a garden and I should care for it properly, and so I did. She had a bit of Sandra in her, that sister; it was hard not to do what you were told.

I've painted the place twice since I bought it. It used to be a pale shade of green, almost peppermint, but I redid it in the late seventies to a toasty brown with rust orange trim. Did it again in the late eighties with heritage colours, muted reds and greens. Haven't had the strength to do it since then, or the money to pay someone else to do it for me.

So anyway, what with all the previous owners' bits and pieces calling up memories of happier times in my little house, family times, it took a while for it to feel like my own. But gradually, bit by bit, it wore down my defences. That other family began to fade into the wallpaper, and the house seemed to curl itself around me like a winter cloak. It began to feel like home. For the first time in my life, I had somewhere I could truly call my own.

The boy's dream had begun by the creek bed. Instead of the meandering filament of silver that he knew, the water of his dreaming was murky and fast, rushing downstream with a force that smashed into boulders and tore small bushes from their roots. He was burying a kookaburra. Its body was stiff and cold, its feathers soaked in blood. Suddenly it came alive in his hands and perched on his arm, its sharp claws digging into his skin. It beat its wings and laughed maniacally at the boy before taking flight, shaking drops of blood from its feathers like water, and disappearing into the cloud-filled sky. When the boy focused on his hands, they were covered with writhing white maggots. He tried to shake them off but realised they were emerging from wounds in his fingers and gaping gashes in his wrists. He plunged his arms into the water, which was not ice cold as he expected, but warm and thick. The viscous liquid sucked at his limbs until he overbalanced and toppled in. The stream pulled him along, the water's rhythm in his ears, steady like a heartbeat. He could see his mother in the distance, her face turned from him, and he called to her as he passed. She merely raised a hand in greeting. He had travelled well past her before he glimpsed her face at last – it was devoid of features, an anonymous mask on his mother's body. The water became thicker, a dense sludge. The boy struggled. The noise grew louder, expanded in his ears until he felt the pressure against his eardrums. He heard voices calling to him, although he could not make out the words.

When he opened his eyes he was disoriented. His arms flailed against the sheets, against the water that he felt sure was about to pull him under. Gradually his eyes adjusted to the dimness; he saw his shoes, his chair, a strip of pale yellow under the door. His left ear throbbed, a dull ache. He could hear people, lots of people, laughter filling the house, the sound of their conversations sliding under the door along with the light. He peered at his clock radio. The digital numbers read 1.37 am. The boy massaged his sore ear in an attempt to relieve the pain; a stab penetrated deep towards his eardrum, like a cottonbud inserted too far. He hoped his mother had stocked up on the Panadol in the bathroom. He slipped out from under the sheets and cracked open the door.

Cigarette smoke and the pungent aroma of marijuana swirled in the air. Twenty or more people appeared to be crammed into the living room, a few bodies spilling into the hall. A man, his shirt unbuttoned, sat spread-eagled, his back against the wall, his mouth open, snoring. A half-full bottle lay loosely in his hand, a trickle of clear liquid flowing onto the carpet. Two women in short skirts stepped over him as they made their way to the bathroom. They squinted at the boy and giggled. Music played loudly but he couldn't make out the tune, let alone the words. The thudding bass boomed in his chest. He ventured further into the hallway, skirting past the man, and waited outside the bathroom door.

By the time the two women emerged, his ear was pulsing with pain, and he needed to pee. The girls were still giggling. They hardly gave the boy a glance as they made their way back towards the party. The boy rushed into the bathroom and closed the door tight.

The room smelt of piss and spew. He tried not to look too closely at the puddle on the floor beside the toilet bowl. He rummaged through the drawers until he found some Panadol. He ran the tap, using the end of his mother's toothbrush to push aside a mushy sludge of toilet paper blocking the drain in the basin. Cupping his hands, he swallowed a deep draught of water and washed down two tablets.

A groan startled him. He froze, afraid to raise his eyes to the cabinet mirror in case he saw someone standing right behind him. But when the groan came again, he realised it was coming from behind the shower curtain, pulled across the bath. His feet planted on the floor, he reached out one arm and gingerly hooked a finger around the edge of the curtain.

There was a naked man sprawled in the bathtub.

He let the curtain drop. He looked from the toilet to the bath and back again. He really did need to pee. He stood at the toilet with his back to the bath, his brow furrowed with concentration, his right leg jiggling up and down. Another groan. The boy spun around, a wet patch spreading on his shorts; he wrenched open the door and slammed it shut behind him.

He stood outside the door to his own room, thinking he would quite like to see his mother, but not wanting to run the gauntlet of her friends and acquaintances. Especially not with the stench of urine rising from his pants. He slipped inside his room, pulled the door to, retrieved a pair of tracksuit pants from a crumpled heap on the floor and changed out of his shorts. He opened his door again and peered out. A large woman in a colourful strapless dress came towards him, crooning his name. He could feel the cigarette in her left hand brushing the back of his neck, while the drink she held in her right sloshed onto his T-shirt.

Look at you! I haven't seen you since you were this high! Come here and give Aunty Leanne a cuddle.

The woman pulled him close until his face was smothered by her large bosom. He had no idea if he had met this person before. She smelt strongly of alcohol and perfume, with an underlying sweaty odour that nauseated him.

He managed to extricate himself, along with one of her nipples, which she stuffed back under her tight dress. The boy staggered backwards and bumped into a couple slow-dancing. The man was at least shuffling his feet; the woman was draped over his shoulder and appeared to be asleep.

Fuck. Watch it, mate.

Leave him, Anthony, he's only a kid.

Well what's a fucking kid doing up this late? Hey, ya slag, I didn't even know you had a kid.

His mother had appeared from the swell of bodies. She gave the man's arm a playful punch.

Watch who you're calling a slag, darling. Had a look what's hanging over your shoulder lately? Sloppy seconds, that one. Would've thought you had better taste.

Piss off. You weren't complaining last month. Couldn't get enough, as I recall.

In your dreams, Anthony. I've moved on to bigger and better.

The man released his hold on the woman and gripped his crotch suggestively.

Doubt you've found better, and I know you haven't found bigger.

His glassy-eyed smirk faltered as the woman slipped from his grasp and collapsed on the floor. She raised her hand to her forehead and groaned, and then was still. The man crouched down and roughly rolled her over beside the wall, out of the way of people's feet.

Fuck. She's out of it.

He wandered off dispiritedly in the direction of the kitchen.

The boy ventured a glance at his mother. She was staring around the room in an unfocused way, as if she'd forgotten he was there. But then her gaze reached him and she opened her arms. The boy dashed across the space between them and burrowed his face into her sweet, familiar warmth.

Come on, baby. Let's get you back to bed.

With her arm around his shoulders, she led the boy to his bedroom. Once inside, she closed the door behind them and helped him under the covers, pulling the blanket up around his chin. She sat down on his hand, but he didn't want to tell her in case she moved. She closed his eyes with her fingers, like he had seen them do to dead people in movies, and stroked his cheek. The boy relaxed.

When she spoke, it was like a murmur of wind through winter leaves.

I'm sorry we woke you, baby. I'll tell them all to be quieter.

I don't like those people, Mum. They drink too much. And everything smells funny.

Maybe I'll tell them all to clear off soon. It's getting late.

I don't like the way they look at me.

He opened his eyes.

Like I'm nothing. Like you're nothing.

OK, baby. I said I'd take care of it.

Why do they have to be here all the time?

A spark flared in her eyes and she stood abruptly.

Fuck. What do you want from me? Aren't I allowed to have friends? You want me to be some shitty, stay-at-home single-mum loser, is that it? Is that what you think of me? You, you, you. It's always about you. When is it my time, huh? When? When do I get to have a life?

He sat up and reached out his hand. *I'm sorry, Mum! I'm sorry! Please don't be angry. I didn't mean it. They're OK. They don't have to leave. You didn't even wake me up. My ear's sore, that's what woke me. I got up to get some Panadol, that's all.*

She softened and sat back on the bed.

Really, Mum. It's OK. I'm sorry, I shouldn't have said anything.

Her hand traced the outline of his ear. *This one? Poor baby. Maybe you should take a day off tomorrow, rest up.*

He nodded. She leant close and landed a wet kiss on his nose.

Night, night. Sleep tight. Watch those bed bugs don't bite.

She stood. Wrinkled her nose.

What's that smell?

She nudged the discarded shorts with her toe.

Shit, aren't you too old to be pissing your pants? Disgust flooded her face.

Sorry, he mumbled. *It was an accident. I'll clean it up tomorrow.*

Too right you bloody will. Don't think I'm doing it.

She left the room and pulled the door closed behind her. The boy wiped the back of his hand across his nose. He pictured a day at home tomorrow, fetching his mum cups of tea, cleaning the vomit from the bathroom floor. The sound of the empties clinking as he dumped them in the wheelie bin. Even now, over the stench of his own pee, he could still make out the stinging fumes of alcohol trailing in her wake.

It was the summer of '79 or '80 and I found myself hunting through the gig guide trying to find someplace different to take a new girl I was seeing.

I saw the ad for an AC/DC concert planned for later that month. 'Course, I knew it was too late to get tickets the conventional way, but I was thinking I might ask Pete whether he could score any on the side when I noticed the support act. In tiny ten-point type, right down the bottom, it said an act called Flower Power would perform before the main show. It seemed so incongruent – a hippy-sounding band supporting cult legends like AC/DC. So I asked Pete about it, and he trawled his mind and said that Flower Power was some one-woman singing sensation from Melbourne.

It's this chick, he said, *writes her own lyrics; she's on the rise down in the southern states. Great voice. Smooth one minute and then gravelly and throaty the next. Sexy combination. Appears on stage in this schoolgirl get-up, short skirt, suspenders, you get the picture. It's not a hippy band, you moron. That's her name. Flower. Sarah Flower.*

My heart felt like it had forgotten to stop beating. I had to sit down. Pete asked me if I was OK and I said no, not really, and so he wanted to know what was wrong, was there anything he could do? And I said there was so much wrong that it could never be put right, and that I didn't think he could help with that.

He went on with his work, figured I was having a weird moment, I guess.

In the end, I did ask him for help. I asked him could he find a picture of this Sarah Flower. He asked Sandra.

Oh, her. Yeah, my friend Angie saw her live a few months ago. Isn't she supporting up here on the AC/DC tour?

Sandra was a wealth of information on almost any subject you could name.

Pretty messed-up kid, from what I've heard. But whatever miseries she's been through she's channelled straight into her music, in the way that only true artistes do – she pronounced the word *artistes* with a French accent – *and the result, apparently, is heaven. Pure heaven. They say you listen to her sing, boys, and either you think you've died and gone to heaven, or* – she put her arms around both of us and smiled knowingly – *or you drift off to sleep with her music in your ears and go to heaven in your dreams.*

I must admit, I was only half-listening to this patter. I tore out the page, made some feeble excuse and left.

That first night I didn't sleep a wink. I kept going over and over it in my mind, what I'd done, who I'd left behind. I could see Edith still, the last image I had of her, huddled on the couch, her mouth a tight, thin line. Mrs E, solid and unforgiving. Poor Old Joe, plain bewildered. And at the centre of it all, Sarah Emily.

I'd done the wrong thing, obviously. Clearly. It struck me as incredible that I hadn't properly realised that until this moment. I'd so successfully managed to pack away that part of my life and put it up high on a shelf – along with my baby sister – that I'd forgotten it was there at all. If some bloke told me that he'd done what I did then, I'd think he was a complete and utter bastard. No question. But somehow that person just didn't seem to be *me*. I couldn't connect that man and his actions with me and my current life. But after twenty-four hours of thoughts and regrets, I made a decision. I had to see Sarah again, and Edith too if I could, and set things to rights. I didn't have the first idea how I was going to do that, but I was determined to try. Never too late, that's what I kept telling myself. It's never too late to fix things, never too late to say you're sorry.

'Course, I know now that adages like that aren't always true. Sometimes things can't be fixed. Sometimes sorry does come too late.

But that month I was full of hope. Full of ideas about how it was going to be. It sounds stupid but I came to believe that things would all work out. That I would get to meet her again. That she would see it in her heart to forgive what I saw as my momentary lapse of judgement all those years ago, a lapse that I had never got around to rectifying. I spent long hours on autopilot at work, daydreaming of her filling me in on her childhood, her aspirations, her hopes. Of her sharing those moments with me, sorry that I missed them. Introducing me to her musician friends, perhaps a boyfriend. And all the time, in these fantasies, I featured as a long-lost but beloved father. Talked about, mourned, wondered about. I saw a reunion, me being reinstated in her life almost as if the last twenty years hadn't happened. The girl I had left behind had been a helpless baby. I relished the chance to get to know her as a creative, vibrant adult.

I fantasised about this scenario so often, in fact, that it became almost real in my mind, even though it hadn't happened. It was as if I was remembering the past, rather than envisaging a future event. It happened so neatly in my head, all planned out and perfect.

The day drew closer until finally it arrived. It was a Friday. I took a sickie from work. I was sick in a way – I was so nervous that I expected butterflies to erupt from my mouth at any moment. I couldn't eat. I was fully dressed and shaved, ready to go, at eight o'clock in the morning, even though I knew she wasn't arriving until lunchtime. Pete had found that out for me. He still couldn't work out why I was so interested in this girl, although he had his suspicions. Anyway, he'd managed to have a word to a bloke he knew working security at the venue, and this guy said he'd turn a blind eye if I arrived during the afternoon rehearsal. Must've owed Pete a favour.

I caught a bus into the city and arrived at Festival Hall in the early afternoon. I must've spent an hour mooching about the side streets, trying to get up the courage to go in. Eventually I got worried that some copper eager for promotion might decide to do me for loitering, and I went round to the side door like Pete had instructed.

His mate, Cuddy, was a burly fellow who could've done a few rounds of fisticuffs in the Hall when it was still a boxing arena. The top of his head was as bald as a snooker ball but he sported a bristly grey moustache and a trimmed beard. Tattoos covered his arms from his wrists to his elbows and disappeared into his shirt-sleeves. I approached him about as confidently as if he was a cut snake. *Cuddy,* I said, and held out my hand in as manly a manner as I could muster. He glared at me like I was a piece of dog shit he'd found on his shoe. *Never saw ya,* he said by way of reply, but he edged a fraction away from the door and I took that as my cue to go in.

I followed a dim corridor. From the depths of the building came the beat of a bass drum. I could hear someone fingering a tune on a piano. A sign saying *Performers* led down some stairs to another long corridor with four or five doors on both sides, mostly closed. A woman in high heels, holding a clipboard to her chest, tapped past me and went round a bend at the far end of the hallway. A cleaner trundled by with his bucket on wheels, whistling tunelessly and barely giving me a second glance. Meanwhile, I stood there like a stunned mullet, not sure what to do next. After a few minutes, the woman in the stilettos clattered past me again. Almost as an afterthought, she paused before ascending the stairs.

Can I help you?

Um, I'm looking for Sarah Flower. I'm her ... I'm here to see ...

But the woman evidently wasn't interested in my reason for being there. *Third door down on the left,* she said, and continued up the stairs.

I straightened my shoulders and ran my fingers through my hair. I started to chew on the thumbnail on my left hand, but stopped when I tasted blood. I hadn't felt so nervous in a long time. Reminded me of waiting outside Mr McCready's office at the Home or when I used to stand opposite Edith's lolly counter and pretend to read. Or – and I realised this with a pang – maybe not since I paced around the waiting room while Sarah was being born. I knew then that I had to do it. I had to go up there and knock on that door. So I did.

It was opened a crack by a fellow who could only have been Cuddy's brother.

Yeah? he growled.

I'm ... I'm here to see Sarah ... um, Miss Flower. I'm here to see Miss Flower.

She's busy. Piss off.

He pushed the door closed, so I knocked again, louder this time.

What?

It was as if I'd awoken a bear in the midst of hibernation.

Um ... I really would like to see Miss Flower.

Listen, pal, you're beginning to irritate me now. Like I tol' ya, Miss Flower is busy. How'd you get in here, anyway? He shoved his menacing square head forward and peered around the door. *Who let you in? Fucking shit security.*

He attempted to close the door again but not before I got my hand around the doorjamb. Through the pain of my crushed fingers, I grimaced and said, *Please, please let me see her. I'm her father.*

138

He seemed surprised then, and released his pressure on the door. I winced.

Orright, pal, hold on a moment, yeah? He looked pointedly at my hand, which I removed, and then he closed the door. I could hear him speaking to someone.

He opened the door again, and I caught a glimpse of the dressing room. There was a mirror running the full length of the opposite wall, spotlights glaring along the top. A woman was seated on a stool with her back to me. She had thick chestnut hair that fell, curling, down her back.

Cuddy's brother stepped out from the room and shut the door firmly behind him.

Piss off, pal.

But ... please ... I'd like ...

This time his words were accompanied by a couple of rough shoves.

Listen, fuck off quietly and we'll forget about it, orright? Believe me, you don't want to make me lose my temper.

But ... please ... please just tell her ... her father's here to see her...

He pointed his finger in my face. *Miss Flower don't have a father, orright? So piss off. I don't know what your bloody caper is, but it ain't gonna work. You're not seeing her. Now go!*

Could you please tell her—

He interrupted me. *I did tell her, OK? I said there was some prick here who was either after an autograph or wanting to get into her knickers, I wasn't sure which, but he said he was her father and he sure looked old enough to be her father, so I thought I'd better tell her. And she said she don't have a father, she said her old man died when she was a kid. SO FUCK OFF!*

His words struck me as forcefully as a blow. I staggered backwards into the wall, and then my whole body crumpled, folded in on itself, and I found myself on the floor. I half-expected him to come at me, to lift me up with one of those hairy, meaty hands and manhandle me out of the building, but he didn't. He just glared at me and closed the door again. This time I heard the click of a lock sliding home.

I realise now how pathetic I was – that whole month of fantasising about some type of reunion, about thinking that somehow those twenty years wouldn't matter, as if we could pick up where we left off.

I still picture her sometimes, my daughter. Sarah Flower. I picture what I saw of her that day. A slim figure on a stool, a dark curtain of hair concealing her neck. One hand raised slightly, like maybe she was fixing her mascara. But not her face. Never her face. Although she was seated before a mirror, she was sitting dead-on straight to me, so all I could see was the view of her back. Sometimes I dream about her. In my dream, I'm always trying to manoeuvre myself into enough of an angle to catch a glimpse of her face in that mirror, or even her profile. But in my dream, my feet are rooted to the spot, and I never see anything but her back.

It's still a lovely image. *Girl Seated at Mirror*, that's what a famous artist would title it. But I can't deny I was mighty disappointed not to glimpse her face. My chance to gaze again into those baby-blue eyes was gone.

The boy was slouched under his desk as far as he could go without actually sliding to the floor. Almost horizontal. Every so often Ms Zibraugh turned around from the copious notes she was chalking on the board and peered at the class over the top of her purple spectacles.

I sincerely hope you're all getting this down.

Yes, miss, they chanted in automatic unison.

Because this will all be in next week's test. Her stare rested on the boy until he straightened himself and made a show of finding his pencil.

She turned away and he slid down again, resting his knee on the cool of the metal desk leg.

His palms were sticky and hot. The few overhead fans did nothing to dissipate the fug of sweat and secret farts magnified by the September sun streaming through the windows. He glanced through the glass. A small green and blue budgerigar pecked at the grass seeds, in between raising its head in jerky, anxious movements. A shadow passed across the grass and the bird was gone in a flutter of wings. The boy searched the patch of visible sky but it was empty.

A soft thud on the back of his head. A pig-shaped eraser rolled under his chair. Mitch, in the desk behind him, began to chant in a quiet, sing-song voice.

Take off ze bra, baby ... take off ze bra, baby ...

The boy glanced up at their teacher's back, the flesh under her arms jiggling as she wrote. He repeated the taunt softly, his French accent honed through days of practice. *Take off ze bra, baby ...*

She swivelled abruptly, zeroing in on the boy with a withering glare.

Would you care to share?

No, miss.

Oh, please do. You obviously find something extremely amusing. It would be cruel not to let the rest of us in on the joke. Her voice was cold and the room was silent. *I'm sure I heard something about a bra. That's a topic your tiny little brain finds funny, is it?*

No, miss.

No? NO? She stamped towards his desk, picked up his ruler and brought it down with a smart slap on his open exercise book. The other students watched in silent awe. Her voice was shrill as she continued to scold him, her face furious, the ruler whacking hard and fast. His book began to slide off the desk. When he tried to catch it before it hit the floor, he felt the sting of ruler on skin. He retracted his hand and held it against his chest, a bruise already forming across his knuckles. Ms Zibraugh faltered for only a moment and then brought the ruler down hard on the desk once more.

Perhaps you will consider the subject of your humour more carefully next time. Choose something more appropriate. Her soft-soled shoes squeaked a path back to the board.

That's bullshit, the boy murmured.

I'm sorry? What did you say?

Nothing, miss.

WHAT DID YOU SAY?

Twenty-four pairs of eyes swung between the teacher and the boy, as if at a tennis match.

The boy was made bold by his anger. *I said it's bullshit.* He sat upright in his chair. Refused to move his eyes from hers. *It's all bullshit. And you can't hit me like that.*

She marched towards him once more and yanked at his collar.

Get up! Get out! Go and see Mr Brady right now! I do not want to see your face in this class again today.

The boy remained silent. He got to his feet, closed his book and headed for the door.

All eyes downcast now, not wanting to meet his, not wanting to be the next target.

...

The deputy principal's office was crammed with stuff – too-large chairs, a desk piled high with papers, framed certificates and awards on every wall, knickknacks and confiscated toys on the bookshelves. The boy perched on the edge of a floral armchair. Mr Brady sat behind his desk, swivelling back and forth, his arms crossed.

This is the second time this week, kiddo. The ... he consulted a desk diary ... *the eighth time already this term. Not a good end to the year, is it, mate?*

No, sir.

Rather juvenile, don't you think? Making fun of someone's name like that?

I am a juvenile.

Arms uncrossed. *Don't try being a smart-aleck with me too now, you hear?* The reprimand a cutting warning.

Silence. Everything waiting for a response.

The boy shifted in his seat, eyes on the floor, his hair hiding his face.

Sorry, sir, he mumbled. At last, he raised his head and met Mr Brady's direct gaze. *Sorry, sir. For swearing. And for making fun of her name.*

The deputy principal's face softened. He took off his glasses and chewed on one end. Sat back in his chair. His voice was kinder now.

Yes, well, I'm glad to hear it. Respect. That's important, isn't it. Show a bit of respect for people and they'll generally respect you back. You'd better apologise to Ms Zibraugh, too, hey?

He winked at the boy.

Not her fault she's got a funny name, is it? Hey?

The boy allowed himself a small smile.

Mr Brady leant forward, his elbows on the desk, his chin resting on his clasped hands. *How are things for you at home? Is there anything you want to talk about? Worried about anything?*

No, sir.

Under the deputy principal's scrutiny, the boy self-consciously fingered the fading yellow bruise under his eye.

Fell off my bike, he said, before Mr Brady could ask.

Hmm. Maybe I should have a talk to your mum. I haven't spoken to her for a while now.

No! I mean, no, she's really busy. She's working.

Well, I need to call her to come and collect you anyway. I don't think you should go back to class today. Give Ms Zibraugh a break. Come in tomorrow, apologise and it'll all be forgotten, all right?

Yes, sir.

And I'll just have a quick word with Mum when she comes. Just to check in with her, make sure we're on the same page, OK?

Yeah, OK. Reluctantly. Sir.

You go and sit outside my office, at that corner desk there, and wait 'til she comes. Here, take this and have a look. He handed the boy a heavy book. *It's got all the special events that have happened every day of the year, all throughout history, see? You can look up your birthday and see*

*what else happened on that day over the years. Off you go then, and I'll
phone your mum.*

The boy went outside and began paging through the book.

Mr Brady called to him. *I've rung Mum, she'll be here soon.*

Yes, sir.

An awful lot of people had died on his birthday over the years.
In 1701, Captain William Kidd had been hung for piracy and
murder. In 1934, Bonnie and Clyde went down in a hail of bullets.
One of those Nazis committed suicide in 1945. And wealthy Sir
Edward somebody or other died in 1925 when he fell off his
penny farthing bicycle. That was kind of funny. Some religious
Italian was burnt at the stake in 1498 and a famous American
boxer died in 1990. He read about a disabled six-year-old English
boy who had sued a newspaper twenty years ago for calling him
'the worst brat in Britain' after he had set the furniture alight, cut
his ear off, killed the cat in the washing machine, painted the dog
blue and swallowed insecticide.

Disabled or not, the boy thought, that was still pretty naughty.

Two divers got married underwater in 1988. The French crown
jewels were sold for six million francs in 1887. Right at the bottom
of the page was a box highlighting famous births that day. The boy
saw *1951 – Anatoly Karpov – Russian chess champion*. That was cool.

Forty-five minutes later, the bell signalled the end of another
school day. Students spilled from classrooms, shouting to each
other, talking, teasing, grabbing bags and cramming snacks in their
mouths. The wooden floor reverberated with the thrumming
of feet. Several teachers passed by, car keys in hand. A group of
Year 6s in identical red jerseys headed for the oval.

Mr Brady seemed just as busy after school as during. He made
several phone calls and spoke to two or three teachers about plans
for the following day. He dealt with a snivelling Year 1 girl who
couldn't remember whether she was supposed to wait or walk
home. He gave instructions to the groundsman and sorted out

some money with Mrs Wainright, the admin lady, who always gave the boy a sympathetic smile. Every so often he would pop his head around his office door and check that the boy was still waiting.

Shouldn't be long now, mate. I'll just give her another ring.

Then – *Can't seem to get a hold of her, but I've left a message.*

And after that – *She did say she'd be right over to collect you. We'll wait a bit longer.*

And then finally, at four-thirty, he came out of his office, locked the door behind him and sat down next to the boy.

Well, champ, I guess it looks like she might not be coming. Must have been delayed. How do you normally get home, you walk, don't you? Or ride your bike? I noticed you had a new bike.

Yes, sir. Ride my bike. The boy stood.

I'm not entirely comfortable just letting you go like this, but I've got a family dinner on tonight and I really should be getting on.

It's fine, sir, really. She probably just … you know …

Got held up, you think?

Yeah … maybe. Or maybe she just forgot or … he whispered, *just didn't want to come.* He held Mr Brady's gaze until the deputy principal looked away.

Right. Well. I see. OK, well you get on home then and I'll …

The boy, released at last, hoisted his bag onto his shoulder.

Mr Brady stared after the small figure. He rubbed his eyes, hard, with both hands.

I couldn't decide which was worse – the fact that maybe Edith had told her I was dead, or that Sarah knew I wasn't dead but had decided to treat me as if I was.

I hit the bottle. Whenever the alcohol wore off and my brain switched on again, I'd sit there, dumbfounded at my own stupidity. How could I have walked off and left that little girl? How could I have walked out on Edith? How could I have given up the first notion I had of a family? *Girl Seated at Mirror* – I had created that sad masterpiece. I had something good and worthwhile and precious, and then I had walked away and left it all behind.

I remembered that visceral feeling I had towards the baby. I had been frightened to love Sarah Emily. Hadn't I? Or had I resented her intrusion into my life with Edith? I felt a flush of shame. I cast my mind back to that other vulnerable small child in my life.

My sister.

The one who would never leave me.

Emily. My Emily. Her sweet, milk-fogged breath. The fine, downy hairs on her chubby arms. Her flawless skin, pale as parchment. Those knowing eyes. I remembered how I had loved her, but also how her arrival had changed my mother. How she removed her attentions from me onto the new baby. No longer fussed over me, didn't seem to notice if I ate my dinner or cleaned my teeth. I was no longer the focus of her days.

Emily had arrived as a small intruder; she commanded my mother's devotion, sapped her energy, absorbed her affection like a sponge, and left not a drop for me.

Thoughts of my dead sister and my lost daughter crowded my mind until I couldn't tell who was who. My motivations were murky; I didn't know why I'd done what I did. I couldn't believe I had been so selfish and crazy and weak. The only way it seemed any clearer was looking back through the bottom of a glass bottle. Alcohol wiped my brain of all thought except the next drink. Wiped it clean. Swept it clear. Got all that clutter out of my head.

And so I drank. A lot. For a while there I barely knew which way was up. I drank, but after a while not even the drink could hold the bad dreams at bay. I dreamt nightmarish dreams of disfigured babies and funhouse mirrors, of garish girls with long chestnut hair, of making love to Edith and then looking down and realising it wasn't Edith at all but some other woman that I didn't recognise.

I dreamt of all that I'd lost.

But mostly I dreamt about children. Perfectly formed babies and innocent toddlers. Children maimed and vulnerable and needy and alone. Sweet little girls with warm breath. Screaming infants, their mouths open wide in furious frustration. Creatures as weak and defenceless as kittens. Children susceptible and exposed and frail, or strong and invincible and impervious to the dangers and pitfalls of life.

My sister. My daughter. The children I once knew.

In my sober moments, I tried to make sense of my actions. I considered my unrealistic desire to reconnect with my daughter. I thought back to her birth, and the shame and fear and self-loathing it had ignited in me all those years earlier. And then further back still, to my sister. To what I had felt towards her.

There was no startling revelation. No moment of truth. Didn't matter how I circled it around in my mind, I found no answers but only more questions. And all I could do was wait.

As time passed, gradually I was able to stop thinking about those children missing from my life. Gradually I came out from under that smothering grey cloud. For the most part.

I drank less. Took up tennis with Pete, when he could drag me along.

That's about when I got my first chooks, too. I took that as a good sign, being able to care for something other than myself.

My dreams of children came less often, and were less intense. I stopped thinking about Sarah Flower. I stopped remembering Edith.

Simple kindnesses pulled me through. I could've ended up much worse. There're people out there merely existing. Scraping by, one day at a time, with such worry and sadness and fury within them that it would kill you to know about it. People with so many of those little compartments in their heads that they spend all their time scrabbling about trying to tunnel through to freedom.

I never did tell Pete why I was so interested in meeting Sarah Flower. Of my connection with her. Never told him, and he never asked. Even later, years later, when Pete and I figured out we were related, I still never told him about Sarah Flower. Figured it was enough of a bombshell already, what with all he knew of my past, my childhood. Didn't want to drag any more skeletons out of the closet to see the light of day.

There's only so much contempt a fellow wants to open himself up to. There simply wasn't any way I could frame my treatment of Edith and Sarah – that whole period of my life – and make it seem halfway reasonable. So that's how it went. From time to time I would clam up, grieve too late and all over again. And drink.

But eventually I would put the bottle away and keep on going. After all, what choice did I have?

Don't suppose it will matter in the end. All our secrets go with us to the grave.

The sounds of early summer filled the air. Black crows cawed and swooped. A lawnmower buzzed in the distance. There was the shrill call of insects, and a hushing as the wind lifted the leaves on the branches and set them down again. The skin on the back of the boy's neck tingled and burned; his eyes crinkled against the dry breeze. He leapt the fence in a practised jump and heard the chickens' squawking intensify to welcome him.

The old man had tried to give him another chick, a yellow one, had even offered to get another baby black one, but the boy had refused. Midnight was gone. The boy had not spoken to him again about how the chick had died, and from then on the old man had kept quiet about it.

He unlatched the gate and the birds ran for the exit, hopping about in the sunshine, making for the leaf mulch under the avocado tree. The boy considered life as a chicken, with your only worry being where the next worm came from or whether or not you would produce an egg that day. He thought he wouldn't mind coming back as a chicken.

He glanced up at the verandah but the old man did not appear. They had lately taken to spending Saturday afternoons together in the garden. The old man was teaching him how to weed and water, how to prune and harvest. The boy was helping him prepare a vegetable garden in the back corner, wired off to protect it from the chickens. Today they were meant to be digging in some fertiliser. Stinky stuff, stored in the woodshed.

The boy lay on the grass, reading and dozing. The shadows grew longer, and dusk crept across the yard. He closed his book, shooed the hens back into their house and latched the gate. The old man had not come. Perhaps tomorrow.

...

Sunday dawned grey and overcast. The boy dressed and headed for the yard. He paused to listen outside his mother's room, then pushed on the door. Soft snores came from the mound of bedclothes. He couldn't tell if the blankets hid one body or two.

He sat on the back steps and laced up his trainers. The old man had made it clear – no shoes, no gardening. *We don't want a shovel slicing off those toes.* The steel-grey sky was studded with ominous thunderheads. It would rain before dinner.

In the old man's yard, he stopped to watch a row of ants as they made their way up the scribbly gum. He opened the henhouse and let the girls out onto the grass. The woodshed door screeched open and he began to pull the heavy sack of blood and bone out into the open. He closed his eyes and grunted as he heaved the bag across the grass, leaving behind a flattened trail. He got as far as the jacaranda and then flopped down on the lawn, his legs sprawled across the sack. The tree was immature, less than two metres high. A dozen purple blossoms crowned the leafy green. Across the old man's back fence, there was another jacaranda, a giant silhouette against the silvery clouds, thick limbs perfect for climbing, and a thousand periwinkle-blue flowers nodding in the breeze.

A bush turkey landed on the fence in a flap and flurry of wings. It balanced precariously for a moment before dropping to the ground. Keeping one nervous eye on the boy, the bird strutted towards the henhouse, each scraggy claw lifted and placed in a precise pattern. With a rush it dashed for the grain bucket inside the door. The boy had forgotten to replace the brick on top; the bird lunged at the lid with its beak, sending it clattering to the ground, and then had its whole head in the bucket, gobbling grain as fast as its gullet could swallow.

The boy flew up and across to the henhouse, waving his hands wildly in the air.

Har! Har! Get out of it, you dumb bird! Go on, scat! Shoo!

The squawking turkey thrashed around the confines of the hutch, too stupid to find the door opening, its beady eyes glinting in fear. After a strange dance in which both boy and bird writhed and jumped and flapped, the disorientated turkey spotted the space through which light flooded, and made its bid for freedom. The boy followed him to the fence with shouts and claps, and then did a victory dance in the weeds.

Surely all that noise would rouse the old man.

But the house stayed silent, the back door firmly shut.

The boy went back to the woodshed and found a shovel. He pulled aside the chicken wire and began to turn over the rich, loamy soil. Every shovelful of earth revealed a tangle of worms – *a good sign,* the old man had said. The boy shovelled and loosened clods of soil; he picked out rocks and small stones, and pulled out the remaining weeds by the roots. It had been only a few days since they had cleared the patch, and already more weeds had sprouted four or five centimetres high.

He worked at a steady pace throughout the morning, stopping only to gulp mouthfuls of water from the outside tap, hot at first from the sun, becoming icy as the flow pumped from deep beneath the ground. The storm threatened and the air remained muggy, clinging to his skin and gathering the dirt in his nostrils. Trickles of sweat coursed down his arms and back, and stung his eyes.

Every so often he would pause and stare at the house, willing the old man to make an appearance, if only to say he was unwell and didn't want to work in the garden that day. But he didn't show. The boy kept digging, unwilling to stop. If he did, he would have to make a choice. He could go home. He could put away the shovel, chase the hens back into their house, and go home.

But he hadn't seen the old man for two days now.

He couldn't go home, not without knowing.

The second choice was to find out what was happening. What was wrong.

He thought of entering the silent house. Usually a glimpse of the old man was enough of an invitation. The boy felt his presence was expected, anticipated. But not today. Today the house squatted mute amongst the profusion of green. No movement at the curtained windows. No footsteps from within. It even smelt empty. Something about the atmosphere of the house gave the boy pause. Today it did not feel welcoming. Today he did not feel invited or expected. Climbing the stairs and entering seemed wrong somehow. Like last time, when he had discovered the old man feverish and shivering in his bed. When he had thought he might be dead.

He couldn't stop, not yet.

He worked for another hour, his stomach growling, his limbs growing slack with fatigue. Finally he threw the shovel onto the dirt and plodded towards the house. He was hot, filthy, tired and hungry. He stamped up the steps, announcing his presence with noise and bluster. He hesitated, then knocked on the door. To his surprise, it yielded to his fist, swinging open to the old man's kitchen. The familiar smell of vomit and alcohol filled the boy's nostrils.

It smelt like home.

Although he had noticed a dusty bottle of whisky in the old man's cabinet, and the occasional beer bottle in the recycling bin, he had never before seen much evidence of him drinking. And this smelt like serious drinking. His mother on a bad day.

The boy peered through the gloom. Dirty dishes were piled in the sink. Flies crawled over a half-eaten sausage on a plate on the table. More and more like home. He counted two empty whisky bottles on the floor beside the bin, three wine bottles containing only the dregs, and a few stubbies lying on the stove or sideways on the floor.

He levered his muddy trainers off his feet and stepped inside. Immediately the smell was stronger, and the source became obvious – a stinking pile of spew, right there on the floor on the other side of the kitchen. The boy looked away.

He tiptoed towards the lounge room, darker even than the kitchen, the curtains drawn tight against the day. The old man was sprawled at a funny angle on the sofa, one leg resting on the floor, one arm thrown over his face. His head was tilted back and – to the boy's relief – guttural noises came from his open mouth. The boy crept nearer, holding his breath against the stink. The old man was a sorry sight. Dried vomit splattered his shirt and his fly was undone. The boy stared at the old man's bare feet – white and hairy, with tough, curling yellow toenails.

So this was it. The old man was a drunk. Like his mum. Like all her boyfriends. Like just about every adult he had the misfortune to come into contact with. Pathetic.

The boy turned away. In the kitchen he kicked an empty bottle against the wall in disgust. Pain soared through his big toe. He grabbed his shoes and slammed the back door.

...

After school on Monday, the boy cycled to the creek. Detritus from the previous night's storm littered the ground. The sky was still grey, and water dripped from disturbed branches. He rode fast and wild through the bush, skidding on loose dirt and patches of mud, and trying risky jumps. He threw flat stones across the water. He ran into some Year 8 boys and sold them the last of his smokes for two bucks each. He waded into the shallows and tried to catch tadpoles with his bare hands. He pulled up great clods of earth and threw them into the water.

He found a fallen nest and smashed the lone egg against a boulder.

He fought a eucalypt, bashing his fists over and over on the bark, until his knuckles bled and strings of snot mingled with the dirt on his face.

Then he sat on the damp earth, hugged his arms around his knees, and cried.

...

Tuesday he skipped school and spent the day re-creating their last chess game in his head. All afternoon, and he still couldn't find a way to beat the old man's last move.

Wednesday he remembered the chickens. As he opened the gate, they rushed to him, scolding him in their shrill voices. When he scattered the grain, they fell over themselves to get at it, the older ones delivering ferocious stabs to the weaker hens. Their water container was almost empty and stank of chook poo.

There were seven eggs in the nesting boxes. In a series of deliberate, calculated throws, he smashed each one against the verandah posts, and watched as the bright yellow yolks ran down to stain the earth.

After half an hour spent watching the ants delight in the unexpected feast, the boy's breathing had slowed and his heart had returned to its regular beat. The broken shells and their glistening contents made a forlorn scene of carnage. He got the hose and tried to wash off the sticky mess that was fast solidifying in the sun, but it was no good; the albumen had dried onto the paintwork.

The boy then spent an hour cleaning out the henhouse. He filled the boxes with fresh straw, raked the dirt and even ran a stick around the corners to catch at the dusty webs. When he was finished, he sat and watched the hens stride around the yard. He pulled aside the wire netting around the patch of earth intended for the vegetable garden. One by one, the chickens strutted over cautiously, attracted by the aroma of fresh-turned soil and the promise of bugs.

Another storm hit on Thursday afternoon. The boy stayed in his room, reading and devouring a king-size block of chocolate he had swiped from the corner store. His mum came to the door about seven-thirty and asked if he wanted pasta, but the boy felt sick in the stomach. He ignored her and eventually she went away.

On Friday morning he made a decision. Bugger school. Bugger the old man too. Be damned if he was going to allow him to drink himself stupid and neglect his chooks. The boy wanted to plant that garden. He wanted to beat the pants off him at chess. He missed his afternoon tea.

He missed the old man.

...

He waited until his mum had left the house. That was after ten o'clock, and she hadn't even asked him why he wasn't at school. He marched into the yard and jumped the fence before he could change his mind. Straight past the henhouse, past the barren vegie patch and up the back stairs. The door was unlocked. The kitchen was in an even worse state than it had been five days earlier. A foul odour emanated from the overflowing rubbish bin; plates crawling with flies sat stacked in the sink and on the table. The bottles had multiplied. The boy ignored it all and stomped into the lounge room but it was empty. He headed for the old man's bedroom and pushed aside the door. More bottles lay on the bedside table and scattered across the carpet. The bed was empty.

After establishing the old man was not lying unconscious on the floor, the boy continued to the closed door of the bathroom. He put his ear against the peeling paint and listened. Nothing. He raised his hand and knocked lightly, suddenly aware of how out-of-place he felt here without the familiar tidiness and biscuits and chess game. There was no answer. He knocked again, the hollow sound echoing in the still house. This time, a groan, just audible. His irritation returned. He twisted the old-fashioned brass door-knob and squinted against the sun's glare streaming through the high window and reflecting off the mirror. It took only a moment to assess the situation. The old man sat on the floor, his head resting against the rim of the bathtub. A mouldy shower curtain was draped like a vulgar headpiece across his hair. The boy raised his hand to his nostrils and tried to breathe through his mouth. Specks of vomit were spattered in the basin, with more of it in the bath. The toilet was filled with the vile stuff, and hadn't been flushed.

The old man was clothed in a ragged pair of shorts and a yellowing singlet. His sunken chest rose and fell in an irregular rhythm. His face was a sickly grey, drained of substance, as if the skin no longer had any structure beneath it and was sagging over his skull. He was unshaven, grey stubble covering his chin and cheeks and upper lip in ugly patches. He had gashed his forehead at some stage in the last few days, and the puckered wound was red and inflamed. He looked old. The boy wondered fleetingly just how old he was. The old man had never told him, and he had never asked.

...

It was a long day. At first the boy simply sat beside the old man, breathing in the stink of him, sullen and quiet. But as his anger ebbed away, he began to make himself useful. He decided not to call the ambulance again, not yet anyway. Instead, he did what he could. He flicked aside the shower curtain, found a clean washcloth, soaked it in cold water, and sponged the old man's face and upper body until he roused and shook his head and muttered nonsense. Satisfied that he wasn't dying, the boy got a pillow from the bedroom and placed it behind his head. The old man opened one glassy eye and stared at him for the briefest moment, then rested his head down and recommenced snoring.

The boy started with the bathroom. He found disinfectant under the sink and used the whole bottle, rinsing out the basin and the tub, flushing the cleaned toilet, and mopping up the vomit crusted outside the bathroom door, working around the old man who slept on unawares.

He found a bin bag and collected the empties from every room, and then dragged the whole lot outside and into the recycling bin. It was well past lunchtime. He found half a block of cheese in the fridge, along with some stale crackers and an unopened lemonade in the cupboard.

He filled a glass with tap water, took it to the old man and held it to his mouth. Most of it dribbled down his stubbly chin, but the boy thought that at least some made it into his mouth. The old man's Adam's apple bobbed up and down once as he swallowed.

Next he went through the fridge. He threw out the week-old milk and the putrid fruit, the mouldy bread and the opened cans of soup. He scraped all the leftovers into the rubbish bin, gagging as dozens of maggots squirmed at the intrusion, and heaved the bag into the wheelie bin. He piled the dirty dishes on the table, filled the sink with water as hot as he could stand and washed them all by hand, rinsing off the suds with clean, cold water. He had to stop three times to dry and put them away to give him more room.

Another glass of water for the old man; this time he drank about half of it. When he opened his eyes, a vague look of recognition passed between them.

In the bedroom, the boy threw open the window, letting a fresh breeze blow through the room. He pulled the sheets from the bed, wincing at the stains, then bundled them up in his arms and set off to find the laundry.

He found the washing machine under the house. It was in a corner with an ancient concrete tub, batons screening them off from empty plastic pots, spilled bags of fertiliser, a rusty rake and several sealed cardboard boxes. He dumped some washing powder in with the linen and started the machine.

Upstairs the old man had stirred and was attempting to crawl out the bathroom door. The boy stood in front of him. The old man stared first at the boy's feet, then his gaze travelled to about the boy's waist before the effort became too much and he sagged to the floor.

Drink, he muttered.

The boy went to the kitchen and returned with another glass of water.

No. Drink. There. The old man gestured towards the kitchen, from where the boy had recently disposed of several full and half-full bottles of booze in addition to the empties.

The boy squatted down so he was at eye level with the old man.

He shook his head, his stare unwavering.

Nope. Sorry. No more drink.

He offered him the water.

With more strength than the boy would have given him credit for, the old man swiped at the glass and sent it clattering across the floor.

Whisky! he said, and tried to get up off the floor. But again it was too much effort; he crawled on all fours towards the kitchen and sank back into semi-consciousness.

The boy collected the glass, refilled it and placed it within easy reach. Then he set about searching for clean sheets.

The contents of the linen cupboard were sparse but organised. The boy found double bedsheets and two pillowcases. In the bedroom, he banged the pillows together out the window, and then jumped on the bed for good measure. He spread his arms wide and the sheets billowed out like sails on a ship. He tucked in the corners as best he could and folded the top sheet over, as he'd seen his mother do.

With a glance at the sleeping man, he surveyed his day's work before slipping outside.

Back at home, he wrote a note to his mum:

Dear Mum, gone next door to help him with something.
I might be back late. Dont worry I ate.
xxx

He found some leftover pasta and an apple that wasn't too soft, and packed them in a bag with a bottle of Coke and his book.

When he returned, the washing machine was silent. He tried to hang the sheets on the rotary clothesline in the backyard, but they kept dragging on the ground. In the end he doubled them over and hoped for the best. He said a quick hello to the hens, threw them some feed, and went back into the house.

The old man was sitting where he had left him, but the glass of water was empty. His eyes opened as the boy approached. He held out the glass. *More?*

Please, he added.

The boy refilled the glass and handed it to the old man, then sat down beside him on the floor and opened his book. He didn't speak. The man gulped the water.

After a while, the old man struggled to stand. The boy held his arm and steadied him, then helped him stagger back to the bathroom. He flicked the switch and light flooded the room, gleaming off the clean surfaces. The old man stood very still. When he turned to the boy, his eyes brimmed with tears.

The old man leant over the toilet, one hand on the wall, the other reaching inside his pants. He glanced over – beseeching, embarrassed – and the boy moved away.

The boy heard the bath running. He fetched a fresh towel from the cupboard and placed it on the side of the bathtub. The old man stood naked, his skinny limbs pale under the fluorescent light, his buttocks pressed flat from sitting on the floor. He looked at the boy in gratitude and contrition. Still the boy said nothing.

He searched timidly through the dressing-table drawers until he found a clean T-shirt and a pair of Y-fronts with the elastic gone. That would have to do for now. He left them folded inside the door.

When the old man came out of the bathroom, the boy led him to his bedroom. He pulled back the sheets and the old man slid gratefully under the covers. The boy gave him more water and set a jug beside the bed. He retrieved his book and made himself comfortable in a chair under the window. The whine of mosquitoes kept him awake for a while, but eventually sleep overcame him.

He dreamt of whisky bottles and billowing bedsheets, of endless glasses of water and droning mosquitoes.

That bloody kid. Why can't he leave a man to get pissed in peace. The taste so smooth, like velvet wrapping itself around my throat. Flowing through my limbs to the tips of my fingers and toes. Encasing me in warmth and softness and forgetting. Taking me to a place where nothing means anything, where the past is more real than the present, where the future is far, far away. When I'm drinking, I'm in a place of nothingness. No pain, no happiness, no regrets. No feelings. Nothing but a void stretching out before me like an unending horizon on a jewelled sea. And when reality begins to prick at your skin, you down another shot and everything becomes blurry again.

Just like when I saw *Girl Seated at Mirror*.

And when I walked out on Edith and Sarah.

But most of all, most of all, it comes back to her. The one who will never leave me.

Love is a fictional place.

But grief and betrayal – all roads lead there.

Life doesn't take kindness into consideration, I've learnt. It's not the natural order of things. Kindness is something that has to be eked out, little by little, dug out of the cold, hard ground like gold out of rock. And when you find it, you'd best pass it on quick smart to someone else, before some other sod sees that kindness and beats it out of you. I'll tell you something for nothing – when you get to my age, you've got a right to a blather. Even a drunken blather. There isn't nobody who can take against you for it. Especially not some snotty-nosed kid with enough life experience to fill a thimble. Especially not him.

When the boy opened his eyes on Saturday morning, he had to turn his face from the sun's glare. At some point during the night, he had slipped from the chair and onto the floor, his head on a cushion, his book askew. He stretched, his body stiff, the skin along his legs and arms patterned with the imprint of the carpet. The old man jerked in his sleep, mumbled something, and then continued his raspy snores. The boy peeled himself off the floor and stood over the bed, watching. The old man's eyelids fluttered. A line of spittle ran from his mouth down the side of his stubbly chin. The boy replaced the cushion on the chair and left the room.

His own house was quiet. He saw from the kitchen clock that it was after eight o'clock. He went into the bathroom and shut the door, stripped off his clothes – caked with dirt and filth from the day before – and stood for a long time under the shower, the cool needles of water piercing his skin. When he was dressed, he returned to the kitchen. The only teabags he could find were all used, tangled on an old saucer. He chose the least disgusting one, brushed off the grey mould and made a cup of tea, adding lots of sugar and a dash of milk.

He knocked on his mum's door. No response. He turned the doorknob. His mum stirred as he crossed the room, and dislodged her arm from under her sleeping companion. She reached for the boy, groping the air as her eyes attempted to focus.

Made you some tea.

Thanks, precious. You're up early, she whispered. *Why don't you go back to bed? Last time I checked, you were sleeping like a baby.*

The boy held her gaze, willing her to ask him, ask him anything, to admit the lie. But she only stared back at him until her eyelids drooped shut again.

Must've been years ago, he muttered. His mother exhaled – a long, ragged sigh – but made no reply.

He fixed himself a Vegemite sandwich and then made a second one, which he wrapped in greaseproof paper. It was after nine by the time he slipped through the old man's back door.

He put the sandwich on a plate and made another cup of tea, this time with a decent teabag and lots of sugar to make up for the lack of milk. He carried the mug into the bedroom and placed it on the bedside table, then went back for the sandwich and a glass of water. He settled himself into the chair and began reading his book, glancing occasionally at the sleeping form in the bed.

After a particularly exciting bit – the first pirates had boarded the ship belonging to the second gang of pirates, taken them all hostage and raided their treasure and were about to make the captain walk the plank – the boy looked up to find the old man peering at him.

Good morning. I made you some tea. And a sandwich. From home. Hope you like Vegemite.

You been home? Good. I thought I remembered you sitting there half the night.

The whole night, actually. Only went home to have a shower.

Bloody hell, kiddo. What'll your mum think?

The boy returned to his book. *She didn't even notice,* he murmured.

Shit. The old man attempted to find some of the bluster he had felt the night before, some of his irritation at the boy refusing him his whisky and curtailing his bender and disallowing him from continuing to wallow in alcohol and self-pity. But the sheets were cool and fresh, the foul taste had all but gone from his mouth, his eyes were less gritty and the pounding in his head had dulled to a subtle ache. He found he couldn't be bothered complaining.

The boy glanced up again, this time with a level gaze, and said, *And watch your language.*

The old man's eyes fell; he stared at his trembling fingers picking at the threads of the blanket.

Thank you, he whispered.

The boy gave an almost imperceptible nod.

...

An hour later, when the boy returned from feeding the chooks, the old man was sitting up in bed, licking the last of the Vegemite from his lips and sipping at his cold tea.

Lots of worms in that weed patch, said the boy. *Be good for vegies if we ever get around to planting any.*

He waited a beat.

Want some fresh tea?

As well as the tea, he came back with a couple of aspirin and a bowl of fruit salad from a tin he'd found in the cupboard.

The old man ate in silence, sipped his tea in silence. The boy sat on the chair and read about pirates.

The old man took a deep breath, his shoulders shuddering with the effort.

The boy focused on one word on the page – *swashbuckling* – his eyes travelling over the letters. The wave of the s, the curve of the c, the straight lines of the l and h and b. The old-fashioned g like a pair of sideways spectacles, not at all like they taught it at school.

The old man started to mumble something, but the words floated in the air, incomplete.

He rubbed the heel of his hand across his eyes. The boy saw them shining. The quiet of the room hung heavy, disturbed by the occasional buzz of a beetle in the corner. The old man stared into the recesses of the room, lost in his thoughts. The boy traced the letters with his eyes. Any word began to seem pretty strange if you stared at it long enough.

A lawnmower started up a few houses away and the room filled with the smell of petrol and cut grass.

I'm sorry you're sad.

The old man turned to the boy's steady gaze, his book propped open on his lap.

When my chick died, I got really sad. And angry. I smashed eggs and stuff.

The old man nodded in acknowledgement.

But you have to stop drinking now. Do you see? You have to stop. I don't like it. I miss our chess games and my special afternoon tea and we haven't even started planting the vegies yet. And the chooks miss you too. They're all squawking and running around like they've lost something. That's you. You're lost. But I came in and I found you and now you have to stop and get better and get up and start being normal again.

The old man reached out and grasped the boy's thin, brown fingers. He took in the boy's earnest stare. He squeezed the boy's hand and felt the small fingers squeeze back.

Took years before the last traces of printers' ink faded from the creases round my fingernails. Replaced by chook poo and fertiliser. Dying art, printing. All done with computers now.

These days I'm amazed at the transformation everywhere. South Bank, the beach, all those manicured paths and well-planted gardens, the ferries coming and going at all hours. Couples strolling hand in hand, kids riding their bikes and scooters at breakneck speed. Mind you, I don't move much from my own suburb and surrounds anymore. Don't see the point. Any change happening further away than my own neighbourhood doesn't affect me. Buildings being demolished, politicians breaking promises or changing sides, luxury apartment developments, riots and protests and people sitting in trees … none of it touches my day-to-day life. Now if the corner store puts up the price of bread by five cents, well, that affects me. Or if the taxi driver can't speak English or doesn't know the most straightforward route from here to Toowong, that affects me.

Or the boy. Anything to do with the boy affects me. Funny, I never would have thought I'd have given a toss. Some skinny kid who steals other kids' lunches, and ciggies off his mother's boyfriends. But he's gotten under my skin, that kid. Stolen into my heart and stolen a piece of it clean away.

...

Pushing fifty, I did an inexplicable thing. Headed south. To this day I can't say why. Maybe I felt myself getting older and wanted to go back to where it all began before I got too old to do it. Truth is, around that time of my life I felt a bit adrift. Like a sail that had come unfurled in a strong wind, flapping about, untethered. I had no ties to speak of. No wife. Apparently no daughter. Parents and sister, all long dead. My friends had all gone on with their lives; they were having grandkids by that time, some of them. So I locked my little house and packed up the car I had at the time, a beat-up old Datsun 200B, and I headed down the Cunningham Highway.

I remember I stopped at the Gap, Cunningham's Gap, the highest spot en route. Beautiful place, up in the ranges. You can pull off the road next to the truckies' rigs – them all sitting there like warts on the face of a princess, having their smoko – and you can take a walk. Which I did. Fresh, crisp mountain air, like a cold shower. And I remember the bellbirds. The sound of them calling to each other, their shrill cries whipping through the air and echoing off the cliffs. I walked for a good hour that day. I wended my way through the towering trees and forged through brush so green it was like a different planet. Flowers I didn't recognise. Smells I couldn't place. I even saw a pademelon. It was getting towards dusk and he was grazing along the path. The sound of me startled him and he looked up, straight at me for a moment, before bounding off into the undergrowth, leaving behind a small pile of brown pellets, the only proof he had ever been there at all.

By the time I returned to the car, the truckies had mostly gone, although there were still two or three big rigs planted firm, no drivers in sight. Maybe they were sleeping in their cabs. I don't know.

I passed through Warwick. And Stanthorpe too. I stayed a couple of nights in one of the pubs in town. The second morning I was there I decided to go for a walk and see if I could find my old house, the one I'd lived in with Mum and Emily and, for a little while, with my father. I didn't hold out much hope. I'd been such a little chap when all that happened and I got whisked away to the Home. There were so many new houses or renovations of old homes. Nothing familiar stood out. I doubted my chances of finding something that I'd lost so long ago, in another time, another world. Another life.

And then I saw it. The huge spotted gum towering into the blue, standing sentry on a three-way corner. That tree brought back a rush of memories – its solid trunk, its branches wide and sheltering, higher even than I remembered. I could almost see the shadow of my six-year-old self hiding behind it, the sharp smell of gum sap, the whirr and clack and chirrup of cicadas rattling like dried beans in a shaker.

I counted two houses up the street and stared.

There it was. My old home. The same low stucco fence. Two leaning poles strung with washing line. Windows shuttered against the wind. A house full of secrets and lies. A house full of the ghost of my baby sister.

The stories that place could whisper through its boards. The families it's sheltered, the truths it could reveal. Tales settle in the landscape of those places and remain long after the characters have gone.

I stood there for quite a while. No-one was about. I thought about knocking on the door, but what would I say? In the end it was a house, only a house. A shell. Its inhabitants been and gone, their stories replaced by new people, new families. Maybe if I kept my distance, whatever bad things had happened in that place would remain only in my memory.

And so I moved on.

In Toowoomba I found my way to the workers' cottage that served as the Historical Society – four or five rooms laid out with dusty record books and glass cases full of farming implements and common household objects from years ago. But it was the walls of photographs that interested me. Every available space on every wall in every room was taken up with black-and-white enlargements from as early as the turn of the century. I found what I was looking for – three photographs of the Home. The first was a close-up of the building itself. It was as I remembered it: the grey stone walls, the enormous willow with its curtain of leaves like a waterfall, the monochrome tones emphasising the dreariness of the place. The second was shot through the bars of the fence into the grounds. The last picture showed a smiling Mr McCready in one of the boys' rooms, one hand pointing to an iron bed made up with stiff white sheets, and the other gesturing as if to show the spaciousness and comfort offered by his establishment. I felt myself smiling right back at him. He hadn't been a bad guy, Mr McCready. The only male role model I had as a boy. Seeing him standing there, in his ancient suit with his hair all slicked back, I got a feeling of nostalgia, like I might have been looking at a picture of my own father.

...

Determined little bugger, that kid. Twice now he's rescued me from the brink – once from the pneumonia and now from myself. Rescued me from myself. I didn't want to be rescued, not this time, that's for sure. I wanted to curl up and forget, lost in the fumes of alcohol and dreams – or nightmares, more like. But that kid, well, like I say, he's a determined little bugger.

Just as well, I suppose. We had a game of chess this morning and, if I'm honest, I quite enjoyed it. Truth be told I'm pretty glad he rescued me.

Life's a long, hard road, but that doesn't have to mean you give up and lie down when things get stony. I mean, have a gander at the kid. He hasn't got an easy life, I know that now, for certain. But I never hear him complaining.

So I think maybe I've learnt a thing or three over these last few days.

About the boy.

And about myself.

The ache sprang from deep between his shoulders and extended along each arm. When he lifted the heavy bucket, or brought the hoe down hard on the loamy soil, or even stretched upwards in an attempt to ease the strain, his muscles burned with fatigue, screamed at him to stop. But he didn't break pace for a moment. He was too happy.

The soil writhed with worms and emitted a rich smell of chicken manure and trapped sunlight. The two had worked side by side for most of the morning, talking only when necessary. *Pass me that bucket, would ya?* Or *Could you hand me the rake please?* Or *I think this bit here could do with some more water.* The bare bones of gardening conversation.

Prickling heat and sweat collected under the boy's hat and through his hair, tickling his ears and dripping from his temples. He could taste salt when he licked his lips. The old man stopped often. Sometimes he leant on his shovel and stared at nothing in particular that the boy could see. Sometimes he turned on the water and lifted the hose to the boy's face; the water was cold and refreshing. The boy could see the weariness in his eyes, the age spots dappling the backs of his hands, the trembling as he lifted the shovel. But he was here, the old man was out here in the sunshine, and the two of them were digging in the garden, and they were happy.

Over jam sandwiches, a cup of tea for the man and a tumbler of lemonade for the boy, the two surveyed their work. Raised mounds ran the length of the neat garden, sugarcane mulch filled in the valleys, and the perimeter was lined with protective chicken wire. It was ready.

The old man pushed his hat back on his head and wiped his forehead on his shirtsleeve. He hawked a ball of phlegm from the back of his throat and spat onto the grass.

This grime gets up my nose and in my throat like nobody's business. You'd think I'd been eating the stuff. So, what are we going to plant?

The boy didn't hesitate. *Beans. Silverbeet. Tomatoes, the normal ones and those little cherry tomatoes too. Lettuce. And shallots and onions and potatoes. And maybe some of those other fancy lettuces, you know, like rocket and those Chinese ones you get in supermarkets. Oh, and carrots, definitely carrots. Hey, maybe we could get some of those purple carrots? You ever seen them, purple carrots? They're really cool. And what about chillies? I like chillies, but not too hot. And herbs ... parsley and basil and coriander and all of those ones. And—*

The old man interrupted him with a barking laugh, his palm held high. *All right, all right, stop! Enough already! We've got a small backyard plot here, not a farmstead. I don't think we can plant all those things, not right away anyway. What about you pick a couple of your favourites and we'll start with them and see how we go? Don't want to get ahead of ourselves here.*

The boy nodded sagely, as if deliberating on this wisdom.

I've been googling, he said with a self-conscious grin. *Do you know how many gardening websites there are? There must be a hundred different vegies. More than a hundred. A thousand.*

He looked up at the old man from beneath his lashes.

Broccoli and eggplant. Can't forget those.

The old man groaned and lay back on the grass in mock exhaustion.

The boy jumped up and did a whooping victory dance around the garden, frightening a bird from the mango tree and scaring the chooks into a cacophony of squawking.

Hard to believe it took Pete and me as long as it did to work it out. And when we finally did, we were that staggered you could've knocked us for six. People always talk about it being a small world – six degrees of separation and all that – but still, it was a helluva surprise. I mean, we'd worked together all those years. Drank together at the pub. Shared the odd meal.

Just never talked much about our families, I suppose. I certainly hadn't.

Wasn't until Pete's brother died a few years ago, and we got to pondering about how many of our generation were falling off the perch, that we got onto the topic of how people were generally living longer, and Pete mentioned how his Aunt Daisy had passed away not too long before at the grand old age of ninety-six, and how she was the youngest of six girls, and wasn't that something, a family of six girls? Not too many families around today with six kids, let alone all girls – it was a different time back then. And something in my mind turned over, like I was peering through smoked glass and couldn't quite work out what was there. Something about the name Daisy.

It's a nice name for a girl, Daisy. Coming back into fashion, I said.

And the smokiness cleared a little. *You know, I reckon I might have had an aunt named Daisy too.*

Could be, said Pete. *Popular name back then.*

I rubbed the sandpapery stubble on my chin. *I seem to recall my mum had a lot of sisters,* I said. *My mum was June, and there was Kath … and I'm sure there was a Daisy …*

Pete stared at me over the rim of his beer glass. He placed it down, slowly.

And Elizabeth and Eunice, he added. *And my mother, Patricia.*

We stared, our bleary eyes trying to look back in time and make sense of what we were saying. He mentioned a few place names and gradually it began to dawn on us.

You're June's boy, he said in astonishment.

Peter, I said. *Peter. You kept rabbits. And … Harold? Arnold? Who died in the war.*

Harold. My oldest brother, Harold. Died in '41. Pacific.

Well I'll be, I said. *Peter. Peter with the rabbits.*

And you're June's boy.

At that moment the reminiscing grew quiet. I could see it all playing out in Pete's mind. What he could remember of his child-hood. His little cousin from Stanthorpe.

June's boy.

I could see him joining the dots.

You had a sister … didn't you have a sister who died as a baby?

I took a big gulp of beer and the glass slammed down on the table heavier than I meant it to. Beer sloshed over the side and onto my hand.

I wiped my fingers on my trousers.

I did, I said. *I had a sister. Emily. Died when she was a little 'un.*

I was wondering how much he would remember. How much he'd been told, all those years ago.

He rubbed his eyes, trying to dredge up the memories.

I seem to recall, he said. *Some tragedy. Family tragedy. I remember*

Mother was upset. And her sister Kath went down to help. And then the baby died and you were … you were sent away. I remember now, you were sent away and we were told we were not to ask about you again.

I'd forgotten, he said. *So many years ago, and I'd forgotten.*

Yeah, well, no sense dragging up the past, I said. I waved at the waitress, tried to get her attention. Anything to take the spotlight off me.

He slapped his hand against his leg.

Your father, he passed away during the war too, didn't he? Like Harold. I remember now. That's why Aunt Kath went to help. And I seem to recall your mother getting remarried.

I concentrated on my drink.

Did she? he asked. *Remarry?*

I raised my eyes to him with as level a gaze as I could muster.

I don't know, I said. *I haven't seen her since I was six years old.*

He gave me a searching look then, but he pried no more. Merely nodded, like I'd answered his question.

He covered my hand with his own and I realised I was shaking.

Steady on, he said. *All a long time ago now, mate.*

Felt so peculiar, his hand on mine like that. An unexpected familiarity. Men our age don't touch much as a general rule, and it had been a good few years since I'd been with a woman.

It occurred to me that this particular man – Pete, my friend, my *cousin* – was the first blood relative I'd sat with in almost seventy years. I don't mind saying, fair sucked the breath out of me for a moment.

What if he knew? What if he remembered – if not now, then surely later – what had happened back then? What if the story had survived in family lore all these years? I wondered what he knew, what he had been told, what he remembered, and I thought: *What must he think of me?*

I've gotta go, I said. I pushed back my chair and fished some notes out of my wallet. Put them on the table. My hand was still shaking. The blood was thrumming in my eardrums.

I've gotta go, I said again. I could hear Pete talking, something about what a remarkable coincidence and how come we'd never worked it out before now, but I couldn't comprehend him over the pounding of my heart. All I knew was I needed to get away before he asked me anything else about Emily.

...

Pete was a good friend. He left me alone for a few days and then when he did mention it – us – again, he was as considerate and charitable as I could have hoped for.

Look, mate, he said. *Whatever happened then was a long time ago. Obviously it's something you don't want to talk about.* He waited. I nodded. *And that's fine by me. But I'm so glad to have discovered we're related. All right?*

I nodded again, relieved.

From then on, Pete would make a point of telling people that we were cousins, but that's as far as it went. Said we'd gone thirty years without setting eyes on each other, and that we'd then worked side by side at *The Tele* for many more years and still hadn't discovered we were related, and how about that. He seemed proud of me, proud to lay claim to me.

And that wasn't something I'd ever felt before.

...

A few months after that, he took me for a beer, said he wanted to talk to me about something.

Now I know you don't like talking about the past, he began, *but I got to thinking. I've been going through a box of Mother's things. Old papers and whatnot. Should have probably thrown it all out years ago, the kids keep telling me to, but you know what a hoarder Sandra was and I can't bring myself to do it. Anyway, I found a few bits and pieces that I think you should have. If you'd like them. I think they belong to you.*

He pushed across an old shoebox and a tattered envelope.

He hesitated, as if he wasn't sure how to say the next thing that was on his mind.

I'm not sure why Mother had all this stuff. There's a whole collection of things from all her sisters, especially after they'd ... you know ... He looked awkward. *I mean, we're in our seventies, aren't we, mate. I assume ...*

No need to state the bloody obvious, I said. *I can assume as well as you can. But I've never been told, so I don't know the details. And to tell the truth, I don't need to know. What does it matter, now? After all this time?*

If it had happened years earlier, I'm not sure I would have taken the news as well as I did. But as it was, I'd marked my seventieth birthday and I finally felt – despite all the odds – that I'd made old bones. I began to think of the past as just that – past. Gone. Finished. Unable to be changed or undone or bettered. I can't say I was too upset or emotional or even very surprised. After all, it didn't matter much anymore. They were all dead, or as good as. Nothing to be done about it now.

Later, at home, in private, I went through the box. Mostly junk. Some old jewellery that had blackened with age, a couple of old-fashioned keys, a cut-glass bottle, a pewter vase and a broken watch.

And the envelope.

The envelope contained a few papers and a photograph. The seal had long since come unstuck and I suppose Pete had read the contents before he passed them on to me.

But he had the decency never to ask me about it. Never mentioned it again. Like I said, he was a good friend.

The photograph, of course, was of me. I must have been about three years old. I'm standing ramrod straight and I've got one of those fake smiles plastered on that kids get when they're told to smile or else. I'm in short pants and there's a kitten curled up on my left foot. Funny, I don't ever remember having a kitten. But I recognise the ivy on the wall behind me, and the cross-hatched door, and the bit of driveway where the policeman slipped in the slush all those years ago.

There was a handwritten letter, probably to my mother, although the first page was missing so I couldn't be sure. It was signed Kath. She referred to the Home, and the war, and there were mentions of Eunice and Daisy.

But it was the second letter that got my attention. It was addressed to my mother, typed on official Australian Army letter-head, and regretfully informed Mrs Lawrence that her husband had been officially declared Absent Without Leave.

Absent Without Leave.

There was another note, folded and refolded until it was a small, hard square. When I unfolded it, the paper was torn and grubby, like it had been handled a lot, and not always gently. The words were scrawled roughly and were hard to read in places; they crawled across the page as if eager to escape over the side. In part the letter read:

You must agree that things have not always gone smoothly between us, and so I am hoping that what I have to say will come as no surprise. I have met a local girl and we are very much in love. I do not plan on returning to Australia and in fact as I have deserted my post I most probably will never be able to do so in any case. I shall miss the boy, of course; please tell him his father thinks of him often. And I am sad to never know the baby, but as we have never laid eyes on each other, I don't suppose she will miss me. She must be twelve months old by now? In any case, I'm sure you will be a good mother to both of them, and are no doubt better off without me. We have spent more time apart than together because of this bloody war and I am sorry that has prevented us from knowing each other properly as man and wife ...

All of this was news to me, of course. There I was, seventy years old and I'd spent my whole life thinking that my father had died

182

in active service in New Guinea. I'd been told he was missing, and even then I knew that when you go missing in those jungles for long enough, they presume you're not coming back, except maybe in a box. Reading that letter – learning that he not only deserted but also took up with another woman – fair winded me. Shone a whole new light on events.

I remember quite clearly the day Mum got the telegram that she said – she said – told her he was missing. I can see her whole body slumping, her hands trembling so much that the piece of paper shook. Her eyes, when she finally looked at me, were unfocused, like she wasn't seeing me at all, like she was staring right through me to the wall behind.

Or maybe I don't remember any of that. Maybe I've re-created that image over the years since. Maybe there was no telegram. Perhaps I contrived her grief, or if not, perhaps the pain I saw on my mother's face was not from loss but from betrayal.

I don't know. I was only six years old. And anyway, the events of two weeks later took over the fact of my father being gone. I mean, he was already gone; he'd been gone for months. Hadn't seen me or Mum since before Emily was born. It was a tragic time. Fathers conceiving children they didn't know they had, or worse, knowing they had a baby coming and not being able to return. Or not ever seeing them at all. I suppose if you've never seen the kid then you don't have any fatherly affection for her. But then, what would I know about fatherly affection.

I got to thinking about all the females in my life – Emily, Edith, Sarah, and of course the first woman in my life, my mother.

I tried to think back to what my mother was like, tried to remember fragments of her and my father, of how they were together. But I'd never had a clear picture of him in my mind – he was absent more often than not, even before he went missing. And with the passage of so much time it was practically impossible. And my mother … I remembered my mother as worn down by life, tired to the bones with caring for me and my sister. Grief-stricken and aching with loss.

I remember her as alone.

It was all such a long time ago. Does it really matter anymore?

Snake was back. The boy recognised his motorcycle in the front yard. He skirted it as if it might spontaneously rev into motion. He paused on the top stair and pressed his ear to the door. Hearing no sound, he stepped across the lounge. His mother's bedroom door was shut. He slipped into his own room and closed the door.

From his pocket he pulled a nugget of fool's gold. It gleamed dully in the dusty shadows of his room. He had noticed it on the deputy principal's desk when he'd been hauled in for fighting with Tommy Brownlow. It was nothing personal against Mr Brady – he just wanted that nugget. He had fallen against the desk on his way out and swiped it before either Mr Brady or Tommy noticed. Now he opened his shoebox and found a place for it amongst his treasures.

The mumble of voices prompted him to replace the lid and slide the box back under his bed as his mother knocked and opened the door.

You're home! Good timing. We're going to have pizza. Want some?

The alarm bells in his head competed with the growls from his stomach. *Um … OK, sure. I'm starving.*

He trailed after her into the kitchen. Snake threw the phone onto the table with a clatter and stared at the boy.

185

Pepperoni with extra chilli all right for you, kid? He smirked.

The boy's mouth was dry. He swallowed. *Yeah. Fine.*

So …

Snake kicked out the chair nearest to him.

Haven't seen you for a while. Sit down. Fill me in on what you've been up to.

The boy silently beseeched his mum to intervene, but she was oblivious.

I'll leave you two to chat then. I'm going to have a shower. Call me when the pizza gets here.

She left the room. The boy was alone, the snake rearing up, ready to strike.

The man drummed his fingers on the tabletop, his eyes never leaving the boy. The corners of his mouth twitched as if he was trying not to smile.

So … he repeated again, *eaten any good chicken lately?*

He guffawed at his joke. The boy looked away.

Snake grabbed the boy's wrist and held it fast. He winced. He concentrated on the man's hand as tears stung behind his eyelids and threatened to spill over his lashes. He concentrated hard. The hand gripping his wrist was a boxing glove in comparison to his own. Thick, stubby fingers, the nails bitten to the quick, the lines and whorls ingrained with grime. The boy waited until the moment he felt the man's grip loosen, and then he twisted free and ran out the door without looking back.

...

He pedalled fast, his legs a blur of motion. He couldn't say – not even in his own head – what he was running from or why it was so necessary he get away. Snake made him uncomfortable, but then so had many of his mother's other boyfriends. One or two had been all right; they'd talked to him like a mate and not some worthless kid, some nuisance who was in the way. But mostly they were rough or cruel, or at the very least smelly and unkind and stupid. Good or bad, they never lasted long. The one thing the boy could be sure of was that whoever he was, he would only be a temporary annoyance. Except for Snake. He'd been hanging around, on and off, for months now. The boy rode faster, as if his furious legs could push away unwelcome thoughts.

He followed the concrete path through the park and skidded to a halt next to a tangle of native bushes. He dragged his bike into the undergrowth and left it half-hidden under a scratchy shrub. He pushed his way through the curtain of foliage that concealed the slow-flowing creek beyond. The overhanging leaves blocked the afternoon sun, dappling its rays into constantly changing patterns. Shadows danced on the surface of the water and on the narrow banks. The air was cooler here, the summer heat fractured through the leaves and branches, relieving its sting. The boy cleared aside a patch of leaf litter and squirmed his bottom into the dank soil like a puppy settling in a basket. He leant against the trunk of a solid gum and rubbed his back against the tree, each scratch creating another itch. He lifted great handfuls of dirt and mulch and watched as the layers of the earth slipped through his fingers – first the muddy clods stuck together with creek water; then the loose soil from which emerged a beetle, two worms and a cockroach; then the dry summer dust on top; and finally the fallen leaves, the detritus and waste of the growth around him. The pungent odour swelled into the air with each sweep of his arm. Ants scurried away in frantic indecision; unseen life rustled outside his arm span. He leant back again and closed his eyes, suddenly heavy with fatigue. Sunbeams played across his face. The drowsy droning of a bee harmonised with the burbling of the creek. He slumped sideways, cradled his head on his arms, and slept.

He dreamt he was flying above the park, his arms outstretched, breeze lifting his hair and billowing his T-shirt into a sail. He could see the oval below, the long grass waving like the roil of the ocean.

He could see the glittering line of water meandering across the lower east side of the park, tracked on both sides by a boundary of brush. On the other side of the creek he could just see the road, glimpses of black asphalt glinting in the sunlight. He swooped lower and lower, feeling the power in his limbs. The undulating grass grew to meet him, until his belly swept across its feathery tips, tickling his skin. He reared upwards and gazed down again. To his surprise, Snake was in the centre of the field, his arms with his large, hairy hands waving at him. He flew a little lower. Snake was gesturing at something on the ground, something hidden in the grass. He fell further, knowing that to cease his forward motion would be to drop from the sky. There was a dark shape amongst the lurid green, and then he swooped, and the old man's face was peering up, frightened and vulnerable. The boy plunged lower, and quick as a flash Snake tripled in height and grabbed the boy's wrist, pulling him to the ground. He landed with a grunt. The old man had vanished. Snake was sucking on a wishbone and held it out, an offering. The boy reached out and hooked his pinky around one side of the bone and pulled with all his strength. He fell backwards, and saw in his hand one half of a black chick, its body rent in two, its tiny heart still beating, pumping out spurts of red from the severed arteries that protruded obscenely into the air.

The boy woke with a jolt and glanced around wildly. The sun had set; the evening glow was soft. Black clouds of bugs hovered. He smacked his arms and thighs, squashing two or three insects with each slap. Small smears of blood dotted his skin. He unfolded his cramped body and inspected it for bites and welts and scratches. He looked directly upwards, into the darkening sky, where pinpricks of light pierced; a handful of diamonds scattered against black velvet. As he pulled out his bike, he saw the rising moon low against the horizon. He headed towards the moon, and home.

I asked the boy today what he was doing for Christmas. *Nothing,* he said. Just like that.

Even at the Home we had Christmas. I said to him, *Surely your mum'll do something nice for you, hey?* Seems it's a counter lunch at the pub every year. With the mother's latest fella. From what I've seen of the blokes that hang around over there, I doubt there would be too much Christmas cheer for the boy.

I've had a few sad and sorry Christmases. Not much chop for a kid. At least at the Home there were lots of us, all in the same boat. We were too busy having a good time with the novelty of it all to be feeling sorry for ourselves. We always had roast pork or lamb, sometimes beef, with gravy and vegies too. Brussels sprouts, carrots, chokos, peas or beans. And roast potatoes, crunchy from the lard. One of the local churches, it might have been the Micks but I'm not sure, always sent over a box wrapped in brown paper and string, labelled *Christmas Gifts for the Lost Lambs of Christ.* We all thought that was terribly funny. *Baa!* We'd all cry. *Baa! Baa!* Then Mr McCready would clip whoever was closest over the ear and tell us we were an ungrateful lot and he had a good mind to return the box unopened, or forward it on to the poor. Then we'd fall quiet and act all remorseful and eventually he'd relent and ask one of the boys to get the scissors. He'd cut the string and open the box and hand out one wrapped gift to every boy.

There was never any left over, and no boy ever went without, so they got the numbers perfect every time. There were a couple of years, though, when the Micks or whoever must've been too poor and underprivileged themselves to give to the poor and under-privileged, 'cause the big brown box never arrived, and at the last minute Mr McCready went out to town himself and came back with shopping bags full of whatever must've been on special that week down at the local variety store. One year, I remember, it was a box of chocolates for every boy. That was a pretty good year. Another year we each got a toothbrush and a ball of twine. We got awfully creative with that string – boys made slingshots, string dolls, kite tails, and of course tied each other up quite regularly.

And the Christmas carols. One of the teacher's wives, Mrs Kabranski, used to accompany us. The ivory piano keys were aged yellow and smooth, and poor Mrs K was tone deaf herself. We had a competition going each year to see who could make up the most disgusting lyrics to each hymn and then manage to sing the new words undetected by Mr McCready. The little kids got the giggles and were usually caught out, but some of the older kids could get along to verse four or five without so much as a snigger.

Like they say, you can't buy memories like that.

The sun beat down remorselessly on the hall's tin roof, and light shot through the windows and played on the tinsel. Half-a-dozen overhead fans turned, so high up they cooled no-one but the geckoes that clung onto the cornices waiting for moths.

The boy's class was performing two songs. 'Grandma Got Run Over by a Reindeer' was a popular rendition that always made everyone in the audience laugh. It was the boy's job to hit the cymbals at precisely the moment the sleigh hit the eggnog-soaked Grandma, leaving her lying in the snow with hoof prints on her back. In each chorus, immediately after his cymbal clash, Carli Rhodes – a pretty girl with laughing eyes and ears that were slightly too big – let out a scream of such pitch and intensity that those in the front row couldn't believe it came out of her delicate mouth. A beat before the duet of clash and scream, Carli's enthusiastic singing would cease for a moment as she gathered her breath for the shriek to come. She would tilt her head towards the boy, watching his arms, making sure her timing would be right. Each time the boy felt her eyes on him, he felt warm and self-conscious; perhaps he blushed. But by the time he had crashed the cymbals and heard her scream, and turned his head towards her, she had already looked away.

Two more classes performed after theirs. By eleven-thirty, the preppies were restless and fidgeting, the older kids whispering together or chattering loudly or punching each other or grabbing someone's elf hat or Santa beard. The principal made his closing remarks and the audience sighed with relief as they heaved themselves out of the uncomfortable chairs, collected their belongings and headed towards the doors. On the way up the aisle, or paused by the door, each mum and dad scanned the room and made eye contact with their child. For some, that was enough – a simple wave and they were out into the sunshine and back to work. Others wended their way through the crowd, finding their children and bestowing hugs or kisses to the tops of heads. The boy heard parents praising their children or murmuring words of encouragement. He saw Carli Rhodes' father pull her ponytail and tickle her nose with tinsel; she laughed and threw her arms around his stout belly.

The boy packed his cymbals into their case and hoisted it over his shoulder. He slipped out the side door, avoiding the crowd of happy families, and went to the music room to put the cymbals away.

...

In the late afternoon, the heat still radiated up from the asphalt and shimmered in a haze around anything metal, blurring the outlines of fences and roofs. The chickens were sprawled in the dust, double their size with their feathers fluffed out and their wings in the air as they attempted to cool down. The plants in the vegie garden lay limp and dejected with the heat. It was too early to water them – the drops would disappear before they hit the ground.

The old man looked hot too. He was reclined on the lounge clad only in a singlet and baggy shorts, his protruding legs like thin straws, his varicose veins almost pulsing. His eyes were glassy, weary. The boy flopped into an armchair and flung his legs up, one over each armrest, trying to make as little contact as possible with the greasy fabric.

It's hot, he said.

It is, the old man agreed.

SO hot.

Yes, SO hot.

Hotter than the desert.

Hotter than the sun.

Hotter than summer on the sun.

Hotter than an egg frying in a pan.

Hotter than Pink, the boy said.

Hotter than red, the old man retorted.

The boy giggled. *Want some water?*

Yep. There's ice in the freezer.

When the boy was in the kitchen, the old man called out, *Fancy a game of chess?*

Nope. Too hot for chess.

Never too hot for chess.

The boy returned, two glasses dripping with condensation. *Maybe later. I can't think. It's too hot to think.*

How did you think at school, then?

Didn't.

The old man looked stern but his eyes gave him away. *Won't learn much if you don't do any thinking, you know.*

I know.

And if you don't do any thinking, and you don't do any learning, you won't turn out to be much chop.

Yeah, yeah, I know.

And you'll never beat me at chess.

I can beat you anytime, the boy declared. *Only I don't want to show you up.*

Oh is that so, huh. That's why you've never beaten me, 'cause you don't want to show me up?

Yeah, too right. Don't want to hurt your feelings either.

The old man hid his laughter behind a cough. *Oh, I see. So …
why is it you keep playing with me, then? No challenge in it for you, surely,
if you know you can beat me anytime you want.*

I do it for you.

For me?

*Yeah, for you. They say playing chess and stuff, doing crosswords and
Sudoku, all that stuff, they say it keeps your mind healthy, keeps your
brain working right. Keeps the Alzheimer's away.*

The old man was a good shot. The cushion got the boy directly
on his forehead.

You cheeky sod. I'll give you Alzheimer's. He threw another
cushion. The boy ducked. He scooped the ice cubes from his glass,
crawled commando-style across the floor, then lunged at the old
man, stuffing two ice cubes down his shorts and rubbing another
up and down one of the old man's legs. He squealed as half a glass
of iced water was dumped on his head and dripped onto the carpet.

Hey! Don't think I'm *cleaning that up.*

The old man lay back in his seat with a sigh. *Doesn't matter. In
this heat, it'll evaporate before you know it.*

And sure enough, as the boy watched, the puddle on the carpet
shrank, the edges fading to the same grey, until you could never
have said where the water had fallen, or even if it had fallen at all.

I headed on down to the Village today. I'd run out of canned soup and bread and there weren't any teabags left either. And the boy goes through my biscuits like there's no tomorrow. But the real reason I made the effort wasn't the food. Thought I might find the boy a Christmas present.

At my age braving the shops is quite a feat. By the time I get moving, get dressed (easier said than done with the arthritis in these hands), and wait for the taxi to show up, it's damn near lunchtime as it is. I get the driver to drop me right outside the doors. I could use the crossing but I have no desire to be scraped off the road with a shovel, so I avoid the traffic as much as possible, especially the lead-foots with letter Ls and Ps displayed. Downright dangerous, these learner drivers. So I lever myself out of the cab and make my way to the lift, which must be the slowest in Brisbane. Still, I don't mind having a gander through the glass to see what's going on in the world. It would be quicker to ride on the travellator but I don't trust myself to get on one end or off the other without causing myself an injury. Getting older seems to consist mainly of keeping watch over your body to make sure it stays in one piece.

The Christmas crowds today didn't help. All over the Village I could barely see for the glare of tinsel and gaudy baubles hanging off every available surface.

Bit overdone, isn't it? I said to the girl behind the counter at David Jones. She waved her hand in the air like she was shooing a fly.

Been up since October, she said. *You wait. Soon as Christmas's over, we'll have hearts and flowers everywhere and before you know it there'll be hot cross buns for sale down at Coles.*

She was a nice enough kid, bit heavy on the make-up though. Bit overdone herself, if you know what I mean, not that I said that to her. At least she's not like most of the kids who work there. Some of them are young enough to have been born this century, and they seem to equate age with infirmity. I may be a touch deaf and a bit slow but that doesn't mean I've lost all my marbles.

I told her I wanted a present for a ten-year-old boy. She assumed it was my grandson and I didn't disabuse her of the notion. She showed me books and board games and weapons, a lot of weapons. They had a whole arsenal of shotguns and pistols and water guns and missiles and darts. Guns with scopes and realistic sound effects. I decided against the weapons. Figured the kid gets enough of that at home. Eventually I settled on a computer gadget that he can attach to his bike to record distance and speed and such. Wasn't too expensive and seems like something he might like. I hope so anyway.

I'm thinking I might invite him out somewhere on Christmas Day. I'm at a loose end myself, what with Pete gone, and the kid didn't sound too excited at the prospect of a pub lunch with his mum and her latest squeeze – called Snake, if you can believe it. When I asked him why, first off he clammed up and wouldn't say, and I thought it certainly doesn't sound like a term of endearment now, does it. But then he mumbled something about the fellow having a tattoo of a snake. Can't say I've noticed myself, but then my eyesight's not the best. Grubby things, tatts. Seem like a good idea at the time, and then one day you wake up at sixty and realise you've got saggy skin covered with bad drawings of skulls and hearts and the names of ex-girlfriends.

Anyway, the guy's been around a lot lately, so much so that the other day I asked the kid whether he was his father. I thought maybe he'd reappeared on the scene.

Who, that dickhead? he said.

Oi, watch your language.

Well he is; he's a complete bastard. No way is he my dad. Why would you even think that?

All right, all right, don't get on your high horse. I only wondered, that's all.

He glared at me like he wanted to say something but couldn't think of an adequate response.

I'm thinking I might take him to the beach. We could get a train to Welly Point or Cleveland, or maybe even a bus to Bribie Island. I haven't been to the beach for ages. And when I asked the boy, he said the only time he'd ever been was when he was about four, and all he remembered was the burning sand on his feet and the ice-cream his mum bought him and how it dripped all down his arm.

Mind you, it'd be pretty hot, whichever beach we went to. I think I've got a big old umbrella in the shed; we could take that. And hats. We could get fish and chips, a cold beer for me and a soft drink for the kid. It'd be a real adventure. Yeah, I think that might be just the thing. Christmas Day at the beach. 'Course I don't even know if the kid can swim. I'd have to be careful about that, 'cause Lord knows I'm in no condition to charge in and save him if he gets into trouble. But that's what they have lifesavers for, isn't it. If they work Christmas Day. I wonder if they work Christmas Day? Maybe the ones without little kids or much family volunteer for it. Wouldn't be much chop, would it, spending Christmas

Day scanning the horizon for drowning tourists, half of whom are probably drunk on Christmas cheer. But then I s'pose if you saved someone, that'd be a good feeling; that'd be a pretty good Christmas present, wouldn't it. Now I'm rambling. Anyway, a day at the beach. That sounds like just the ticket.

The boy couldn't believe it. The beach! He was going to the beach! He hadn't been to the beach – any beach – since he was four years old. The old man had it all planned out. They would take a bus into the city, then the train to Caboolture, then another bus to Bribie. An island! Apparently there was a huge bridge linking the mainland to the island. Then they could decide to go to the calm side, with shallow water and a picnic area, or the surf side, with real waves. And they'd get fish and chips and sit right there on the sand and eat.

Now all he had to do was persuade his mother.

He waited until she was home from work. He had cooked up some two-minute noodles and thrown in some tins of tuna, corn and peas. When she arrived, he made her close her eyes and go straight to her bedroom and change. By the time she emerged, he had cleared the table of everything except cutlery, salt and pepper, and two clean glasses filled with iced tea. He had plated up the meal – it was colourful and appetising. He pulled out her chair like he'd seen them do on the movies, and placed a clean tea towel on her lap with a flourish.

Wow! This is amazing! Did you do all this yourself? It smells delicious. Thanks, love.

The boy sat too, and they ate in silence for several minutes.

Mum.

Yeah?

It's nearly Christmas.

I know. How much school have you got left?

This is the last week.

Huh. So how long 'til Christmas then?

About two weeks.

She lifted her glass and peered at him over the rim. *Yeah, well don't be expecting too much this year. I'm still paying off that bloody bike.*

No, I'm not! I mean, the bike was a great present. I don't need more presents.

Good. Well, so long as you're not expecting anything. Haven't had much work this month, you know. Still, we'll have a good time down at the pub, hey? Slap-up lunch they do. Remember last year? Turkey and all the trimmings, Christmas pud for dessert.

The boy remembered the pudding. He remembered his mum had tipped half a glass of brandy over it and the man who was with them had set it aflame with his cigarette lighter and the smoke alarms had gone off. He remembered her getting pissed in the bar afterwards and the security guard manhandling her out at closing time, threatening to call the police if she didn't leave quietly. He remembered the long walk home, the boyfriend swearing blue murder as he tried to half-carry the boy's mum, while she kept stopping along the way, twice to vomit into somebody's flowerbed, and several more times to collapse, crying, into the dirt, mumbling words that the boy didn't understand and that the boyfriend clearly didn't care to hear.

Actually, I wanted to talk to you about that.

He placed his fork beside his plate and spoke steadily.

I was wondering if you'd mind if I didn't come with you this time, to the pub I mean.

His mum continued to shovel noodles into her mouth, waving her fork around as she spoke.

What do you mean? You love that Christmas lunch! We do it every year! What are you gonna do, sit at home by yourself? No, no way. You're coming. The three of us are going together. It'll be fun. A real family outing.

The boy picked up his fork and they ate in silence again.

Then he had an idea.

It's just that, I thought you two might want to go out together, you know, just the two of you. For something special. For Christmas.

Oh, love. His mum reached across the table and stroked his hand. *That is so sweet. Really thoughtful. But I couldn't leave you alone at Christmas. What sort of a mother would that make me, hey? No, we'll all go together. We don't do enough things together. And besides, he's always saying he wants to do more stuff with you. He likes you, you know.*

Well actually, Mum, I wasn't thinking I'd be alone. I was thinking I might do something. With someone else.

His mother's smile faded from the bottom up – first her mouth turned down at the corners and then her eyes grew hard. She dabbed her mouth with the tea towel.

Someone else? What would you do with someone else?

Um … maybe … go to the beach?

She emitted a short, sharp laugh. *Go to the beach? On Christmas Day? Sit in the hot sun, sand everywhere.* She shuddered. *Who on earth would want to take you to the beach on Christmas Day?*

The man next door. He's already asked me. He says we can get a bus to Bribie and eat fish and chips and go for a swim. He said he'll take really good care of me and you don't need to worry. I don't even need to bring any money. He said he'll pay and everything.

His mother continued to stare at him in silence.

The man next door? she said finally. *You want to spend Christmas Day with the old guy next door.* It was more of a statement than a question. *You'd rather spend Christmas Day with a complete stranger*

201

than with your own mother? Her voice was escalating now, getting louder with each word. *You selfish little shit. And here's me thinking you wanted me and Snake to have a romantic day and all the time you want to go off with some old pervert.*

He's not a pervert, the boy murmured.

What?

I said he's not a pervert. He's nice. He just … he's all alone, and he hasn't been to the beach for years, and neither have I … and he thought it might be nice if …

His mother continued to stare coldly at him.

Well, I want you to come to the pub. With us. Her voice was deliberate and she enunciated each word with care. *With Snake and me.*

The boy hesitated, staring into his noodles. He looked up and met his mother's steely gaze.

I don't want to go. I want to go to the beach.

You're coming with us, to the pub.

No, I don't want to. I'm going to the beach. And you can't stop me, he added.

His mother was so still. Only her nostrils quivered. Suddenly she pushed her chair back and overturned the remainder of her meal. The dish clattered to the floor. Bits of corn and straggly noodles stuck to the cupboard doors. The boy sat fixed to his chair. His mother gripped his chin in her hand so hard that he could feel the inside of his cheeks cutting against his teeth. He closed his eyes against the pain but didn't try to pull away. Her face was close enough that he could smell tuna on her breath. Drops of spittle flew onto his nose as she shouted.

You're an ungrateful little shit! I do everything for you. I work my fingers to the bone for you, so you've got somewhere nice to live and food to eat and a fucking bike to ride around on. And what do I get in return? Nothing. No fucking respect. Snake treats you like his own son and what does he get? Nothing.

She pushed his head, hard, against the back of the chair.

Fine then. Fine. Go to the beach. Go and spend Christmas with some old pervert who you don't even know, instead of with your own mother who loves you and cares for you and does everything for you. See if I care.

She marched off towards her room.

But don't come crying to me when Christmas is finished and all you've got to show for it is sunburn and sand up your bum crack.

She paused at the doorway. *And clean up that mess! I don't even like fucking noodles.*

She slammed the door so hard that a picture fell off the wall.

Only a week to go 'til Christmas. Only a week 'til our big beach adventure. I don't know who's more excited, me or the boy. I haven't looked forward to an outing this much in ages. I've got the route all planned out, and what we'll take and what we'll eat and where we'll sit and swim and maybe even walk a little, as long as these old legs hold out.

I told the boy I'd like to go over and speak to his mum, make sure it was all square with her, but he said she was fine about him going and I wasn't to worry. When I tried to insist, he got all angry and practically forbid me to go anywhere near his mother. Well, of course I told him that only made me more worried that he hadn't asked her permission at all, hadn't even spoken to her about it. And how would that seem then? Me taking off with the kid and her not knowing where we'd gone? He changed his tune then, went from angry to sad and quiet-like. He told me that his mum hadn't wanted him to go although she'd agreed in the end, but she wasn't happy about it. I said, *Maybe we shouldn't go then,* and you should've seen the kid's face. He was about ready to burst into tears. He said he'd never wanted anything as much as this trip to the beach, and his mum was only pissed off 'cause he wouldn't traipse along with her and Boy Wonder to their *shitty boring lunch* (*Oi,* I said, *watch your language*), and she didn't even care about him and so what if he missed their stupid lunch, there would be dozens more stupid lunches but only one trip to the beach, this one, and he really wanted to go and if I liked him at all I would just shut up about his mother and take him to the beach. Well. I was so surprised by that outburst that I didn't even say *oi, watch your language* again. That kid hardly strings two words together, let alone a monologue like that. But I'll say this for him: when he feels strongly about something, he says so. In any event, I figured he truly wants this trip. His speech had that whole frustrated tone to it – I remember feeling that way myself at his age, like no-one would listen to me. And I decided, maybe it's time someone did. Start listening, that is. So it's off to the beach we go.

The middle of each day was a strange time, still and hot. The chickens too hot to squawk, the dogs spread out in the dust. Mothers with babies sprawled under ceiling fans for sticky afternoon naps. Children sat indoors playing board games or watching TV, sniping at each other and eating chocolate that melted in their hands. The turgid air captured sounds and held them a moment too long. As the afternoon wore on, the adults pressed themselves to move, to get up and do something before the day was gone, to bring in the washing or at least pack the tools away. It was too hot to cook; salads and cold meat would do. The crickets would start up at the first sign of the cooling air; the cats' whiskers quivered with every suggestion of a breeze, and they stretched and licked their paws and found the energy to purr. The birds found their voices – the kookaburras cackled at the foolishness of the heat, of the passing of another day. As the heat dissipated, the smells returned: the sweetness of cut grass, smoke drifting from a burn-off over the hills, sausages spitting on somebody's barbecue.

The boy passed these days of early summer in a drowsy funk of inactivity. The chickens were fed, though – he threw handfuls of grain on the ground and the hens strolled over and pecked desultorily before retreating to the shade – and the garden was watered. Only in the late afternoon, cautioned the old man, or the very early morning, or else the water would burn the leaves, and seep into the soil without leaving a trace. So, late in the afternoons the boy would hose the garden and himself in equal measure, occasionally directing a cold spray towards the old man, who complained and laughed and batted the water away with his hat. He weeded too, with the evening encroaching and the soil moist and pliable.

Better get onto those weeds, the old man said. *They're growing like weeds in there.* He chuckled at his own joke.

It was true. They sprang up overnight: wispy fronds of asparagus fern, curling vines sprouting from invisible seeds, dainty leaves on stalks decorated with miniature flowers.

Mind the beans, son, don't pull them out. And the coriander, don't you step on those coriander seedlings. They're popping up everywhere.

Yeah, yeah, I know. I'm being careful.

And mind you don't squash those capsicums we put in – do you know the difference between them and that weedy thing?

The boy remained crouched, shook his head. *I know, all right? Jeez. I helped you plant them, remember? I'm not stupid, y'know.*

No need to get like that. I never said you were stupid. The old man took off his hat, scratched his head and rotated the brim of his hat through his hands. *'Course,* he muttered, *you* did *pull out all those baby bok choys.*

Jeez, I said I was sorry, how was I to know they were proper plants? They looked exactly like those other things that you're always telling me to pull out, how am I supposed to ... He trailed off as he saw the mischief in the old man's eyes.

Ha ha. Very funny. He plucked a leafy intruder and threw it, clod of earth and all, towards the old man. *Least I can see the difference between the two. You'd be lost without my perfect vision.*

The old man grunted. *Very funny yourself. So long as you watch where you put your big feet,* he said, as he brushed off his shirt.

Later, they sat in companionable silence on the grass, the old man leaning against the fence, the boy scratching his back against a tree trunk. He had collected half-a-dozen fallen mangoes from the old man's tree; the piquant smell grew stronger as he peeled one with his teeth and sucked at the flesh of the fruit. No matter how many he ate, dozens more littered the ground beneath the tree, their smooth yellow skins disfigured by bite marks from the greedy fruit bats.

I would too, you know, he said.

Would what? said the boy.

Be lost. Without you.

He paused.

And it's not only your vision I'd miss, either.

The boy wiped his hands on the grass. *Yeah, whatever.*

I'm serious, kiddo. I'm kinda used to having you around. And you're right about the garden. It wouldn't be half as good if you weren't around to do the watering and the weeding and what not.

So you're the brains and I'm the muscle, is that what you're saying? The boy's tone was jesting, embarrassed.

The old man allowed the quiet to settle between them. The insects had softened to a background hum. The clucking of the hens was subdued and intimate.

You're a good kid, you know that?

Yeah, whatever.

Whatever, whatever … what's with the whatevers? I'm trying to tell you something here, something good about yourself.

Nothing that good about me. Only a kid, hey. In the way most of the time, that's what my mum says.

The sun had disappeared behind the horizon and the sky was the discoloured purple of an old bruise. Dense clouds drifted overhead, swollen with the rain of an evening storm.

Sometimes I think she'd rather I wasn't here. Like, maybe her life would be different, better, if I wasn't around. She'd be free.

Free to do what?

I dunno. Stuff. Go out. Not worry about me. Boyfriends and stuff, you know.

The old man gathered his assurances.

I'm sure that's not true, kid. I'm sure your mum loves you. All mums love their kids; it's a fact of life, isn't it? It's nature, the natural order of things.

The old man heard his own words and wondered if he had ever believed them himself.

He shuffled over to sit closer to the boy, reached out and ruffled his hair. *You need a haircut, kid. You're starting to look all bedraggled and neglect—* His words stopped abruptly. *Might take you down to my barber. Does a pretty mean number four.*

The boy shook his head out from under the old man's touch. *Get out of it. Anyway, it's the holidays. I can have my hair as long as I like.*

They turned simultaneously to the rustle in the avocado tree behind them. A possum was clumsily making its way through the branches and landed with a thump on the deck railing. The sensor lamp clicked on and a blade of light cut across the back stairs, illuminating a wedge of grass. A flurry of night insects became visible, dancing. The old man heaved himself upright with a grunt and staggered in a bow-legged waddle towards the patch of garden. He placed one hand in the small of his back and bent over, fumbling amongst the foliage with the other. Miniature capsicums glowed red; inky globes of eggplant dangled from their stems.

Whatcha doing?

Hold on a second and I'll show you.

The old man straightened up, groaned again, and shuffled back to sit beside the boy. He opened his outstretched hand. In his palm lay a tiny ball no bigger than a matchhead.

Go on, take it.

What is it?

The boy rolled the ball around his own palm. It was rough to the touch, striated with delicate lines.

Have a guess, kid. What do you think it is?

Um … it's a seed, I guess.

Correct. What type of seed?

How should I know? Could be anything, a weed or anything.

Nope, not a weed. You're right about it not looking like much, though. Just a muddy-coloured seed, bit rough around the edges. If you didn't know what it was, you might overlook it, hey. Throw it away, even.

So what is it then?

Guess, I told ya.

Um … not tomato, I remember what they look like. And not carrots. We planted mostly seedlings; we didn't have many seeds straight into the ground.

Correct.

I dunno, I give up. What is it?

That, my boy, is two things. The first thing is, it's a coriander seed. Come straight from the plants we put in. Remember that tall one that I said was going to seed? Well, that's the result. Our own coriander seeds, falling on the ground and sprouting themselves up again without any encouragement from us.

Yeah? Coriander, huh? The boy raised it to his nose and inhaled. *Smells like the spices at the curry place down at Rosalie. Mum took me there once.*

Yep, it's a different smell to the leaves.

How come you never told me before that these were growing straight from seeds?

Waiting for you to notice, wasn't I.

The boy pinched the seed between his nails and inhaled again. *So, what was the other thing?*

The old man was staring off into the dark. *Hmm?*

The second thing. You said it was two things.

Oh, yeah, I did.

He took the seed from the boy and held it up between them. A cloud changed shape in the breeze, revealing the moon.

It's you, kid. This seed is you.

The boy remained silent, focused on the seed and the moonlight.

This seed is just like you. Initially it's not much to look at. A tiny lump, a bit coarse and rough, to be honest.

The boy shot him a glare, but still said nothing.

But you know what, kid? This seed is bursting with possibility; it's a seed full of promise. It might be dormant now, quiet, waiting and watchful, biding its time, but when the time is right, it will open up and come to life, and sprout into that beautiful, aromatic herb that's loved by millions all over the world, and it will serve its purpose. All it needs is the right environment. Water, good soil, nutrients, bit of sunlight. Keep the weeds away so they don't strangle it before it's got a decent chance to develop. Doesn't need much.

His voice was vague now, and dreamy.

Nope, doesn't need much for this seed to fulfil its promise, to reach its potential.

He reached out his shaking hand and took the boy's hand in his own. He placed the seed once again onto the boy's palm, and enfolded his fingers over it. They sat like that for a moment, the boy and the man, their hands loosely gripped, the moonlight flooding the garden.

Eventually the boy released his grip and stood up.

I should be getting home.

He bent towards the old man and helped him to his feet.

I'll put the seed into my treasure box.

The old man nodded, grunted, and began to tread unsteadily towards the house. The clouds had closed over the moon.

The boy reached the fence.

Is everyone a seed, then? he asked.

The old man paused but didn't turn around. *I reckon so, kid.*

A beat.

What about you? the boy said.

The old man emitted a short, sharp laugh, or perhaps it was a cry.

Me? Me … yep, I guess even I was a seed once. Not anymore though. Now I'm just a husk.

And with that the old man moved again towards the stairs, almost seeming to float on the breeze and the shadows; an empty husk, light, and drifting gently.

Sometimes I dream about her. Emily. Not Sarah Emily, *Girl Seated at Mirror*. No, I don't dream of my daughter. It's my sister – the original Emily – who comes to me when I inhabit that other world of sleep. Not often, maybe once or sometimes twice a year. And always when I least expect her to appear; when I have almost – but not quite – forgotten her existence. And then she comes, creeping softly, a persistent ghost, entering my head through the portal of sleep. Arriving on a comforting sigh; leaving footprints on my soul.

I always used to dream of her as a baby, the age she was when she died. But lately, she has been older – a child, a young girl of eight or nine. Yet I recognise her. She looks fragile and delicate, with wispy long hair and knowing eyes. All deception. I know that beneath the surface lie courage and determination, a steely resolve. I know this because she has been coming to me for seventy years. A loyal friend, a trusted keeper of family secrets.

I dreamt of her again last night. At the instant she slips into my thoughts, when I become aware that she has arrived, I am always a little startled – *Oh yes,* I think, *of course, it's Emily.* I am never surprised to see her, just momentarily bewildered that I could have forgotten her, like the bafflement you feel when you remember something after losing your train of thought – it seems impossible that you could ever have not known.

She was quite ethereal. Her outlines were smudged, her movements slow and insubstantial. Sometimes she's solid, you see, solid and dense and very … *there*, if you know what I mean. But last night she looked as if a light wind would not only blow her away, but actually blow right through her, so that she would disintegrate like a handful of ash.

She never speaks. Her mouth opens and she gestures like some people do when they're talking, when they're trying to make a point, but I never hear the words. It doesn't seem to matter. I don't feel frustrated by the fact that I can't hear her, and she doesn't seem agitated by my incomprehension either. She talks continually, like I've seen mothers do to their infants – nonsense words, made-up songs, comforting noises for babies too young to understand. Maybe that's it. Maybe I'm not an advanced enough being to understand her language.

The location of the dream changes. Sometimes we're in a proper place, somewhere I clearly recognise – the backyard, the Home, my own living room; once the local corner store, though why she chose that spot I never could fathom. And sometimes we're just … somewhere. In the sky, perhaps, surrounded by cloud. Or submerged in a substance like water, but viscous and breathable. Sometimes there's merely space, a huge empty nothingness. Just Emily. And me. Brother and sister again.

I am never frightened by these dreams. Not even in the period immediately after she died, when I was a youngster. I suppose that's why I've never been afraid of ghosts. I figure I've known one my whole life, and all she's ever brought me is a sense of peace, though God knows she'd have reason to do otherwise, if any ghost would.

People speak of unsettled spectres, of ghosts trapped between this world and the next, eager to frighten the heck out of us mere mortals. But that hasn't been my experience at all.

I'm unsure why she's visiting me now as a small child. It did cross my mind that it's 'cause of all the time I'm spending with the young fella next door. But that would mean that how I see Emily is dependent on what's going on in my waking life, and that thought doesn't sit comfortably with me. I like to think that she is real, you see – well, as real as a dream can be. I don't like to think that I'm conjuring her. Seems wrong, somehow. Disloyal.

So then I started to think that perhaps ghosts age much slower than we do, you know, like one human year is seven dog years or whatever that ratio is. Maybe one lifetime – seventy years or more – equates to only seven or eight ghost years. That would be something, wouldn't it? Though the truth is, I wouldn't mind a visit from an elderly Emily. A little old lady with powder-soft skin and wrinkled jowls and merry crinkled eyes. What must she think of me, after all these years. Grown old and saggy, bits not working, hard of hearing, eyesight not much chop. What must she think.

Last night she hovered around in my dream, talking nineteen to the dozen, and with me as usual not understanding a single word. Not that it mattered. When she arrives, a feeling of stillness and serenity settles over me. I feel rested.

After so many years of her visitations, I recognise when it's time for her to leave me. It's like the moment when you rise out of a warm bath, and the water runs in rivulets down your body and the chill of the air brings goosebumps to your skin.

A shiver of loss.

Last night she laid her hand against my cheek, her soft touch like fingertips on velvet, a chick's down, the stroke of a child's eyelashes. I struggled to hold on. I pushed my face against her palm, willing her to stay. And in that split second of consciousness, when I was aware of waking but had not yet opened my eyes, I fully expected to see her cool, pale hand pressed against me.

But it was only the corner of the pillowcase brushing my face. Or maybe the idle play of the night breeze, masquerading as my dead sister's caress.

The evening sky was lowering its curtain across the sun as the old man and the boy headed home. The cool air felt delicious on the boy's nose and shoulders, pink and tender from the day's heat, the burn that had reflected from the shimmering water and the sparkling sand. He was half-walking, half-skipping, every so often completing a happy little circle around the old man who shuffled forward in a weary but steady pace. In one hand he clutched the old man's gift, meticulously rewrapped. The boy delivered a chirpy monologue, dissecting every aspect of the day since the second they had boarded the beach-bound bus.

I can't wait to put this on my bike. What a great present. Thanks so much. Again. I really like it.

You're very welcome. And thanks for the water bottle. I haven't seen metal ones since we used to get those aluminium cups in plastic holders. Used to give us Alzheimer's, apparently.

Yeah well not these ones, these ones are the safe stuff. Plus it's got your name on it, so even when you do get Alzheimer's, you'll still be able to remember who you are.

Watch it, you. If I wasn't so exhausted you'd get a clip over the ear. Anyway, it'll be good for when I'm out doing the gardening.

What about that seaweed? Wasn't that weird? I wish I could've brought some back. Would've been so cool to shove that down the girls' dresses.

I told you, it would've smelt something horrible.

Yeah, I know! That's what's so good about it! Smelly and slimy, perfect. And how about that jellyfish? I've never seen a jellyfish before. I didn't realise they actually looked so much like jelly. You could see all its insides, its brain and everything.

I don't think jellyfish have brains. I don't think they're that advanced.

Well, it sure had something in there. Maybe it was its nervous system.

It was right to be nervous around you. I'm surprised it survived the experience.

I only wanted to see what it looked like! I couldn't see it properly in the water.

I think that's the whole point.

The bus was great. Wasn't the bus ride great? All those huge houses. Who do you think lives in all those humungous houses along that road we went along? They must be millionaires for sure. Maybe even billionaires. Really rich, anyway. Some of them had their own horses! And driveways as long as our whole street! Imagine having to go through that huge gate, probably you'd need your own key, or maybe the kids have a secret gate code to let them in, and then they ride their bikes all the way up that driveway before they even get to the house. Damn, that would be something.

Oi, watch your language.

Well, it would be, wouldn't it?

Sometimes being rich isn't all it's cracked up to be, so I'm told.

I'll bet it's only the poor people who tell you that. The people in those houses would be laughing.

Yes, but are they happy?

Probably. Yep, definitely I'd say. Very happy.

Hmm ... maybe you're right. Living the dream.

And thanks for the fish and chips. That was the best fish and chips I've ever, ever had. Ever. Even better than that fish place at Rosalie.

It was pretty good fish and chips, I'll agree with you there.

Wasn't that dog cute? I wish I had a dog like that. What kind did the boy say it was again?

Umm … I think he said a spoodle. Or maybe a labradoodle. Possibly a cavoodle. One of those newfangled breeds. Can't see the point, myself. Nothing wrong with a mutt from the pound.

But it was so cute and really smart. It wasn't scared of the water at all. It came right on in after me. The water was so warm. You should've come in deeper. You hardly got wet at all.

Up to my knees was plenty for me, son. I'm too old to be cavorting around in the waves.

There weren't any waves! That's what was so good about it. You could swim out for ages and it wasn't even deep.

Yeah, I noticed you swimming out for ages. If you remember, I had to keep calling you to come back in.

The boy fluttered his hand in a dismissive gesture. *I was fine. I'm a good swimmer. I told you. Better than that other boy. He couldn't even keep up with his dog. And what about when that car pulled up and all those guys got out and they were all pissed and that one was dressed like Santa and then he went in the water and his friends had to rescue him?*

Oh hilarious, that was. Stupid louts. Full as googs, the lot of them. Lucky they didn't drown themselves. That waterlogged suit must've been heavy as lead.

It was the best day. The absolute best day. We have to go again. Can we go again? Soon?

Well, we'll have to ask your mum about that.

The mention of his mother deflated the boy. He stopped skipping. Stopped altogether. The old man turned back.

Thank goodness you've stopped bouncing around like Tigger. Making me tired just watching you.

He walked a few more paces then stopped again.

Well, come on, we're almost home. I don't know how on earth you've got so much energy left, 'cause I'm done for. Ready for a hot shower and a cup of tea and bed.

I don't want to go home.

The old man squinted through the last of the sun's rays. The boy was slouched against a fence, his head bowed; his long hair flopped over his face. In places his skin was starting to develop an angry hue. A smattering of sand adorned his hairline, as well as the inside of his ears and the backs of his calves. A chocolate ice-cream stain all down the front of his shirt. The old man thought how young the boy seemed, how vulnerable.

Sorry, mate, not much choice about that, I'm afraid.

The boy met his gaze. *Can't I come home with you?*

Me? I think your mum'd have something to say about that, don't you?

Nope. Actually I don't think she would.

He kicked at the gravel.

I don't think she'd care at all, actually. Probably be glad. His voice was louder now, indignant.

The old man shuffled towards the boy and put his hand on his shoulder. The boy winced.

Ouch.

Sorry. Guess we should've reapplied the sunscreen like the bottle said.

He leant his weight back against the fence and stood beside the boy, both of them staring up the road towards their two houses squatting next to each other in the gathering night.

We've had a pretty good day, haven't we? he asked.

The boy nodded.

Let's not spoil it now, hey? We can go again, sure we can. Once I recover from this episode. Maybe ... maybe your mum would like to come too?

No! The boy's vehement response echoed against the house opposite and bounced along the empty street.

220

No. No way. That's our place. Our special place. Just for us. You have to promise!

OK, OK, it was only an idea.

You have to promise!

All right, I promise.

Swear.

I swear, all right? We'll go again. Just us. Now come on, let's get home before she sends out a search party.

As if. It'd be no search and all party, muttered the boy.

On our way up the hill towards home, the boy and I passed fences and decks strung with Christmas lights, and glowing trees framed by illuminated windows, winking with festive sparkle. That Greek family that arrived a few years ago was having a barbecue with about thirty of their relatives. Kids and dogs all over the place. The old Mitchell place was quiet, but I could see Amy Mitchell baking through her kitchen window, and I could smell her mince pies from the street. Old Amy, she must've been ninety if she was a day. There was a stretch of three or four houses in a row where I didn't know the people. Bought and sold, renovated. In one I saw a very pregnant lady putting her feet up in front of the telly. In the next yard, a dad played cricket with two small boys while their mum sat on the stairs, fanning herself with junk mail. Families eating dinner and talking. I paused for a moment to get my breath.

I looked at the boy and I thought about the families in our street, and I thought about *my* notion of family. Fathers defined by their absence rather than their presence. Mothering a state of benign neglect. Home the place you were barely noticed. Or ignored. Manipulation and self-preservation acting as poor substitutes for unconditional love.

222

I thought about the luck of the draw in where you're born, and where you end up. You draw the short straw, and what shred of hope do you have of a normal life? If you're born someplace with none of the advantages that others take for granted, how do you get along in life? And if you don't know any different, how can you hope for something better? How can you have a shot at what's possible if you don't even *know* what's possible?

The families I saw around us gave off the simple comfort of loving and being loved. Of having the security to hope and the confidence to dream.

My sister had no chance to hope. No opportunity to laugh and grow and play. To love, to mourn, to take risks, to try. And my wings were clipped early too. No choice in the matter.

The boy ... what does he hope for? Where does he dream? How high will he fly without someone to show him the way?

Snake and the boy's mother were sitting at the kitchen table. The air was thick with a potent combination of tobacco and marijuana, trapping the day's heat. Half a bottle of rum stood next to an empty one. The Christmas decorations that his mum had put up the day before were now drooping, the humidity loosening the sticky tape. On the table, still in its unopened box, was the fancy cigarette lighter the boy had given her that morning, swiped from the shop counter while the girl was busy with another customer.

After spending all day in fresh air and sunshine, the house was dull and slow and oppressive. His mum's eyes were red-rimmed. She had a discoloured mark on her left cheek.

The boy stood in the doorway. For a few moments, no-one said anything. The tick of the wall clock sounded unnaturally loud.

Eventually the boy spoke. *I'm back.*

His mum swung her head in his direction. The thought occurred to him that she looked like a doped-up cow.

So you are. Back. Back from your adventures.

Her head nodded in slow motion, as if confirming something to herself.

Yes, she said, to no-one in particular.

Snake went to the fridge and rummaged around. As he stood there in the light of the open fridge door, guzzling a beer, the boy examined the lines and scales of the tattoo that came together to form the reptile. The ink was mostly faded. Some places had been touched up recently, dots of brighter blue highlighting a curve. One spot near his underarm flared red and inflamed. An infection, the boy thought. It looked sore.

The serpent's eyes glittered from the back of the man's neck, almost like they'd had flecks of gold added. With a shiver, the boy realised that despite the man's movements, those eyes seemed fixed on his own. It was like one of those pictures in a horror movie, where the people in the paintings on the walls have eyes that follow the unsuspecting victim, watching him as he carries on unawares.

The effect, the boy understood, was that no matter whether the man was facing towards you or away from you, there was always a pair of eyes following you, observing your every move. If Snake the man couldn't see you, his tattoo certainly could.

He shivered again, imagining that they were one and the same thing, but finally managed to drag his gaze away.

Well, I'm gonna have a shower. The boy walked through the kitchen. He could feel Snake's human eyes burning into his back.

He shrugged out of his clothes and a spray of sand fell to the floor. He examined his sunburn. The worst bits were across his shoulders, the tops of his thighs and the backs of his arms. And his face, which sported red warpaint stripes. He stood under the cool water of the shower. Now that he was home, he realised how tired he felt.

He pushed the shower curtain aside and listened. Raised voices in the hall. He remembered, too late, that he hadn't locked the bathroom door. It banged open and Snake stamped into the room, grasped the curtain and pulled it from the railing. The boy couldn't tell if the jagged sound was the tearing plastic or a cry from his own throat. Snake grabbed the boy's upper arm and pulled him over the rim of the bath. The boy's knee banged painfully against the enamel. He started to crawl across the floor but the man stood on one outstretched arm before pulling him up and marching him across the hall towards his bedroom. Puddles of water marked their way. The boy saw his mother disappearing into the kitchen.

He was thrown on the bed, onto a coil of rope and two belts. Where had they come from? Snake pulled back his right arm and delivered a solid punch to the boy's temple. A shower of stars twinkled across a red sky, and then nothing.

...

The first slice of pain woke him from his unconsciousness, bringing him back to harsh, ugly reality. The second stroke whistled through the air before the belt cracked across his shoulders. The shock of the third brought tears to his eyes and ensured he was fully awake to his surroundings. His cries were muffled by whatever was covering his mouth. He was still naked, lying face down on his bed. His arms were tied with the rope to his bedhead. His legs felt crushed. The weight lifted as Snake rolled off. He raised his arm and then the discomfort of the boy's crushed legs was abruptly and spectacularly drowned out by the agony of a belt buckle slicing into his sunburnt flesh. He could feel throbbing welts across his back and shoulders.

The man stood beside the bed. The boy whimpered, his eyes squeezed shut. He could hear Snake pacing. Out of nowhere, another stroke of the belt, this one harder and stronger due to the man's extra leverage from his standing position.

The red swimming again in front of his eyes ... the pinprick of stars ...

Oh no you don't, you little shit. Don't you black out on me again. You're gonna listen to what I got to say, you hear me?

The man grabbed a handful of the boy's hair, wrenched his head back and slapped his face until he came to. He heard the belt drop to the floor.

As the man spoke, he pinched the boy's skin, a painful twist behind his knees or on his earlobe or in that tender place under his arm.

You ... little ... shit, he repeated.

You ungrateful little shit. You left your mum alone on Christmas Day. Christmas fucking Day!

The twists became harder. The boy could feel nails biting into flesh, drawing blood.

I told her, I said that boy needs to learn some respect. That boy needs to learn some discipline.

The boy sensed the man's face coming closer, smelt the foul fumes of alcohol rise into his nostrils. Snake spoke in a growled whisper.

And I intend to teach you some.

He reared back; all at once he had the belt in his hand once again, and he brought it down full force onto the boy's bare buttocks. This time, even the stars were gone, as a crimson ocean washed over his pain and his thoughts and his fear, and carried him away.

...

He awoke to the reassuring touch of a washcloth on his brow. He held his breath as the pain flooded through his limbs. When he opened his eyes, it was Snake sitting beside him, stroking his forehead with a gentleness that was surely impossible. Maybe it was all a nightmare, thought the boy. A terrible nightmare. A movement beyond the figure of the man caught his eye. His mother, watching from the doorway. She came towards him.

He's awake.

And to the boy, *How're you feeling, love? You want a drink?*

'Course he wants a drink, after the day he's had. Get him one of those cold Cokes.

His mother didn't budge, just stood there fingering her bruised cheek.

Move it, woman!

Her absence hovered between them. The boy flinched slightly and a great tremor of pain swept across his body. He shut his eyes.

Best to keep still. You've got some nasty marks. Must've been a bad fall. You've grazed your whole back. Or maybe it was a jellyfish that stung you? Horrible, isn't it, the dangers that are out there. If you're not careful.

His voice was oily, taunting. A warning, an edge as sharp as a knife.

But don't you worry. Me and your mum, we're gonna take good care of you. She's put a heap of salve on those cuts and the bruises'll fade in a day or two.

On his wrists the boy could see bracelets of red rubbed raw. One side of his head throbbed with a dull ache, like the background beat of loud music. He shifted his weight and found the sheet stuck tight in places by a crust of dried blood. He tried to roll onto his side and the pain seared across his back like it was on fire.

He vomited in a sudden, violent retch, and the man sprang from the bed, cursing and wiping his trousers, flicking wads of half-digested fish and chips onto the floor.

You little fucking bastard!

Calling to his mother – *Clean up that mess! Ungrateful shit. Try to help and get spewed on.*

And he was gone.

His departure mobilised his mother into action. She returned to the room with cloths and a bucket of warm water.

Come on, love, let's get you cleaned up. You'll feel better.

She helped him to a sitting position, rolled up the dirty sheet and threw it into the corner. She spread out his doona and helped him lie face down again. She wetted the cloth and wiped his mouth and his hands, then rinsed it and began to pat gently, oh so gently, at the dried blood that had collected across his skin.

The boy relaxed into her touch. All at once he was crying, silent tears wending down his cheeks. She pushed his hair back and daubed at the tears.

Oh baby, I'm sorry. I'm so, so sorry. Please don't cry. It'll be fine. We'll all be OK, I promise. Snake doesn't mean it, baby. He likes you, he does. He only wants to make sure you grow up right. He doesn't like it when I'm upset. I was so sad we didn't spend Christmas together. Maybe I shouldn't have got so sad to him. He was angry for me, really. Don't cry. We'll work it out.

She pulled his head against her chest, her hands stroking his hair in a soothing rhythm. She was careful not to touch his back. The boy allowed himself to slacken into her embrace, allowed her sweet perfumed smell to erase the metallic tang of his blood. She was rocking back and forth, and stroking, and humming something, and for a moment he imagined he was two or three years old again, and being held by the most important person in his small life. He remembered the feeling: absolute dependence and trust, unwavering safety and warmth.

His tears dampened his mother's breast as she rocked him to sleep.

...

It was the smell that woke him. A sour odour that clung to the inside of his nostrils, stronger with each breath. He lay unmoving. His eyes remained closed, heavy-lidded, stuck with sleep. He wriggled his toes and arrows of pain shot up his legs. He tried flexing his arms, one at a time, but each attempt brought a fresh tide of discomfort. Nothing unbearable, though. At least nothing seemed broken.

But that smell. What was that smell?

His eyes refused to open. Concentrating hard, he raised one arm to his face. His fingers prised his eyelids apart and came away sticky. As he lowered his hand past his nose, the smell intensified.

He peered through his slitted eyes. There was no moon, and it took a few minutes of blinking before he was able to discern the familiar shapes of his room. A sinister mound in the corner materialised into his chair with his jacket slung across the back. An odd structure squatting on the floor became his schoolbag topped by a pair of trainers. His bedroom door was closed, bordered by a sliver of light. He twisted his head on the pillow, slowly, painfully. The window was partly open to the night. A weak gust of hot air fluttered the mobile of paper cranes strung from a nail. Outside, in the gloom, a nightjar called.

A figure lay across the bottom of his bed. At first he thought it was his mother, fallen asleep during her vigil. Gradually, as his eyes adjusted, the shadow of his mother realigned, reshaped, morphed into the form of a man. Snake. A bead of sweat formed on the boy's forehead and dripped into his eye. He blinked rapidly, hoping the silhouette on the bed would change into some items of clothing or a bunched-up doona. But his eyes picked out more details as the dimness receded. The shock of black hair. The tattoo across his chest and left bicep. The reptile's tail that vanished into a springy dark tuft. The boy's eyes widened as his brain registered what he was seeing. Nested on the tuft of hair. A thick, fat slug, slightly bent, obscene against the coarse hair and the tanned skin.

The sound came from his throat as though from someone else's voice. He was acutely aware of the need to remain silent, and yet the noise came … a frisson of fear, barely stifled. He knew, too, the impossibility of movement, and yet his body was backed against the bedhead, his feet pushing against the sheets, stinging stripes pulsing across his torso.

Snake woke. Woke to the sound of the boy's cry. He stared at him and then stretched, luxuriously, nonchalantly. As if the world hadn't just stopped spinning. As if the air hadn't become water or smoke or acid. As if he could breathe and move and function without pain or fear. As if the tableau in that room, on that bed, was normal. Slowly, watchfully, he rolled towards the boy. One hand reached out, tenderly. The boy was stricken, unable to move, unable even to take a breath. The man lowered his hand onto the boy's groin.

It must've been only a second, maybe not even that long – a fraction of a second. But in that short time, three things happened in rapid succession. Snake managed one tentative stroke, the boy's penis stiffened, and he recognised the sour, sticky smell covering his face. He rolled off the bed in an agony of movement, flung open the door, pounded down the hall, wrenched open the back door, and ran, naked, fleeing into the night, tight sobs of fury and humiliation echoing in the emptiness and rousing the chickens from their sleep.

Just when you think you've seen all life has to offer, when you believe that you've passed enough years to have served your time and paid for your sins, they throw something else at you. I think of that expression: *Things could be worse. And probably will be.* Never a truer phrase. You'd think an old man would be entitled to some peace. You'd think I'd have seen enough pain and distress in my years that I'd be allowed a few quiet ones, some time at the end of my life to reflect and wallow in my own regrets, and not have to deal with some new indignity. But that is not the case. No sir. Whoever's doing the organising up there, they're just sitting around thinking up new ways to get at me, novel methods of abuse. Why can't an old man live out his last years in peace, hey? That's the question I asked the Detective Sergeant, but he merely looked blankly at me and pretended he hadn't heard. *Ramblings of an old guy,* I could almost hear him thinking. And then he got back to the business of interrogating me.

So you don't deny that you took the boy to the beach yesterday?

No sir, I don't deny that at all. That's exactly what we did. We went to the beach.

On Christmas Day? You took a ten-year-old boy, a stranger, with you

232

to the beach on Christmas Day? And you don't think there's anything odd about that?

First off, the kid's not a stranger. He's my neighbour. And my friend. And second off, what's so strange about spending Christmas Day with a friend?

He's not your grandson. He's not related to you in any way. You took him away without his mother's permission and against his will.

Now hang on, that's not true. His mother knew. The boy told me she'd given her permission. And it most certainly was not against his will. He had a great day. We both had a great day. We ate fish and chips on the beach. He saw a jellyfish.

Detective Sergeant Logan appraised me from under his bushy eyebrows. *I have no doubt at all that YOU had a great day.*

He leant forward and rested his arms on the dented metal tabletop. It was grey, like the rest of the room. Grey walls, grey folding chairs, grey light shifting through grey shadows. He moved his face close to mine. His skin was pockmarked with decades-old acne scars. His left eye twitched involuntarily. His breath smelt of peppermint and Fisherman's Friend throat lozenges. When he spoke again, he whispered, a low growl that frightened me more than I cared to admit, even to myself; certainly more than his loud posturing of the last hour.

That poor kid, on the other hand, he didn't have such a great day, did he now? Huh? Those welts on his back, they weren't that much fun. Those belt marks on his legs, they probably weren't a barrel of laughs either.

I stared at him, mutely, like the idiot I am. Like the idiot I must be.

I began to wonder about the wisdom of my choosing not to have a solicitor present.

And fondling his privates, that was the icing on the cake for you, wasn't it. But I'm guessing for him, not so much. No, I reckon that was pretty unfunny for him by that stage. But then, you've always had a penchant for little boys, haven't you? All those years in the Boys' Home, does funny things to a bloke. Only a matter of time before your natural instincts came out. I'm only surprised it took so long. But then, I've heard grooming the kids is the best part. The an-ti-ci-pa-tion. He drew out the syllables.

My eyes met his. I couldn't look away.

The payoff must almost be an anticlimax, huh? His honeyed tones became a screech. *Especially when you get caught, you dirty bastard!*

I looked down long enough to see my hands trembling like I was having some sort of seizure. They seemed not a part of me, some strange restless creatures at the ends of my arms.

And then I passed out. I must've hit my head pretty darn hard on the corner of that metal table on the way down, 'cause I had an egg-shaped mound on my temple that lasted a full week.

...

The police medic saw to my head, pronounced the egg a *minor injury*, and declared me *fit to continue interview.* She clearly couldn't feel the pounding behind my eyes or the throbbing above my temple.

But back to the grey room I went.

The detective with the cratered face was waiting, the smell of cigarettes wafting from his pores. Another man sat in the shadows. I hadn't noticed him before, but now that I had, it seemed he had been there all along, silent and listening. I lowered myself gingerly into the grey chair, trying to avoid any sudden movements that might aggravate the pain in my head. The detective sat with his forearms crossed over his paunch. He stared at me, daring me to look away, saying nothing.

The other bloke stood and made an elaborate show of lifting his chair and placing it at the table before clearing his throat and addressing me.

I hope your head isn't troubling you too much, sir.

Clearly we had entered the realm of good cop, bad cop.

We understand all this must be very troubling for you, sir, and now on top of that you've had a fall and got yourself a nasty bump on the head. We don't want to keep you here any longer than is absolutely necessary, all right?

I begrudged him a nod, merely to acknowledge his politeness. The place above my ear jangled.

You must understand our concern. The boy's a friend of yours, you say, so surely you can see we want to work out what's happened and make sure he's OK. All right?

All right, I echoed.

Are you still saying you haven't seen the boy since you returned from Bribie Island yesterday?

That's right.

So you haven't seen his injuries?

I flinched. *No, I haven't.*

I had heard them described, though. Heard the foul words bandied about as if they were speaking of a stray dog. Made me sick to my stomach.

And you still deny having anything to do with those injuries?

Yes. Through gritted teeth.

Has he ever seen you naked?

The change in tack took me by surprise and it must have showed on my face, because bad cop leant forward in his chair, eyes ablaze with interest.

An automatic *no* quivered on the edge of my lips, waiting only for the puff of air to expel it from my mouth and become real. But then my mind tracked back to that day, the afternoon the boy found me covered in my own vomit and urine, drunk as a skunk and smelling like one too. I saw him peeling off my clothes and running the shower. I saw myself hunched over the toilet bowl, trying to pee; heard myself telling him to go out and shut the door so I could piss without an audience. Saw him glance at my sorry nakedness with disappointment.

It wasn't in me to be dishonest to this fellow, not when he was making such an effort to be polite.

Yes.

Sorry, yes? Did you say yes?

Yes. Yes, he has seen me naked. Once, just the once.

I began to babble. I knew I was babbling, could feel the words tripping over themselves in their hurry to get out and explain themselves, but I couldn't seem to stop.

Only the once. He was helping me shower. I was drunk. I mean, I was drunk and upset. The kid helped me. He saved me, really, saved me from myself. I was in a bad way. He fixed me up, he … he … I mean, it was innocent enough, he …

I stared at the two men, at the disbelief on their faces. My monologue petered out and I slumped back in my seat.

I was embarrassed to discover my eyes had filled with tears. My voice came out meekly as I whispered, *It's not how it sounds …*

Bad cop's hands, white-knuckled, clasped the edge of the tabletop.

You dirty bastard. He spat the words at me like poison. *You filthy, dirty bastard.*

I don't know what came over me then. All at once it was too much – his language, my fear, my concern for the boy, my confusion, the ache in my head.

Oi, watch your language, I said. The phrase rolled off my tongue. *I'm old enough to be your father. Show some respect.*

Good cop leant forward, his hands together under his chin as if in prayer. *All right, grandpa, calm down.*

Calm down? CALM DOWN?

I shouted the words as I pushed my chair back and stood to my full height, concentrating all the anger I could into my glare. I enunciated my words as slowly and clearly as I was able.

You two bozos listen to me. That kid is my neighbour and my friend. If he's been hurt in any way, it has nothing whatsoever to do with me.

You should be out there finding out who did it instead of wasting your time interrogating an old man. He's a good kid. Smart, and funny, and clever too.

My eyes betrayed me again. This time the tears coursed down my cheeks unchecked.

If he's hurt, I need to see him. I should be with him. He's been there for me. I need to … to see him. To make sure he's OK.

I never touched him, I added, for extra emphasis.

Bad cop swore at me again but good cop held my stare. And then, in a very quiet voice, so quiet that I had to strain to hear the words, he said, *So how come the boy said that you did?*

The boy huddled into the sagging vinyl of the armchair, his legs pulled to his chest, his arms wrapped around his knees. He was trying to take up as little space as possible. His back still hurt; he could feel the raised welts with every slight shift. So he tried not to move, or to look at the woman opposite him, or to think. Especially not to think. If a stray tentacle of thought even attempted to make its way into his head, he chopped it off before it had a chance. He pictured a miniature axe inside his skull, ready to lop off any intruders. He'd seen an octopus once on a documentary, watched how the creature sneakily stretched the tip of one tentacle into a crack in the rock, the gross arm wriggling back and forth, forcing its way in, until before you knew it another and then another had penetrated the tiny crevice, and the animal's whole body had insinuated itself right through the crack and into the space beyond. He pictured the possibility of that happening inside his head. He did not want the thoughts crowding his brain. He couldn't afford to let a single one slip through. He didn't know how it had all gone so horribly wrong; all he knew was that he must not think about it. Not think at all.

He concentrated instead on the details of the room. It was

spacious, as big as three rooms of his house put together. One wall was almost entirely panes of glass. Despite the air conditioning that he could hear humming away behind him, several of the windows were open to the breeze, which swept through in irregular gusts. He imagined the lady kept them open to air the room, to sweep away the words no-one liked or wanted to hear.

He could hear the rumble of a train. Two pigeons landed on some unseen perch in a flurry of feathers, squabbling over the best spot. The sunlight poured through the glass, pooling on the floor, throwing the remainder of the room into shadow. Behind him was a wall, blank except for a large painting done by a child. He'd noticed it right away when they came in. To his right were three straight-backed chairs around a table. Coloured pencils and textas spilled across its surface. A blue pen had fallen and leaked onto the beige carpet. Beyond that were cane storage cubes housing the greatest assortment of toys he had ever seen. Picture books, chapter books, puzzles and boxes of games vied for attention on the cramped shelving. Soft animals, blocks and pull-along toys lay scattered across the floor. Two lifelike dolls sat together, a girl and a boy. She had long blonde hair and chubby arms, while he had short brown hair and a mischievous grin. The boy suspected they were completely lifelike under their clothes too. He looked away.

To his left was the door through which he had been ushered an hour earlier. It was closed. His only escape route, sealed shut. There was a couch that didn't match the armchairs, and a small kitchenette in the corner. He could see teabags and a kettle, an under-bench fridge, a packet of plain biscuits. He had refused one when the lady offered. She'd said she wouldn't eat them either, *too boring*, and had suggested they ask for chocolate cake, but the boy had shaken his head to that too. He didn't think his stomach would hold anything, not even a plain old biscuit. He didn't think he would eat anything ever again.

At first the lady had tried to talk to him. She'd spoken about the weather and school and sports. She'd asked him if he liked reading and what he enjoyed watching on TV. She'd asked if he had any pets, but the boy had curled tighter into the armchair and stopped looking at her, so she hadn't asked about that again. Eventually she stopped talking. She simply sat, patiently, silently. Every now and then the boy snuck a glance at her: sometimes she was picking at a fingernail; once she was adjusting her shoe. From time to time she would gaze right back at him in a questioning way. The boy wondered if her look was accusing, but decided it wasn't. She was older than his mum and dressed much older still. While his mum favoured short skirts that showed off her legs, and low-cut tops and strappy sandals, this lady wore a loose printed dress and comfortable shoes. Her earrings jangled against her cheeks when she spoke. They were made from seed pods. The boy focused his attention on the patterned material of her dress. At first he'd thought it was an abstract design, but now he saw the outlines of birds and flowers hiding amongst the randomness. The known hiding in the unknown, the familiar in the strange.

The lady straightened in her chair and rose stiffly to her feet, arching her back and clasping her hands.

I don't know about you, but I'm starving. I'm going to slip out and order us some sandwiches before we fade away. What's your favourite?

The boy remained silent.

Well, I'll order a selection. Egg and lettuce, some ham and cheese — maybe some corned beef and pickles; that's what I feel like myself. You sit tight. I'll be right back.

She pointed to a door beside the kitchenette.

You remember that's the bathroom, right? You go ahead and use it if you need to, while I'm gone. Make yourself at home.

She studied him a moment before turning away. At the door she paused.

Maybe you'll feel more like chatting when you've got some food into you. I know I just can't think at all on an empty stomach.

And she was gone.

The boy released a sigh like a balloon deflating. His ribs hurt from the tension of shallow breathing and trying not to move. He got up, his legs tingling from being cramped into the one position. Pins and needles pricked his left leg and his foot landed heavily on the floor, numb and unfeeling. He rocked to and fro on the spot, trying to get the circulation back into his limbs, and then made his way to the bathroom.

He closed the door behind him. There was no lock. He lifted the lid and aimed into the centre of the bowl, then flushed. He washed his hands under water that was ice cold and splashed some onto his face. He raised his eyes to his reflection in the mirror above the basin. A stranger peered back at him. A tired boy with red-rimmed eyes and messy, tangled hair. A bruise darkened one eyelid. The yellow of an older bruise circled his jaw and disappeared under his ear. The boy in the mirror seemed worn out and sad. And guilty.

How did it all go wrong? The boy felt the octopus tentacle groping inside his head; he closed his eyes and conjured the axe, imagined with all his might the blade falling sharply onto the horrible, slippery thing, severing it, halting its progress. But the axe was blunt and the water was icy and the bathroom light was harsh and confronting, and although the boy tried and tried, he failed to stop the probing thoughts. They entered his head in a tumbling rush; they ambushed his skull and took over his brain. He saw the ropes and the dark curly hair and the sand glistening on the beach. He saw his skin peeling from his nose and the welts on his legs and felt someone else's hand touching him. He saw a blue tattoo and a battered hat and green shoots pushing through the soil. He saw the innards of the jellyfish pulsating and a sodden Santa suit; he saw a red blanket of pain. It was all mixed up in his head. So many thoughts colliding.

What had been said could not now be unsaid. But that didn't mean he had to say it again.

He pictured his mother, her arms grasping him to her, covering his nakedness. He felt her rocking him there in the grass, holding him so tightly he couldn't breathe. Her hands had rubbed the wounds on his back, causing him to bite his lip to stop from crying out. Her sobs, terrible heart-rending sobs, as she clutched at the boy as if he was a life raft in a stormy sea. Her words, he had tried to make sense of her words, to understand the meaning underneath her cries and her moans.

I'm sorry, baby, I'm so sorry. I love you so much. Please forgive me. Please, please forgive me. You're all I've got. You're my whole world. We've got to take care of each other. We've got to stick together. It's you and me, baby. I'm sorry, I'm sorry, I'm so sorry.

Listening to the word – *sorry* – the sound of the letters as she sobbed and groaned, as she dragged the word from inside herself, the word becoming a mantra, a symbol. Not a word anymore but a prayer, an incantation, a cry for help. *Sorry, sorry, sorry,* over and over until the word itself sounded strange and new, another language.

And then her anger, sharp and furious. She had grabbed his shoulders, hard, her grip so strong it hurt. A vice. An animal caught in a trap.

He's special, special, do you hear me? This is my chance for happiness. Don't mess this up for me, all right? Don't do this, don't ruin this for me. He doesn't mean anything. He only wants you to be good. He wants us to be a family. God, he's the first one in how long to show you any attention, any affection, and this is how you react? Huh? This is how you repay everything he's given us? Everything he's done for us?

Her face melting, the anger draining away, replaced again by sorrow and regret. And something else – fear.

Oh baby, please, please, let's start again. Please? For me?

The voices from the darkness, the beam of a torch falling across his mother's shoulders. Two policemen in uniforms, solid boots and pale blue shirts with creases ironed in. Questions thrown about in the night, crowding overhead in the humid air. Questions and responses jumbling together, like night insects buzzing around uncovered skin. Queries about nakedness and injuries and bruising. About anonymous phone calls and reports of a disturbance. About minors and domestic violence and child abuse and unsafe environments. Questions he couldn't answer. Questions he didn't want to hear. *Who? When? Where?* And *Why?* and *How?* Questions sucking the oxygen from the atmosphere and doing his head in.

And in the midst of it all, his mother, his only mother, his dear mother who loved him and wanted him and was clutching him to her breast with the ferocity of a tiger protecting her cub. His mother's eyes, beseeching, asking him, begging him. Demanding his loyalty.

His mother talking about Christmas Day and the beach and the old man. His mother gesturing to the house next door and crying and holding him close. His mother speaking of unnatural relationships and too much time together and inappropriate touching.

And the boy. His silence. At first. And then his mute acquiescence. Agreeing. Questions pushing down, answers required.

His mother. Begging. *Begging*.

Simple words to release the pain. To stop the questions. To take away his mother's hurt.

Yes. The old man. Yes.

Him.

Yes.

...

The boy had forced down an egg sandwich – it lay like a rock in his stomach – and the lady had allowed him to leave the room. He could hear the policeman speaking to his mother in low, controlled tones and gesturing with what the boy interpreted to be impatience.

His mother appeared to be interested in a spot on the floor. Every so often she would shake her head. Eventually the policeman gave an exasperated sigh and presented his mother with a piece of paper. She did not read it, but signed at the place he indicated, with the pen he handed her. She eyeballed him then – the boy thought he heard her say *thank you* – and the policeman watched her retreating figure as she made her way over.

Thank God that's over. I thought they'd never let us leave. Come on, let's get out of here.

Her hand wavered in the air, then smoothed his fringe and tucked a stray bit of hair behind his ear.

How about we get ice-cream on the way home? Huh? What do you say? You and me?

Sure. Ice-cream sounds good.

He followed her down the hallway, past the room where the doctor had inspected his back. He'd checked other parts of his body too and the boy had held his breath in embarrassment, wishing he would finish, hoping it would all soon be over. When they passed the room with the toys and the biscuits, the lady was standing in the doorway, watching. Waiting for them. She gave him a sad smile.

You've got my number, right? You can call me anytime. Anytime at all. Even just to talk.

The boy mumbled a reply. Her eyes were kind. He hadn't noticed that before.

As they headed into the main corridor, and the lady vanished from the corner of his vision, his mother muttered, *Should mind her own fucking business, stupid bitch.*

He followed his mother into the darkness, his pupils dilating, trying to make sense of the shadows.

The female police officer was pleasant enough. She drove me home when good cop and bad cop decided to release me. *Don't leave town,* bad cop had warned, as if I had anywhere else to go even if I wanted to. I needed to get back to my own house and close the door on the world and all its madness.

I stumbled a little going up the stairs and she put her hand under my elbow and steadied me.

Sorry. Bit light-headed.

No worries, you take it easy. That's a nasty bump you've got on your head.

Then I couldn't seem to get the key to fit in the door and I mucked around with the jolly thing for a good few minutes before she took the keys from my hands and did it for me. Her hands were quite large for a woman, but soft and smooth. It almost did me in, that softness. Especially after the day I'd had.

Once we got inside she started flapping around, opening cupboard doors and offering to make me a cuppa, but by that stage I wanted to be rid of her. Didn't think I could stand any more kindness. When she'd gone, I sank into this chair and haven't moved since.

To be honest, I don't know what to think. The inside of my head's buzzing with thoughts and questions. I feel mixed up. Angry, that's for sure. And scared. Sad. Confused. And betrayed.

I keep thinking about our day at the beach. It seems impossible that was only yesterday. I see the boy digging in the wet sand at the water's edge, his shoulders going pink in the strong sun. I see those larrikins larking about, and the dog bouncing around the kid and barking fit to kill.

I see the expression on the kid's face as he lifted that jellyfish and poked it with his small fingers, trying to decipher its insides.

And then I see the grey room, with bad cop spraying my face with his peppermint spittle as he spews out the most disgusting filth, taunting, goading, accusing me.

And I can't reconcile the two images. They won't fit together.

Something is terribly, horribly wrong.

They wouldn't let me see him. Not even after they let me go. Good cop spouted some gobbledygook about *not pressing charges* and *lack of evidence*. Huh. Hard to find evidence when there isn't any, I told him. But even then they still wouldn't let me see him.

To be honest, I'm not sure I want to. See him, that is.

On the one hand, if he's hurting, then I should see him. Simple.

On the other hand, those detective's words keep ringing in my head. *How come the boy said that you did?* How come, indeed.

I should never have got mixed up with the kid, him and his crazy mother. Lord only knows what tales he's been spinning. I'm too old for this palaver. I'm weak pickings. Ready to be taken advantage of.

A man should have more sense.

Don't think this is over, bad cop said before I left. *We'll be talking with you again.*

I heave my tired bones out of the chair, flick off the switch and

246

drag my sorry self to bed. Don't even bother unlacing my shoes. Just lie on the bed as I am and pull the covers up. Close my eyes against the late-afternoon light.

They were sitting at an outside table under a gigantic red-and-white-striped umbrella that blocked the worst of the sun. The boy sucked noisily on an icy frappé through a straw. His mother fanned herself with a menu and sipped her white wine. A plethora of shopping bags littered the ground around their feet. His mum had really gone to town: she'd taken him to Dogstar and City Beach, and then got him some awesome skate shoes from Skatebiz. They'd popped into Mossimo where she'd bought him three T-shirts and a pile of undies with the label around the band. She'd wanted to get him a *Star Wars* doona cover from Target but he'd baulked at that, saying he wasn't a kid anymore. She'd shut up real quick and not mentioned sheets again.

She hadn't bought herself a single thing.

And now they were sitting here eating burgers and fries, just the two of them. The boy tried to think back to the last time they had done something together, without anyone else. He couldn't remember.

What's your face all screwed up for? You look like your brain's thinking too hard.

He relaxed his features and was surprised that a smile had found its way onto his face. *Just thinking about how nice it is here.*

With you, he added.

His mother's phone trilled. She glanced at the display and then snapped it shut.

Bloody cops. That's the third time since yesterday.

The boy drew his finger across the frosted glass. *What do they want?*

Jeez, what do ya think? They want to know what the fuck happened, don't they. Can't leave a family alone. Gotta poke their noses into everybody's business. They let that pervert next door go home, so now they need a different name to put on their fucking paperwork.

She cupped her hand under his chin.

Don't worry, love. You did good. They can't prove anything. They'll get tired of it eventually and go catch some real criminals, and you and I'll be left in peace.

So … they let him go.

Yes, baby, they did. And you stay away from the old perv from now on, all right?

Yeah. All right.

His mother's cool hand on his face. Her smile a red gash.

And … Snake?

She leant forward and lowered her voice.

Snake? she said. *Snake wasn't there. You didn't see him, and I didn't see him.* Her tone became smug. *The cops know nothing about him, baby. They don't even know he exists.*

The boy's heart almost burst with relief. It wasn't the old man. And it wasn't Snake. The boy tried to imagine that he had woken in the night to an intruder, an escaped prisoner who had beat him and hurt him and then run off into the night.

It could have happened. Perhaps it did happen that way.

His mother adjusted her sunglasses and tipped her glass towards him, her fuchsia nails gripping the thin stem.

Well, we should do this more often. Maybe we will from now on.

She took a long swig and placed the glass down. It rocked unsteadily.

Maybe we will, she repeated.

The café was filled with the holiday crowd. Tired women snapped at toddlers or sighed with exasperation at teenagers. The boy felt special, alone with his mum. No school for another few weeks, a mango frappé, and his mum all to himself, all day. He stirred the dregs with his straw.

He took a deep breath. *Wanna see a movie later?*

His mother sipped her wine and stared across the bustling tables.

Actually, I have plans for later. We were … me and …

She lifted her sunglasses and peered at the boy. He was aware of her gaze but sat immobilised, concentrating on the ice crystals, thinking about how quickly they melted in the heat. Finally he raised his eyes to meet her quizzical stare.

Sure, she said. *Why not. A movie would be fun. What do you want to see?*

The boy's insides felt like the melting ice; warmth coursed through his veins. He felt he might dissolve with happiness.

. . .

Night had fallen by the time they arrived home. No motorcycle in the driveway. The boy was comfortably full of popcorn and Coke. He glanced at the old man's house as he passed. A single bulb burned from the bedroom. The boy contemplated hopping the fence to check on the chickens. He could examine the lettuce leaves under the moonlight and find the juicy caterpillars that liked to come out at night, find them and wake up the hens with a tasty surprise.

But a swathe of clouds scudded across the moon, and it was late, and he needed to pee. And his mum was already in the house. She'd mentioned hot Milo. The boy made a silent promise in his head to check on the hens in the morning. He followed his mother inside.

It's been nearly two weeks now and real quiet without the kid around. Didn't realise how much I'd gotten used to his visits. The girls miss him too. They were all bunched up this afternoon, over by the side fence, scratching as if their lives depended on it. Fretting, I'd reckon. You'd swear they were trying to make a break for it. *The Great Escape*, fowl-style. Looking for the kid and his tendency to overfeed and spoil them, I suppose. It's gotten so I'm a pretty poor substitute. But I'm all they've got now. So they sit in the dust and wait.

Buggered if I know what's going on over there in that house. I've spotted the two of them, the kid and his mum, going in and out a few times. In fact I've seen them together more times in the last few days than I've ever noticed before. Maybe she's got some holidays. Maybe they're getting along better. I hope he's OK. It doesn't matter about me. I'm not important. It's the boy I'm worried about. Like the police said, I'm only a neighbour. Not even a friend, not really. Not so as you'd notice.

I suppose I should've known it wouldn't end well. Fancy an old guy like me thinking he could be friends with a kid like that without someone taking offence. *Unnatural,* they said, down at the cop shop. *Not normal.*

And yet …

I miss our chess games. The board's still set up from our last match. He was winning too, and not because I was going easy on him. He was getting better all the time.

I've got a cupboard full of chocolate chip biscuits that nobody's eating.

School'll be starting again soon, I suppose.

I see him by himself every now and again. He belts out of the house, jumps on his bike and he's off down the road like a rocket. Won't make eye contact. Don't blame him. Sometimes I think I should be angry. But then I think about all the mistakes I've made in my life, and I figure it all comes out in the wash. In the end, you get what you deserve.

And besides, the kid's got his mum. That's important. It's good for a boy to have his mum. I should know. I remember what it was like to not have mine. Like the kid would say, *It sucked, big time*.

I miss telling him to watch his language.

Down by the creek the light played through the trees, trespassing on the surface of the water. In its depths, the creek was the colour of steeped tea. A magpie carolled. A kookaburra landed on an overhead branch, fluffed its feathers and perched in perfect still- ness, the silhouette of its beak stabbing the painted sky. The boy stared, willing it to move. It cocked its head, glared at him, and let out a laugh that echoed through the branches and over the water before disappearing along the track. Its mate gave an answering call, and soon the bush was full of their chatter.

And then silence again. The bird so still that the boy wondered if he had imagined the movement, the laughter.

In a sudden diving blur of brown and white, it dropped to the ground like a stone and was back on its branch in a moment, the only difference being the thick tail of a lizard hanging from its beak. The tail jerked back and forth and then disappeared as the kookaburra threw back its head and opened its gullet. What must it be like, the boy thought, to be eaten alive? To know – in those last few precious seconds – that the end was near, that you were trapped, and could do nothing to escape?

As he scanned the sky for the bird's mate, he picked at a scab on the back of his thigh. Not yet healed, still tender. He worried at the wound until his fingers felt sticky, then he gaped at the red smudges staining the ridges of his skin.

He winced as he unfolded his legs and stood. His shirt still stuck to his back in places where the cuts had been deepest. At least it didn't hurt to walk anymore. And the bruises on his face had almost faded. Only a pale yellow tinge hinted at what was there before.

His mum had been pleased. Said he'd be all healed up by the time school went back. *Nothing to make anyone start asking nosy questions.*

The boy touched his wrist: no sign of the angry red welts. It was amazing how the body healed itself. Cells multiplying, creating a new layer, closing over ugly injuries and making his skin smooth and new again. As if the wound had never existed. As if everything was the same as before.

The canopy of green had concealed the state of the sky beyond. As he emerged from the foliage and retrieved his bike from its hiding place, rain began to spit into the earth. The boy doubted that the old man had remembered to put the hens away. He'd noticed more and more often lately that they were out of their routine – locked in their hutch when they should be out pecking the ground; or wandering all over the garden at dusk, when they should have been snuggled up inside, safe against foxes and the dangers of the night. A couple of times, the boy had snuck through the darkness to visit, and on one occasion he'd found them – well past midnight! – huddled together under the avocado tree, each one trying to push into the centre and away from the unknown. The poor things had seemed confused and lost. He had unlatched the gate of their enclosure, trying not to make any sound that would disturb the night air or frighten the chooks, and then bustled them inside, where they swiftly found their favourite perches and clucked at him in an admonishing but contented way.

He didn't like to see them like that. Not neglected, exactly, just … not cared for like they were used to. But if he thought too much about it, he began to feel guilty that he wasn't there either, and so he restricted himself to his sporadic late-night sojourns.

The garden was pretty pathetic too. Clearly not enough water – the plants were wilted and droopy. Weeds had sprung up into every available spot of earth, and a possum had lifted one corner of the chicken wire and helped itself to the parsley. All that remained was a bunch of stubby stalks.

The old man had dropped the ball. But, as with the chickens, if he started thinking too much about the old man, he got a pain in his chest and a burning feeling behind his eyelids. So he tried not to think about him.

That chess game, though, that was the thing. He'd been winning, too. He could see the board clearly in his mind; he could remember his last move, and the positions of all the pieces. Sometimes he'd try to think ahead, to plan the old man's move, and then his next move, and the old man's response.

He wondered when he would get a chance to finish the game. If he would get a chance.

He was over here again last night. I noticed straight away. First off, the water container was filled to the brim, and yesterday it was at low tide. And secondly, I had to properly unlatch the gate and I'm pretty sure I only pushed it to last night. Tempting fate, I suppose. It'll serve me right if a fox gets in and has a meal. I know I'm being careless but it's calculated carelessness. I'm hoping if I leave enough things undone, the kid's sense of responsibility will kick in and he'll march over here all piss and vinegar and tell me off for neglecting the girls and inform me he's taking over chook duty from now on. That's what I'm hoping for.

But I'm not holding my breath.

At least he's moving more easily now. I guess whatever happened has started to heal up. I try not to think about it. 'Cause if I start to consider what might have happened, what must have happened, the space in my head becomes a muddled grey cloud and I'm about driven spare by what my mind conjures up. I can't bear to think of him hurting. It's like someone's got a knife in my guts, twisting it slowly.

I've come close to going over there. To see how he is. Once I even got as far as the front door, but then I spotted his mum hanging clothes out the side and I followed my own footsteps back home again before she knew I was there. Most of the time I see the faces of those two detectives, one scowling and mean, the other cajoling, and I tell myself, *What the bloody hell do you think you're doing? Why don't you just paint a bloody great target on your stupid mug and call the cops yourself and beg them to take you away?* So after I've given myself a good talking-to, I hunker down at home and try to forget about it. Forget about him.

It's a worry, though, isn't it. I mean, obviously *something* happened. The kid was hurt. From what the cops were saying, he was hurt in ways I don't even want to imagine. But maybe that was only them winding me up, trying to make me admit to something I didn't do. But if he was hurt, why hasn't somebody done something about it? I mean, he's still over there with his mum. No-one's been to the house that I can see, except for that one lady, probably from the Department of Children's Services or Child Safety or whatever they're called nowadays. Anyway, whoever she was, she didn't stay more than fifteen minutes. Maybe one-off incidents like this don't raise their radar. Maybe a kid's got to be smacked around a few times before it's worth them doing anything about it. Huh. Some investigation. If his mum's hitting him, you'd think they'd bloody well do something to stop her. Or maybe it's one of her boyfriends. Some of them are built like brick shithouses; the kid wouldn't stand a chance. I remember one day a year or so ago, not long after I met the kid and before I knew who was who over there, I spotted this mountain of a man sitting out the back. Just sitting there, having a smoke, like he owned the place. So I go back to my tea, and next thing I know, I hear the sound of wood splintering, and I go out on my back deck to have another gander, and here's this bloke attacking the kid's treehouse with an axe. Bit of an eyesore it was, to be honest, only a load of old boards that he'd nailed up into a platform in the branches of the fig tree, but still. So the next time I saw the kid, I said something like *So, I see*

your dad got rid of your old treehouse, hey? Too big for it now, I suppose?
And he stared at me with this real flat expression, a mix of sadness
and wary contempt.

He's not my dad, he said.

Oh, I said. He spoke those four words with such … shame,
and, I don't know, such relief.

I said *oh* again, for want of anything better to say, and it was
such an inadequate response for the resolve and remorse I saw
reflected in his eyes. That's the second or third time the kid's been
at pains to point out to me who *isn't* his dad.

Didn't like the fucking thing, anyway, he said, and he stalked off
towards the fig tree, picked up one of the splintered boards the
fellow had left lying around on the ground, and then whacked it,
hard as he could, against the tree trunk. Hit it so hard he stumbled
backwards from the rebound.

I saw him wiping his eyes with the back of his hands as he
marched off into the house.

Snake hadn't been around since that day. His mum hadn't mentioned him. The house was a haven of calm. After riding his bike or mucking about near the creek, the boy actually looked forward to going home. For the last few weeks, that feeling of dread was absent as he approached the front gate. The unnerving fear of who might be home with his mother or what they might be doing had been replaced by the certainty of a quiet space.

His mum wasn't drinking as much either. She still had enough to get tipsy but the boy didn't mind that so much; she would become affectionate and chatty. It was a thin line between tipsy and drunk, but so far – lately – she hadn't crossed it. She had teetered on the tightrope of coherence and lucidity, but maintained her balance.

The boy was keen not to push her too hard. He was trying to be useful and helpful. Trying to return her wet kisses and her clumsy embrace. With the fine-tuned antennae of prey, he would sense the moment she became distressed or irritable, sense her need to be alone, and he would hightail it outside and go off on his bike for an hour or two. When he felt enough time had passed, he would cautiously re-enter the house, calling out to announce his arrival.

And every time he would find his mother alone, and welcoming, even glad to see him.

He cooked fried eggs and bacon, made tea and toast and served it on a tray in her bedroom. He cleaned the bathroom and hung out loads of washing, stumbling out to the yard with the basket of waterlogged clothes. One day he even began to pull out the weeds that had sprung up around the front verandah, but the simple action reminded him too much of the old man and he stopped. His mother never noticed the garden anyhow.

Sometimes he closed the door of his bedroom and took out his box of treasures. His fingers would roll the marbles and stones, stroke the feathers, and fit themselves inside the gold ring that he was hoping to give to her sometime soon. He would pinch the coriander seed between his fingers, raise it to his nose and inhale deeply, trying to catch a whiff of the hidden spice. In the end his hands always found their way to the metal letters that the old man had given him: cold and smooth, their sharp edges worn by time. He would press them into his palm, fold his fingers over and hold on tight, until his fist tingled. And when he opened his hand again, the imprint of a letter would be seared into his skin, like an old scar.

. . .

He should've known it was too good to last. Evenings of sitting together on the couch, munching popcorn and watching re-runs of *Seinfeld* or *Friends*. Making dinner together. Eating the meal with her at the kitchen table, cleared of cigarette packs and junk mail. The comfort. The absence of fear, of doubt.

The first time he came home to an empty house, he wasn't anxious. It was Thursday: his mum was probably late-night shopping. In a way it was even comforting to slip into his old routines. Letting himself in and being enveloped by the house's stillness. Cobbling together a meal from whatever he found in the fridge. Eating in front of the TV and deciding alone what to watch. But after several hours, he began to get restless. It was like getting a new tooth knocked out: he had gotten used to the presence of something that had grown gradually and imperceptibly, and then, all of a sudden, the hole was there once again, painfully familiar.

And so it was with the boy, alone in the house. He tired of the television and instead lay on his bed, reading a library book. The story was dull and not at all what he expected. He flipped the pages listlessly, hoping for a surprising twist, a death or a vicious crime. Nothing. His eyes grew tired as the print swam before them. A couple of times he jerked awake and re-read a page he was certain he hadn't read before, until he struck a recognisable sentence and realised it was the third or fourth time he had seen the words. Finally his eyelids could no longer support the weight of encroaching sleep. The book landed with a thud on the floor. The boy sank deeper and deeper into slumber, and was soon entangled in his dreaming. Images of snakes and dragons crept through his unconscious, scales gleaming, fire dancing, jets of poison spurting from sharpened fangs. He became ensnared in his bedclothes and kicked with the furious energy of nightmares at the sweat-soaked sheets. Once, he cried out, a single mournful plea. No-one was in the house to hear. A cockroach scuttled from under the boy's bed, crossed the rectangle of sallow light thrown down like a mat, and feasted on a crumb of scab that the boy had picked off his back and flicked on the floor. Outside, a tawny frogmouth sat in the black wattle tree, an extension of the branch, indistinguishable, its head tilted back at an unnatural angle. A fingernail of moon hung low in the night sky, waiting for the dawn.

Like they say, life goes on. I never thought I'd make old bones, but here I am. I drag my sorry self out of bed each morning, try and get through the day without forgetting something important or staining my underpants or falling over and breaking a hip. I try to remember to eat enough and drink enough, to put out the wheelie bin on the right day and to change the sheets occasionally. If the milk smells bad, I resist the urge to add it to my tea. I make the effort to stay mobile, even if it's only to walk down to the mailbox and back.

I should get into that garden but I just can't summon the energy.

At the end of the day, I switch off the lights and crawl back under the covers and think what a wonder it is that I'm still here. After all that's happened.

It's a funny thing, life. When I cast my mind back over my days, I can't help asking what it's all about. It didn't start off too well, that's for sure. And I suppose you could say things went downhill from there. I can't say I ever felt like I got a decent break. But you've gotta make the best of what you've got, work with what God's given you. Take opportunities when they arise. Take a chance. I think back on my life, and it's like a story that I vaguely recognise. That kid in the Home – he doesn't seem to be me so much as someone very like me, or someone I used to know. That man who walked out on his wife and baby girl, surely that wasn't me, but some stranger I've heard of, some fella with no sense. I suppose that's why this palaver with the boy hasn't knocked me for six like it should have – it merely seems like one more slap on the face. I don't pretend to understand it. Can't make head nor tail of the whole damn situation, to be honest. But I can accept it. And that's about all I can do. Accept it and wait to see what happens next.

Morning, love.

Morning, he replied warily. She was nursing a cup of tea and had an open box of painkillers on the saucer. The lines around her eyes were more pronounced than usual. Her mouth was turned down in a scowl and her hair, lank and greasy, lay flat against her scalp. A fat summer blowfly buzzed in a slow circle above her head before alighting on her toast and treading across the thickly smeared jam. His mother glanced at the fly but made no effort to shoo it away.

So ... where were you last night? he asked.

What is this, the fucking inquisition?

He noticed she was slurring her words. When he studied her mouth more closely, he could see a swelling on her upper lip.

Where were you? Where were you? she parodied in a sing-song voice. *What's it to you? You my keeper now?* She pushed back her chair, stumbling as she stood. *I'm a big girl, you know.* She swayed in a brief, unsteady dance. As she shifted away, she caught her foot on the table leg and fell heavily, landing with a thud on one knee.

Oh shit. The boy rushed to her side, knelt and peered anxiously into her face. *Are you OK? Did you hurt yourself?*

She laughed then, the maniacal laugh of the beaten. *Did I hurt myself? Did I hurt myself? No, baby, no. Wasn't me that did the hurting.*

She rocked forward on all fours and made a clumsy attempt to rise. The boy stared in disbelief at the patch of skin revealed as her thin blouse separated from her jeans. Her back was covered in spots. Small, black spots each about half a centimetre across, each rimmed with red. He was not sure of what he saw. The thought flitted through his mind that his mother had caught chicken pox or measles, or some sort of nasty rash.

She got to her feet and he rose too and stood beside her. He was not aware that he had asked a question, but perhaps she had read his thoughts, because she muttered, *Evil little fucker used me for an ashtray, didn't he.*

The boy blinked. He had nothing to say to this. No words.

She winced as she moved towards the sink. The boy noticed a streak of dried blood in her hair, and then saw a gash in the back of her head. It was deep, a grinning mouth, brown and crusty.

Mum, he whispered. *Mum, you're hurt. Your head. You've got a cut on your head.*

S'all right. She brought up her hand behind her as if to prove her point, but thought better of it and fluttered her fingers at him in a dismissive gesture. *S'nothing. Can't even feel it anymore.*

The kitchen was suffused in the pale light of morning, despite the insect-spotted grime on the window. The boy watched her and saw how terrible she looked. How old. How resigned. How much it hurt her just to move.

She reached for the tap and a grunt escaped her lips. She lowered her hand to her side.

Be a love and get me a wet washcloth, will ya?

Her voice was hollow. She shuffled to the chair, sank down, closed her eyes and moaned.

The boy went towards her and stared at the front of her shirt. A smudge of blood stained the white fabric. Unable to resist, he stretched out his fingers. For a moment he thought she might tell him off, or move out of his reach, but she submitted to his ministrations as he tugged on her shirt, and she flinched only slightly when the material was wrenched from the wound beneath, lifting a layer of skin and dried blood.

The crude carving was on her stomach, above her belly button. The wound was the size of a jar lid. A mess of ruptured skin and blue ink and smeared blood. As the boy stared, the rudimentary image swam into focus. The rough head of a snake, its mouth open wide, its long forked tongue licking his mother's navel as if it intended to swallow it whole.

He met his mother's eyes, forced her to look back at him.

He thought he could do it himself, she said, her voice a monotone.

Something like a hiccup escaped her lips, a snatch of a laugh or the end of a sob. She took the boy's fingers in her own and moved them away from her mutilated stomach.

It's OK, baby, it's OK. The boy didn't know if she was speaking to him or to herself.

She folded him in her arms in a tentative embrace, smoothed his hair and laid her chin on the top of his head.

You're my best boy. My very best boy. He didn't mean anything by it. It's a symbol, that's all. Of our togetherness. We belong together. He wanted to make sure I remember that. That's all.

She brought her face alongside his.

That'll teach me to drink too much, hey? Get into all sorts of trouble.

A smile trembled around the corners of her mouth, lopsided because of the swollen mound on her top lip.

We'll be all right. You'll see, she crooned. *Snake's coming round for dinner tonight, baby. How about we cook up something special together, huh?* Her voice had taken on a bright and brittle note. *He's missed you these last few weeks. Said he can't wait to see you again. Catch up before school goes back next week.*

The room fell away and the boy hurtled through space, his feet scrabbling to find purchase, tendrils of hope slipping through his grasp.

It's just after eight o'clock. I'm sure about the time, because the news has started not ten minutes earlier. I'm at the sink, washing up my one bowl and one cup and the small saucepan I used to heat up some soup. My hands are all sudsy, and I can hear the tick of the kitchen clock and the chirruping of crickets, even though it's well past their bedtime. The summer day is slow to relinquish to the night. Someone's lit a fire and I can smell the woodsmoke, carried on the easterly breeze that's sprung up.

At first I think it's a cat, yowling for its mate, maybe a female protesting the amorous advances of that randy tom from up the road. But something in the tenor of the cry gives me pause. I go to the open door and listen. Nothing, bar a couple of muffled noises that could be the chickens settling. I'm about to bolt the door for the night when it comes again. This time, unmistakable. A cry of chilling force. It fills the night and echoes around the room in which I stand. A visceral, primal wail.

And then, abruptly, it stops. Breaks off mid-howl. I listen intently but hear nothing but the wind and the clock, ticking its steady rhythm … *tick* … *tick* … *tick*. The choir of crickets resumes.

Perhaps I imagined it, I think. Yes, I must have imagined it. Because if I didn't imagine it, I would have to do something about it. Far better to ignore it and it will go away.

You stupid, cowardly old man, I tell myself. *Who are you kidding? That was no cat.*

I un-snib the screen door and make my way down the back stairs, my ears quivering with the strain of listening for any unfamiliar noise. I advance across the lawn, the dry grass whispering under my feet. For reasons I don't quite understand, I head towards the boy's house, which is lit up like a Christmas tree. I skirt the bordering fence and stop in the kid's front yard at the rim between light and dark. I remain for a moment in the shadows, unwilling to cross the verge. Part of me is content to remain unseen. I know that as soon as I take one more step, I will become a part of this and the spotlight will be on me.

I'm not sure I'm ready for that.

An owl hoots in the distance. A car rolls down Boundary Road; I see its headlights bouncing off telephone poles and the bus shelter before disappearing towards Mt Coot-tha.

Oh, bugger it, I think, and I take the plunge and shuffle forward through the overgrown weeds.

The front stairs could do with some maintenance. One or two seem like they might not hold my weight. I tread with care and avoid the most rotten-looking boards. When I put my foot on one near the top, it creaks and I freeze, waiting for my presence to be noticed. Nothing. The wind continues its quiet errand. The meagre noises of the night carry on.

Once I am on the porch, I stop and listen. I can hear sounds from inside the house but can't identify what they are or who is making them. The front door is ajar. I take a cautious step towards it, and then another, until I am in a position to peer inside. Through the sliver of open door, I see the outline of a couch, a coffee table piled high with magazines. A movement beyond the perimeter of the room catches my eye. I take a deep breath and push open the door.

I smell something burning on the stove and have a momentary thought – *that pan's going to take some soaking.* I contemplate calling out but decide against it.

The room is bathed in bright white light from an unsheathed ceiling lamp. I take two paces across the grimy carpet and my line of vision – until now obscured by the couch – opens up to reveal a scene that king-hits me harder than any punch.

The kid and his mother are there, and someone else, a man, is curled up on his stomach on the floor. Everyone is very still. I realise that the man is not wearing a bright red shirt. The colour is spreading as I watch. Blood has pooled around his naked torso; fingers of blood are reaching out across the lino.

A large kitchen knife is protruding from the lower part of his back. It's pushed in almost to the hilt, with part of the large blade still visible, and angled upwards. Maybe it's punctured a lung or sliced his liver. The boy's mother is kneeling beside him, her hands attached to the knife. I can't tell if she's pulling it out or pushing it in. She's just sitting there, holding it, with a very strange expression on her face.

The boy is standing behind her. He has blood on his hands and on the front of his shirt where he has wiped them. He stands close to his mother, either to protect her or to shield himself, I'm not sure.

Behind the boy's head, a halo of steam and smoke as that pot is scalded beyond repair.

I take a step closer.

A little fountain of red gurgles from the man's back at the place of the incision. His eyes are open and staring at me. I think he must surely be dead, but then he blinks, his eyelids lowering and raising again as if in slow motion. He has a smudge of blood on his forehead and down the side of his face, covering a tattoo. He makes a small noise, a wet sort of cough. This seems to rouse us all from our inertia. Like a spell has been broken, my senses return to me in a rush of sound and smell. I can taste bile in the back of my throat and think for a second that I might vomit.

There is so much blood.

The mother begins to wail, a high-pitched keening. She keeps one hand on the knife and clutches at the boy with the other. He cowers ... from her? From me? She meets my eyes at last, a mask of sheer desperation and fear.

Instinct takes over. All at once I am kneeling beside the man, my joints creaking, the warm blood soaking my trousers. I grip her hand and prise her fingers from around the handle of the knife. I have to use quite a lot of force; they are gripped tight like an arthritic's claw.

Leave it, I say. *Leave it in. It may stem the bleeding. If we pull it out ...*

My voice trails away. We are both thinking the same thing – leave it in, take it out; neither will make much difference now.

Nevertheless, I feel for a pulse on the man's neck, my hand slipping and sliding. His neck is slick, beads of perspiration running into the blood. I can't think what to do. Should I give mouth-to-mouth? Has he stopped breathing? I'm not sure. Should I try to stop the bleeding? My indecision goes on for what seems like minutes but is probably only seconds. In the end, the man decides for us. He emits one final splutter, covering my arm in a spray of bright red droplets, and then becomes still.

I'm not sure what I expect the woman to do – wail again maybe, or tear her hair, or try to bring him back – but she just sits back on her haunches and stares at me. She doesn't say anything. The boy doesn't say anything either, although he does slide onto the floor and lean his head into his mother's shoulder. He looks so weary.

So the three of us sit there like that for a time, until I realise they are waiting for me to say something, to do something. To make a decision.

We must seem a strange sight, our tableau of four. Like something out of a gory horror movie.

It is all clear to me now.

The boy stares at me with such pleading in his eyes.

I speak as gently and quietly as I can, like you would speak to a skittish horse so as not to spook it.

I understand why you did it, I say to the woman. *After what he did to your son. Any mother would have done the same. No mother could have stood by.*

She looks up at me, relief coursing across her face. She weighs my words, tries them out herself.

No mother could have stood by. I am his mother.

Yes, you are his mother, I repeat. *You were protecting him.*

I was protecting him.

You had no choice.

I had no choice, she parrots. Her face is full of wonder, as if I've explained some great truth to her.

You did what you had to do, I say. *As his mother.*

Yes, I am his mother. I really am his mother.

She grabs my wrist. *This proves it, doesn't it? This proves how much I love him?*

I'm not sure what she's getting at, but I nod and fold my fingers over hers.

Yes, I say. *Yes. People will understand. You were defending your son.*

She looks around wildly at her boy, and I realise she has no-one else. There is no-one else. It is her, and the boy, and this man on the floor, and me.

I'll tell them, I say. *I will explain.*

Hot, grateful tears began to flow. She releases my arm and encircles the boy in her embrace, as if he might float away if she doesn't hug tightly enough.

The boy's eyes peer at me over his mother's shoulder, his expression unreadable. He still has not said a word.

I get on all fours and try to stand but my feet keep slipping and sliding on the bloody floor. I crawl towards the carpet and pull myself up onto an armchair, watching my tracks stain the pile. Then I reach for the phone.

...

By the time the police find us, the mother is angry and unrepentant in equal measure.

I did it! she cries. *And I'm not sorry! I'd do it again in a heartbeat! He beat my son. He bashed me.*

As if to prove the point, she wrenches her shirt up over her breasts. Her torso a canvas of hatred and pain.

He deserves everything he got. He touched my baby. He was evil – evil, do you hear me? I'm not sorry he's dead. I had to protect my boy. That's what a mother does. She protects her child. I'm his mother. I'm his mother!

A constable with crooked teeth puts a blanket over my shoulders. I realise I'm shivering. He keeps touching the back of my hand.

I answer his questions as best I can. He seems to think I'm in shock. Perhaps he's right. I feel disconnected somehow, like we're all underwater, each breath requiring great effort. I catch glimpses of the boy's face and search for a sign, but I'm not sure what I'm hoping for. The situation, the blood, what he said about me, the things he said to me, what his mother has done – it all comes swirling together and rushing like a waterfall, drowning out sound and reason. I feel I understand nothing. Seventy-four years old and I don't understand a goddamn thing.

The biting August wind funnels through the space under the house, gathering strength, then howls out the other side and into the yard, catching leaves and papers and the empty milk containers that the boy hasn't properly secured in the recycling bin, whirling the lot higher and higher into a dirty gust. The boy huddles further into his corner and closes his eyes against the grit. The chick sits in his cupped hands, its silky feathers tickling his fingers. It bobs its pom-pom of a head. The boy thinks the bantam is like something out of the imagination of Dr Seuss. He snuggles it closer to his chest.

He hears his foster mum calling his name through the wind. He doesn't move, and soon enough she peers at him over the side railings.

Hey, she says.

Hey.

You OK? It's freezing out here.

Yep.

Your visitor's here. You want to come inside? I'm not sure the cold concrete's a good place for a man his age to be sitting.

The boy strokes the chick. He feels the insistent beating of its small heart.

He's here?

Yes, mate, he's here. Come on now, we've talked about this.

She descends the stairs and squats before him. Her eyes are directly in line with his, and she waits until he looks up.

It'll be fine, buddy. It'll all be good. She reaches out as if to pull him towards her, but hesitates, and settles for smoothing a lock of his hair. *He seems like a nice man.*

The boy nods.

He's brought you something too. A present. She stands and wipes her hands on the back of her jeans. *I'll tell him you'll be up in a sec, OK?*

Could we … sit in the pergola?

She smiles. *'Course you can. You'll be out of the wind there. I'll light the brazier, should be quite cosy. He said he'll have a cup of tea, and how about I bring you some hot Milo?*

Can I smell Anzac bikkies?

You can indeed. I'll pop a couple on a plate.

When the boy makes no move to rise, she clears her throat in mock admonition. *Well, come on, get off your backside and go say hello and take him down the yard yourself. I'm not bringing him out. Who was your servant last year?*

The boy smiles up at her from under his fringe.

And don't be too slow about it either. Leave him too long with those three upstairs and they'll have him on his hands and knees pretending to be a horse or something.

The boy puts his bobble-headed chick back in the cage. When he reaches the top of the stairs he hovers like a ghost. His foster mum is balancing Amber on one hip and a tray of biscuits in one hand. She pushes the oven door shut with her foot. Bailey is tugging on the leg of the old man's trousers and babbling something about the truck he is waving about. Five-year-old Jemima is twirling her best ballerina twirls, decked out in her frothy tulle, with the old man's hat perched on top of her head.

He watches as the old man reaches down and fingers Bailey's truck.

Those Anzacs smell wonderful, the old man says.

He turns then, and their eyes meet.

The last six months have aged him. The boy sees the old man of his memory, but a little more stooped, his legs a little more bowed, his belt cinched tighter around his waist. A couple more wrinkles on his face but fewer wisps of hair plastered across his pate.

Hello, mate. Long time no see.

Hey, says the boy.

The old man holds out his hand. It hangs there, shaking. The boy steps forward. The cool, dry skin envelops his own. He can feel calluses and the stiff hairs on the back of the old man's hand. Sees the sunspots, brown stains of life. Then in a moment he is encased in the man's embrace, his face against the thin woollen jumper, inhaling his musty smell, arms encircling his bony ribs, eyes screwed shut against the rush of emotion.

...

The pergola is sheltered on three sides. Dry leaves eddy past the opening. A large web adorns one corner, caught between wall and roof rafter, and an industrious golden orb spider picks daintily over the grey threads strung with dust. On the floor, three of Jemima's dolls sit around an eclectic collection of teacups half-filled with dirty water, and miniature plates piled with pretend food of dirt and stones and small sticks.

The brazier emits a circle of warmth. Small sparks crackle and sputter. The boy blows on his Milo.

Here, says the old man, and he pushes the parcel across the slatted table. *Wrapping's not my forte.*

The paper is covered in fishing rods, dogs, golf clubs and old men's slippers. Taped together by a crazed person with access to an entire roll.

Didn't they have any more tape?

Oi, don't be cheeky. You're lucky it's not in newsprint. Just open it, will ya.

It is a red velvet box with an old-fashioned fastener. He levers open the lid. Each piece sits in a velvet indent. Knights, pawns, bishops. White onyx streaked with grey, or black onyx marbled with rust red.

The board's under the bottom there, see, you slide it out.

Squares of timber, light and dark, bordered by iridescence.

I think it's mother-of-pearl or paua shell or some such.

The boy runs his fingertips over the smooth surface. He touches each queen.

Go on, take a piece out. They're weighted. Feel good in your hands.

He sits the two queens side by side on the board and twists them to see every detail.

Well ... say something. Do you like it? It's not new, mind. I found it at that secondhand store in Paddo. I think a couple of the pawns might have a chip or two, but otherwise it seems in pretty good nick to me.

Still the boy is silent.

'Course, my eyes aren't so sharp, so maybe it's got more things wrong with it than I picked up? His voice quavers, uncertain.

No, says the boy. *No. It's perfect. It's just perfect. I love it. Thank you. Thank you so much.* He wipes his eyes with the back of his hand.

Yeah, well, don't go getting all emotional on me. Are we gonna sit out here mooning about all day or are we gonna play? Set those pieces up.

The boy places each piece on the board. The old man takes two pawns, one white, one black, and holds them in his closed fists; the boy taps the right and the gnarled fingers open to reveal white.

Lucky choice. He smiles as the boy moves his first pawn. *You're gonna need all the help you can get.*

The two settle into the pace of the game.

I've acquired a moggie, the old man mutters. He answers the boy's questioning gaze. *A cat. Or rather, he's acquired me. Arrived one day out of the blue, sitting there on my porch, bold as brass. I opened the door and he marched right in without so much as a do-you-mind.*

What colour is he?

Black. Black as coal.

Black as ebony, says the boy.

Black as the inside of a dog, replies the old man.

Black as midnight. A shadow falls over the boy's face.

Hmm. The old man's hand trembles in indecision above the board. He moves a bishop.

The boy's face clears. *Mistake,* he says cheerfully. *So, you kept him?*

Don't count your chickens yet, kid. We'll see if that's a mistake. And yep, he drank the milk I gave him, stalked into my room and curled up on my bed like he'd been sleeping there every day of his life.

Doesn't he bother the hens?

Not a bit, that's the funny thing. He mostly keeps his distance. But one afternoon I saw the strangest thing. Just on dusk, it was, and I went down to pop the girls in their house, and there he was, flopped in the dirt, chooks all around, and one old girl — you remember the one with the wonky eye? — she was perched right atop his head. Funniest thing I ever saw.

The boy giggles in delight. He moves his castle. *Told you it was a mistake.*

They miss you, you know. The girls. Didn't lay for three weeks after you left. Even now I swear they still keep strutting near to your old side fence, wondering where you are.

He smiles wistfully. *They wouldn't remember me.*

The old man took a knight. *You're probably right. Chooks aren't the sharpest tools in the shed. Probably miss all those broken biscuits you used to sneak over when you thought I wasn't watching, though.*

A guilty glance.

Huh. Thought I didn't know about that, didn't you. Spoilt 'em, you did. Have to make do with grubs now. He nods in the direction of under the house. *Given that one a name yet?*

Nope.

Probably just as well. Weirdest-looking chook I ever saw.

The boy begins to protest before he senses the mischief behind the old man's words.

The afternoon wears on. His foster mum brings more tea, and a plate of fruitcake.

Your new family seems nice. Young Mrs Standing, especially.

Yeah, she's all right, I s'pose.

Bakes a mean Anzac.

Uh-huh.

Got her hands full with those littlies.

Yep.

I expect you find them a trifle aggravating at times.

Oh … they're OK. I'm at school mostly anyway, so … His hand wavers between his castle and his bishop.

How is your new school, anyhow?

Big. Five Year 6 classes. Got a cool playground.

You made some friends?

Yeah, some.

The boy studies the board with a fierce intensity, as if it might flap away. The old man folds away the boy's pawn in a sweep of his arm.

You seen your mum?

The boy is quiet for so long that the old man thinks he hasn't heard the question. The mournful cries of crows ride the wind. The boy shivers, zips up his hoodie. Outside the pergola, the day is fading.

I said …

I heard what you said. He squints up against the glare of the overhead bulb that has clicked on automatically. He bats at the insects swarming in its beam, throwing themselves against the light. *There's only one of us here with a hearing problem and it isn't me.*

The old man blinks, slowly, then his face creases into a crumpled grin.

All right, all right. Keep your hair on. I apologise, OK? I should've given you more time to think.

Nothing much to think about. Just deciding whether or not to answer you.

The old man laughs then, a full-throated sound that bounces off the flimsy walls and returns as an echo even as he is shuddering to a hacking cough.

I got to hand it to you, kiddo. You've still got cheek. He fishes a handkerchief out of his pocket and blows his nose loudly.

The boy's face relaxes and he sits back. He picks up a cake crumb and flicks it at the old man, who retrieves it from his shirt and pops it into his mouth. The boy laughs, and the laugh reaches his eyes, and for a moment he seems a different child.

He looks down and moves another pawn. *Yeah, I've seen her. Not much. A couple of times. She was in hospital for a while, and then she was … she said …* He glares defiantly at the old man. *She said she didn't want to see me. That's what the social worker said. She said Mum was having a hard time and needed a rest and couldn't see me for a bit.* He emphasises the words *hard time.*

The old man sucks air through his teeth and stretches out his legs. *She said that, did she?*

Yep.

But you said you've seen her a few times since?

Yeah. Only in the last two months or so. I've been to visit her at the Contact Centre. She hasn't been here, though. Don't think she's allowed. Anyway, she told me she didn't want to see some other mother looking after me. Said it wasn't right. I should be with her. That's what she thinks, anyway.

And what do you think?

The boy concentrates on the remaining pieces, and settles on his queen. *Check,* he says.

I guess I think I'm OK here for a while. It's kinda nice having Bailey and Jemima hanging around, even if they are a bit annoying. And the baby's cute. Mrs Standing's a good cook. You'd never believe how much food she piles into me. And Mr Standing's all right. He's pretty strict but he's at work 'til late so I don't see him so much.

A cockatoo flaps low across the sky and lands on the pergola roof.

He takes us to Newmarket Pool every Saturday. That's pretty fun.

The old man moves out of check. *But you miss your mum?*

Yeah, I guess. I mean, she's my mum. 'Course I miss her. The boy glances up. *I s'pose your mum's dead.*

The old man pushes back the brim of his hat and scratches his forehead. *I suppose you might be right.*

Don't you know?

I never heard about it. That's all I know.

But she'd have to be, wouldn't she. I mean, you're ancient so she'd have to be more ancient than ancient. She'd have to be almost a fossil.

The man laughs. *I guess you're right. Let me see now. I think she was about in her mid-twenties when I was born, so if she was alive today, that would make her … what … about more'n one hundred or one hundred and five years old.*

The boy grins. *Well, that's hardly likely, is it?*

No, the old man says. *Hardly likely. Although not impossible, I suppose.*

The boy stares.

What?

Nothing. I was just thinking. I almost said to you, how come you don't know if your mother's dead or not, but then I thought about my dad, my real dad, and how for the longest time I didn't know if he was alive or dead. Didn't even think about it, actually. He just wasn't there. He'd never been around. And Mum never mentioned him. It was almost like he never existed. If you'd asked me a year ago whether my dad was alive or not, I'd have said the same as you – I don't know. And that wouldn't have seemed strange to me at all.

The old man considers the weight of the boy's words. Eventually he asks, *And now?*

281

Now I know. Know he's alive. The social worker found him. He lives in Cairns. He's got a whole other family. A wife. And four kids.

You don't say. Four kids, hey. That means you've got four half brothers or sisters.

The boy smiles. *Yep. I know. Pretty cool, huh. Instant family.*

You going to meet any of them?

I don't know. I mean, I think so. The social worker said my dad took a while to take it all in, everything, you know. Me. The last time he saw me I was only a few weeks old. I think he'd forgotten about me. And then ... there was all the other stuff that happened. I don't think Dad wanted to know at first. The social worker said he was a bit shocked. But he must've come around, 'cause she said he's told his family about me now, and he's planning to come down and visit in a month or two. By himself.

Hmm. Well, that would be ... cool.

The boy slaps his palms against the tabletop and rolls his eyes. *You saying cool is like, so not cool. It's like the uncoolest thing ever.* He moves a piece. *And check. Again.*

The moon has risen early and now hangs low in the darkening sky, a sharp scythe surrounded by a glowing halo.

The old man studies the board for a long time, as the smell of cooking meat wafts down from the house. The night sounds are magnified in the dusk: the baby crying; the slam of a window; a dog, streets away, howling in misery.

The old man sits back and places his hands on his knees. *You know what, kiddo? I resign. You win.*

What? No way. You can't give up yet. Keep trying.

There are occasions, kiddo, when no matter how long or hard you look at a thing, it just doesn't get any better. And despite your best intentions, and even using all the talents God's given you, on occasion you just can't win. Sometimes you have to know when to resign.

He pushes his chair out. It scrapes along the floor like fingernails on a chalkboard. He straightens up and holds both hands to the small of his back, then shuffles across the concrete to stare out into the evening. A passing fruit bat throws a shadow across the pergola opening. The air smells of woodsmoke. The freeway traffic sounds a steady hum, punctuated now and again by a squeal of brakes and, once, ambulance sirens calling. The old man wonders who they are hurrying to tonight, what crisis they will discover, what pain, what despair, what loneliness. He rubs the rough pads of his fingertips on his temples, and shakes his left leg, which has fallen asleep from being too long in the one position. Pins and needles flood his nerves and shiver up his spine. He figures the boy is brooding on the game, maybe has the board swivelled around, trying to see a way the man could've continued. Or perhaps he is already packing up the pieces.

The old man speaks into the night.

I've still got that last game set up, you know. Our game. Haven't touched a single piece. Can't bring myself to dismantle it when I know what a thrashing I was going to give you.

He expects a sassy response.

But when he turns, the boy is huddled on his chair, hugging his knees to his chest, his hood obscuring his features. His small body shakes. When the old man steps closer, he feels the shuddering before he hears the sobs. When he reaches out to push the hoodie back from the boy's face, the child looks up at him with an expression at once defiant and frightened and unutterably sad.

Can you keep a secret? The boy's voice is reedy thin.

The old man pauses, his hand still hovering above the boy's head. *I reckon so.*

He drags his chair closer and sits, his knees touching the boy's trainers, curled up on his seat. He waits.

It was me.

The man waits some more; for what, he can't say.

It was me, the boy repeats. *Mum told the cops it was her and it wasn't, it was me, and I just sat there and I didn't say anything.* He gives a hiccupping sob. *It was so sharp. And he was so soft. I should've told you when you first came in the house, but there was so much blood and I was so scared and Mum was crying and that bastard was finally quiet and he'd stopped shouting at Mum and ...*

His voice trails off into the night, sucked up by the breeze and spirited away.

Well, that sure gave a shape and colour to the elephant in the pergola. I stare at the poor little bugger, sitting there hunched over himself on that garden chair, shivering, cowering from the truth of the matter. As if it might get up and bite him. As if the words themselves, once uttered, might gather together and become a physical thing of malice.

I consider the little chap. And I think about myself.

My whole life stretches behind me, a continuous punishment. Each incident of regret leading only to more sorrow.

In the boy's eyes, I see the promise of youth, the promise of my own lost youth reflected back to me.

I make a decision.

His mother is gone, or as good as. And what has she done, what's her legacy? Has she doomed him? Or saved him? His life will be hard enough. If anyone knows that, I sure as hell do.

I don't want the kid to have my life, even if he did kill that bloke.

I imagine the seed sprouting a hopeful bloom, shooting upwards from the cracks of his short and troubled existence.

I can see his future stretching before him and sense the cross-roads at which he stands.

I think back to that morning so long ago. The morning Emily died. I close my eyes, almost trance-like. I can see my six-year-old self in that cold, dank house. I was playing on the kitchen floor, near the warmth of the wood stove. Emily was crying. She'd been crying for ages. She'd gone from lusty, full-throated cries to tired, hiccupping sobs. Mum had started off walking around the rooms of the house, in and out, trying to calm her. She'd stood near the stove and she'd sat in the quiet of the back room. She'd even taken a turn around the garden, despite the cold, where Aunty Kath was bringing in washing, cloth nappies that nearly snapped when she folded them, and my T-shirts that still felt clammy and damp.

I had built a ramp for my truck from the firewood, and I was zooming it up and down. I could hear Aunty Kath in the backyard, cursing the arthritis in her fingers, cursing the bats that had left streaks of sticky black poo on the sheets, cursing the height of the clothesline (too high) and the height of the laundry basket (too low). The shepherd's pie she'd made earlier was still in the oven, and the delicious meaty smell filled the kitchen.

I heard the embers popping in the stove, and a muted thud as a piece of wood surrendered to gravity. I pushed aside the hanging tea towel that obscured the smoky glass, in time to see a shower of sparks explode.

Emily was quiet.

I don't know how long she'd been quiet, but I realised she was no longer crying or else I wouldn't have heard the wood fall.

The silence was deafening. It boomed through my head. I strained my ears to hear Aunty Kath, who was now humming a hymn, an activity in which she partook with a great deal more confidence and enthusiasm than her talent merited.

I parked my truck next to the stove and went towards the sleep-out.

My mother was sitting in the rocking chair, with Emily in her arms. She was rocking very gently, and crooning a lullaby, and stroking my sister's fine, fair hair. When I approached, she stopped singing. Stopped rocking. She looked at me and she had not a shred of light in her eyes, not a shred. They were like drops of ink in her pale face.

I edged closer.

My sister didn't cry. Didn't fuss. Didn't move at all. I went closer still and I could see her blue eyes, the translucent lids only half-closed, the veins crisscrossing her delicate skin like a roadmap.

I reached out a finger and brushed it against her downy cheek. I still recall the feel of it, soft and pliable. I bent my head and let my lips graze her forehead. She smelt of Johnson's Baby Powder, with a whiff of sour milk. I placed my pinkie into her tiny fingers, which were curled up like petals. Usually, even in her sleep, her hand would grip mine, a reflex action. I looked askance at my mother. She stared dully off to the side of the room. I lifted Emily's arm then, and let it fall.

I'm not sure what marked the moment I realised. There was no blossoming bruise, no telltale blotch.

Mum didn't try to stop me when I took Emily from her arms. They went slack and she started singing again. A tune I didn't recognise.

Emily was heavy. She was heavy and awkward and she flopped around in her rug. I put her head against my chest and held her close. The side of the cot was down so it was easy enough for me to reach. I laid her in her crib. I like to remember her appearing peaceful, but maybe that's only the guilty memories of an old man. I adjusted her wrap and pulled the blanket over her head. It was pale pink, with bunny rabbits along the edges.

Thinking back on it now, I wonder how on earth I thought to do that at six years of age. And of course, I often wonder about the outcome if I hadn't done it – that simple act of drawing the blanket over my dead sister's face. Of the incident. Of my whole damn life.

But in any event, that's what I did. Great Uncle Ron had passed away in his bed only months earlier; perhaps I'd seen someone do it then. And I seem to recall walking past the scene of an accident, too, sometime around then, a kid on a bike losing the contest with a car. I imagine I saw the kid lying on the road, all bent at funny angles, blood pooling around his head, one shoe thrown clear across the road. I can see Mr Templar, the old pharmacist from down the street, taking off his jacket and placing it over the dead kid's face. Knowing he wouldn't wake up. I can see that, still, clear as a bell. But maybe it's all in my head. Maybe it's a false memory, as they say now, conjured by my mind to make sense of my own actions that day. Pulling the blanket over Emily's head. I guess it doesn't matter either way now. 'Cause that's what I did.

I sensed my mother leave the room behind me, still whispering her song.

And that's when Aunty Kath came in.

And all hell broke loose.

And now, here I am, almost seventy years later, contemplating this boy beside me, with the shadow of my sister at my shoulder. He's an echo, this sad child, an echo of my own childhood self. Unspeakably betrayed, both of us, by those we've loved.

I sense a chance. A chance to save this boy, to save him from himself. And maybe a chance to redeem the boy I once was.

I pull him towards me and lower my face to his tousled hair, matted by the wind. I grip his slight body to mine and I can feel the bones of his spine beneath my fingers, sense how insubstantial he is, as if he's not quite there. One false move and he might float away from my grasp, the instrument of his own undoing. So I tighten my grip, and I hold him close, and I whisper to him.

I tether him to his future life.

Acknowledgements

Heartfelt thanks to all the people who helped bring this story to life: to my friends and early readers for their enthusiasm; to the judges of the Queensland Literary Awards for seeing promise in the tale; to industry professionals Catherine Drayton and Farrin Jacobs for their generous encouragement; to the Queensland Writers Centre, in particular Meg Vann for her guidance and advice, to Katherine Howell for her early support, and to the Brisbane Writers Festival; and to all the team at UQP, especially Madonna Duffy, for giving me a chance. Particular thanks to the wonderful Judith Lukin-Amundsen for her sage mentoring and for asking all the right questions; to my fantastic UQP editor, Ian See, for his keen eye and his thoughtful restraint, and because he cared for this manuscript as much as I did; and finally to all those in the writing community who urged me on. And of course, to my husband and my children, who began telling everyone I was a writer long before I believed it myself.

More fiction from UQP

GRACE'S TABLE
Sally Piper

Grace has not had twelve people at her table for a long time. Hers isn't the kind of family who share regular Sunday meals. But it isn't every day you turn seventy.

As Grace prepares the feast, she reflects on her life, her marriage and her friendships. When the generations come together, simmering tensions from the past threaten to boil over. The one thing that no one can talk about is the one thing that no one can forget.

Grace's Table is a moving and often funny novel about the power of memory and the family rituals that define us.

> 'A wise and tender novel about food, friendship and marriage.'
> Kristina Olsson, author of *Boy, Lost*

> '[A] beguiling novel. *Grace's Table* is involving, moving, amusing and genuinely entertaining.'
> *Books+Publishing*

> 'Delightfully insightful … a highly credible and readable story.'
> *Good Reading*

> 'A wonderful book reflecting on love, relationships, friendship … all of it centred around food.'
> *The Big Book Club*

ISBN 978 0 7022 5004 0

THE ASH BURNER
Kári Gíslason

Growing up with his father in a small coastal town, all Ted knows about his mother is that she died when he was a boy. His father has brought them halfway across the world to start anew, but her absence defines and haunts their lives.

When Ted meets Anthony and Claire, an intense friendship begins, carrying them to Sydney and university. They introduce him to poetry and art, and he feels a sense of belonging at last. But as the trio's friendship deepens over the years, Ted must learn to negotiate the boundaries of love, and come to terms with a legacy of secrets and silence.

Written with extraordinary grace and sensitivity, *The Ash Burner* explores beauty and desire, grief and loss, and the search for one's true self.

'At once contemplative and precise, *The Ash Burner* is an exquisitely written novel that left me deeply moved by its tender exploration of beauty and grief.'

Hannah Kent, author of *Burial Rites*

'This is a beautifully written novel … Its characters are vivid, its landscapes evocative, and its narrative given shape and power by the revelation at the end.'

The Age/ The Sydney Morning Herald

'A thoughtful work that should leave an impression long after it's been put down.'

Readings Monthly

ISBN 978 0 7022 5342 3